THREE-DAY WEEKEND

Ron Skelton

This is a work of fiction. All of the characters, organizations, and events portrayed in this novel are either products of the author's imagination, or are used fictitiously.

Copyright © 2019 Ronald Skelton
All rights reserved.
ISBN 9781798853887

For Suzygirl

The only woman who would put up with me. Fly toward the light my sweet angel.

Av8or

Acknowledgements

Thanks to all the people I based my characters on. A special thanks to my editor, Kim Catanzarite. I learned a lot.

Chapter 1

11:00 a.m. Thursday, July 2

I stood in the doorway of my wife's home office. Suzy was on the phone, giggling at someone on the other end of the line. I was a little jealous. My favorite thing in life was to make her laugh. She was facing the television that hung in the far corner of the room, and hadn't noticed me yet. She looked cute sitting in her wheelchair, wearing powder blue pajamas and pink slippers.

"I'm outta here, Suzy," I whispered.

She didn't respond. Hearing loss was unavoidable with her disease. She wore hearing aids, which helped, but she usually turned one off while talking on the phone. She tucked the handset between her ear and shoulder, then turned her fingers loose on the keyboard. The girl could multitask. I guessed her typing speed was eighty, sometimes gusting to ninety words a minute. Suzy honed her business skills at a major computer manufacturer before getting jammed up in a global downsizing campaign. Their loss—an internet company hired her two weeks later for more money. She never looked back.

Suzy looked up at the TV when the weather segment came on. She kept the muted flat-screen on CNN throughout the day to stay in touch with the outside world. I stepped into her office, which had once been the smallest of our three bedrooms, and nudged her lightly below the ribs. She jumped a little but never made a sound. Her smile lit up the room when she turned around. She held up a finger, indicating she'd either be off soon or find a way fit me in. The latter was probably the case since she was rolling her eyes and making mouth gestures with her hand. She didn't use sign language, but that typically meant she was on a conference call.

She chimed in and then covered the mouthpiece.

"I can't talk you into phoning one in?" Suzy asked, winking at me.

"Blackout day—before and after the holiday," I said, bending down to kiss her goodbye.

"Riiiight, I forgot about that. It's not like there's a chance you would anyway," she said, giving me a quick smooch.

To ensure all the jobs at the auto-assembly plant were covered, my company had a rule; certain prime days had to be preapproved—no last-minute call-ins. My team already had one person off today, the day before the Fourth of July weekend, and another who was upset because she couldn't get approved at the last minute.

Suzy and I were driving to the Smokey Mountains the next morning. She came up with the idea months earlier. There had been a tense moment when I brought up trying to get the emcee slot at *Zanies* that weekend instead. I'd be asking far enough in advance that

I thought I had a shot. I had opened the show a dozen times on Sunday nights—getting the crowd fired up for the paid comics.

The manager at the biggest comedy venue in Nashville promised to put in a good word, paving the way for my first comedy paycheck. The only problem being I had to perform on both Friday and Saturday night. One, and sometimes both those nights were mandatory shifts at my factory job.

During a short conversation with the club's booker, I got rejected, and my Fourth of July weekend was free. The headliner that weekend was a well-known comedienne and star in several straight-to-video movies. She had an emcee and middle act touring with her. The booker told me to keep killing with new material and try again another time. At least I was on his radar.

Suzy comforted me for half a second, then let her boss know she would be out of town that weekend. The company Suzy worked for was a 365-day-a-year operation, especially the customer support department she ran. Technically she was entitled to three weeks' vacation but rarely went a day without spending a portion of it putting out fires for the company.

I hid my disappointment. Twelve-hour days pounding on a computer were exhausting for Suzy, and I was putting in a lot of overtime myself. We both looked forward to relaxing in the mountains. I knew without asking that she would bring her laptop. She usually toiled away while I stood waist deep in a trout stream.

I lingered in the doorway, watching her in action. I tended to forget she was disabled. Suzy's disease left her small in stature and unable to walk. Through spunk and determination, she accomplished more every day than most people. With her Quickie wheelchair and custom van, she had few limitations. The one thing I constantly worried about, though, was how fragile she was.

Suzy was born with *Osteogenesis Imperfecta*, commonly referred to as Brittle Bone Disease. As a child, she had numerous broken bones and surgeries to insert rods into bones too porous to heal. Suzy began using a wheelchair at an early age. She lived an active and adventurous life, but we were always mindful that even a minor accident, car or otherwise, could cause multiple broken bones—or worse.

Chapter 2

"Shopping list?" I whispered when she noticed I was still there.

Suzy cupped the phone again. "I thought you were coming home after the class."

"I plan to, but I may not have time."

"I'm putting the list in your wallet now, remember. Oh, and read the note on the back," she said, blowing me a kiss before responding to someone on the call.

Suzy preferred to do the shopping. She hated that I rarely used the coupons she scoured the internet for. Our small town had a family-owned grocery store she visited almost daily, allowing her to buy only as much as she could carry in her lap—not that the friendly employees didn't offer assistance.

We liked to shop local when possible. Centerville, Tennessee, the town we lived in, had a few vacant buildings on the square, and the one chain grocery store had shut down years earlier. We worried the trend would continue until there was nothing left. If the only remaining grocery store closed, I'd take some of the blame. Since the SaveMart opened across the street from my plant, I was volunteering to stop once or twice a week. In my defense, if the local grocer were open at four in the morning when I drove by, I would have given them more business.

Suzy moved from Atlanta six years ago when we got married. We'd both recently turned forty at the time. We had met the old-fashioned way—on the internet. She had a little trouble adjusting to living in a small town. I knew she missed her friends and having giant malls nearby. In my mind, the main advantage of small-town living for Suzy was that she was sheltered from the crime and other dangers associated with living in a large city.

I grabbed my gear out of the hall closet and went into the kitchen to collect my wallet, keys, and cell phone—a featureless flip phone my wife called a dinosaur. Curious, I removed the list and read the message on the back. I remembered the other reason Suzy didn't like me to shop. I had a tendency to purchase items *not* on the list. *I'm getting season five for your birthday,* was written in large letters on the back of the neatly folded sheet of paper.

My wife knew there was an excellent chance I would wander into electronics and buy another season of *MacGyver*. I had nearly every episode on VHS, recorded off the television. I started buying the DVD sets so I could watch in the original order, without having to fast-forward through commercials. I was well aware that VHS is obsolete, and I was probably the only person on the planet who still had an extensive VHS library.

I was halfway to the door when I realized I'd forgotten my small notebook and went back for it. I kept it in my back pocket to write down any bright ideas that popped into my head. Most of the notations were concepts or phrases I might be able to work into my comedy act. Soon after some major surgery I had a few years back, I experienced a midlife crisis and got on a first-name basis with God. After that, I had an urge to do something meaningful with my life.

Working my bucket list, which also included starting a small business, I gave stand-up comedy a shot. I attended classes at Zanies and was getting stage time there ever since. I wrote down anything funny that popped into my head. I discarded 90 percent of it on second look—or after I received groans from an audience. So far, none of my bright ideas were making money.

"Don't forget your phone," Suzy called when I opened the front door.

"Got it," I yelled back, wanting to say something smart.

"Tell Zeke I said hello. Love you, darling."

"Love you too, sweetheart. I'll tell him," I said, before closing the door, then double-checking that it was locked.

Running out of the house an hour after getting out of bed wasn't normal for me, and because of the holiday, I had a few extra tasks to squeeze in before getting to work. Doing them all in one day, instead of pushing them back until I returned, made sense when I had planned it out. I wondered how I would feel about it when I got off work at three o'clock the next morning.

The Fourth of July fell on a Saturday this year. The post office and banks were closed tomorrow, the Friday before. The car company I worked for the last twenty-eight years, shut down most of its plants the first two weeks of July for model changeovers. Our plant was deemed "critical" due to the high demand and short field supply of the popular models we were producing. We only had the three-day weekend.

Which was fine with me. I'd rather use that vacation time in smaller increments, enjoying three and four-day weekends throughout the year. We were fortunate: a lot of workers didn't get any paid days off when the Fourth fell on the weekend. It's like my dad told me when I spent the summer before my senior year working in a sweatshop for minimum wage, "It pays to be in the union."

The first thing on my agenda was a visit to the doctor's office. I took blood thinners and had to check my coagulation rate once a month. I could've waited until I got back from our trip, but I wanted to know the results since I'd be playing with sharp hooks and hopefully a fillet knife.

The next stop would be at my local fitness center to get a workout, something I had done faithfully since my surgery. My cardiologist stressed how important elevating my heart rate on a regular basis was to a long and active life. I heeded his advice and perhaps exceeded his expectations. The weights were my idea. The more muscle I had, the more low-fat calories I could eat without my stomach falling back over my belt.

Then I'd make a mad dash into Columbia to catch my two o'clock gun class, which I ordinarily attended on the first Saturday of the month. Because I was going to class on a workday, I had to take my gun home and then drive back, right past the gun club, to go to work. There was enough time to do all of this, but little to spare.

My instructor at the gun range today would be Tom Parker, or "Parker" as he insisted on being called. He was a Nashville police officer who moonlighted at the range. I hadn't seen him since my concealed-carry class. Sandy Green taught the advanced class on Saturday, which I attended since I got my permit. Parker taught a class during the week, which I might have attended, except for the extra miles I would have to drive. It wasn't feasible on a regular basis.

Also, Parker made me nervous—too aggressive for my taste. He taught the carry class like we were soldiers in boot camp. I was more comfortable with Sandy, who was laid-back but thorough enough. I was making steady progress with my accuracy, and I was more comfortable with a gun in my hands. It was Sandy who suggested I see Parker when I called to cancel. Seemed like a good idea then, but I worried now what Parker's advanced class would be like. If pushups were involved, maybe I could skip the weights today.

Chapter 3

I walked into my doctor's office, and the receptionist slid her window open.

"How long's the wait in the lab?" I asked. "I may have to come back next week."

She leaned in and whispered, "Don't bother with the *Field & Stream*. You'll be out of here in ten minutes."

She came around and opened the door, then led me down a long hallway toward the lab. One of the nurses smiled and asked how Suzy was doing. I replied that she was grumpy as ever. She said, "Yeah right" as I kept pace with the receptionist. My wife knew everyone in the office by name. If she were with me, it would take an hour to get out of here because nurses and other staff would be walking out of doorways to chat when they heard her voice.

"Have a seat," the receptionist said, pointing to a small waiting area where four people read magazines.

She went into the lab and came out a minute later, "Say hi to Suzy for me."

"I will, and thanks for your help."

I knew I was given special treatment because of my wife. Life with Suzy came with many perks. We rarely had to wait in lines at the airport or just about anywhere. She would never ask for preferential treatment, but someone would usually notice my always smiling wife sitting in her wheelchair and insist we jump the line. I wouldn't have accepted the special treatment here, but I was in a hurry. I decided before I came in that I couldn't wait more than fifteen minutes.

As I sat outside the lab, my doctor walked past studying a chart.

"Hey, Zeke," I said, "Suzy said to tell you hello."

He looked up and smiled.

"Hello, Steve. How *is* my favorite patient these days?"

"I'm fantastic—oh, you mean Suzy," I said grinning. "She's doing great. I'll tell her you asked."

"How's the Bone Growth Stimulator working out?"

"She puts it on her leg every night. She thinks her stress fracture is healing faster than the last one. Hardly any pain at all now."

"Excellent, between that and her calcium regiment, I'm expecting her next bone density test to show some improvement."

"Thanks, Dr. Jackson. I appreciate all you do for her," I replied, not sure if *I* was on a first-name basis. He'd told Suzy to drop the "doctor business" one day when we were in his office discussing her treatment.

"You're next, Steve," the lab technician said, waving me in. I followed her, unwilling to turn and see if I was getting dirty looks.

"So, you're in a hurry," she said as I sat in the chair and put my arm on the wide armrest.

"Sorry, Millie, I should have waited until next week. I have a lot going on today."

"No problem. How's Suzy?"

"She's well, thanks for asking. We rented a cabin in the mountains this weekend."

"You be careful with that sweet lady," Millie said, wiping my fingertip with alcohol.

"I'd lock her in a plastic bubble if it were up to me," I said, as she poked my finger with a lancet and put a drop of blood on the test strip. "Yesterday Suzy asked if I knew any streams I could get her close to. She wants to learn how to fish a fly rod."

"She's something else. You're a lucky man."

"I don't know why she puts up with me."

"Me either. Uh-oh, somebody's eating broccoli again," Millie said, reading the display on the machine.

"1.7, that's not too bad . . . for me."

"That's a little thick. The goal is a range between 2.5 and 3.5. Not 1.2 and 6.8 like you keep bringing me. I'll let the doctor know."

Millie saw me glance at the clock.

"Don't you dare leave while I'm gone. I'll have Connie chase you down in the parking lot," Millie said, referring to the doctor's sweet but iron-willed nurse.

Dr. Jackson had raised my Coumadin dosage over the past months. I was eating a lot of salads—and broccoli—to knock off the fifteen pounds I gained during the winter. Green vegetables affected my coagulation rate somehow. Millie came back a few minutes later.

"Your doctor said to take ten milligrams a day and return next week for another test. Also, limit your intake of foods with Vitamin K, like he told you last month."

"How much vitamin K in a sack of cheeseburgers?" I wisecracked before I rushed to the exit.

Chapter 4

I pulled into my next stop precisely on schedule. The fitness center was big, three floors, and much nicer than most small towns have. The top level contained a state-of-the-art aerobics studio, with a padded hardwood floor and a sound system rivaling any dance club. The main level held every type of cardio and weight machine available. The power room, exclusively free weights, was in the basement.

My goal was to spend one day a week down there getting my pain on. Weekday mornings, there was rarely anyone downstairs. At night and on the weekend, it was a different story. Power lifters and bodybuilders ruled the roost. They tended to make guys like me uncomfortable. This was particularly true on days leading up to a competition, which the gym routinely sponsored.

I hated asking for help with the huge iron plates those heavy hitters left on the equipment. I wasn't sure if that was something all rookies endured or maybe the big guys were getting tired of my Arnold Schwarzenegger impersonations. I was currently bench-pressing 230 pounds, which was respectable for a middle-aged guy but bush league compared to the 450 pounds one of the power lifters had benched at a recent contest.

Today, I was sticking with the weight machines and treadmill. My cardiologist had warned me against power lifting when he observed I'd bulked up since my last appointment. Something about blood pressure spiking on low rep-heavy weight routines. I'd seen enough red and veiny faces downstairs to understand his concern.

I spent thirty minutes running on the treadmill and another half hour going through the machine circuit, which was more calisthenics than actual weightlifting. The leg press was the one activity I excelled at. Even the boys downstairs were impressed when the "old man" hoisted 600 pounds on the iron-plate version they used.

I did my usual fifteen reps on the leg machine and then put the pin at the bottom and raised the whole stack, 475 pounds, then grunted out five additional reps. Afterward, I showered and put on my work clothes: Thick, fire hose material shorts and a T-shirt stenciled with my union's local number and logo. Then I put my running shoes back on. I chose that particular shoe because they were the only pair I could find produced in America.

I typically bought a caffeinated beverage out of the machine on my way out, but today I gulped down some water from the fountain. I didn't want to be shaky during my class. I was more concerned about dealing with Parker than my accuracy with the gun. I'd seen him correct class members, severely in my mind, during my first encounter with him. I got my own rebuke delivered over a megaphone that day.

Having my name blasted out broke me of ever repeating the same mistake. I guess that was the idea. I recognized he was trying to maintain discipline and a safe environment, but his voice, even unamplified, made me vibrate a little.

Chapter 5

Standing behind the open door of my truck, I took my Glock 26 out of the bag behind the center console and hooked the holster over my belt. Thirty minutes later, I turned into the gun club on the outskirts of Columbia, a town that swelled significantly when my employer built the assembly plant just across its northern border in Spring Hill. The range is officially closed during the week, but range officers and class instructors have keys to the farm-style gate, which now stood wide open.

Parker was already there. He was prompt if nothing else. Sandy was notorious for arriving a few minutes late on Saturday mornings, causing a dozen cars to wait at the gate during the winter months when the skeet range opened an hour later. I appreciated Parker's punctuality, especially today. I had little time to spare.

I cringed when I saw only one vehicle parked at the outdoor pistol range. Parker had his back to me as he set up targets. I thought about slipping out before he saw me. Too late, he spotted me and waved. I was expecting other students, but that was unlikely now, five minutes before the hour. Parker was a stickler for arriving on time. One student arrived a minute late for my initial training and was told to reschedule when he could get there before the class started. Parker said he didn't like to disrupt the class, but I supposed it was part of his strict police, and possibly military, discipline.

I pulled out my bag containing a fifty-round box of ammunition, two fully loaded spare magazines, and my hearing protection. The instructor always supplied the targets. With Sandy, I would need another box of ammo, but when I phoned Parker to see if he could fit me in, he told me I had plenty of bullets.

I grabbed my canvas jacket even though it was ninety degrees outside. The night before my first class, Parker called to let me know what to expect. He told me to be sure to bring the concealment part, to train as true-to-life as possible. I grudgingly put on the jacket and headed to my lesson.

"Steve, glad you could make it. All three of my students canceled. It's just the two of us today," Parker said, shaking my hand.

"Must be my lucky day," I said, which was the exact opposite of what I was thinking.

I set my bag on a bench and took out the items I needed.

"I had a lesson planned for my regular students, but since they came up lame . . . is there anything specific you'd like to focus on?"

"I'll be getting my money's worth today," I stalled, trying not to stutter. "I think my balance is a little off. Maybe my accuracy would improve if my stance were better—more relaxed," I said, hoping he would get the hint and go easy on me.

"Great, we'll work on that. Hitting your target is important, but I've got to tell you, most shots taken by police officers 'in the line' are five feet or less. I would imagine the distance is even shorter for a citizen trying to stop a carjacker or armed robber."

"So . . . what, I ought to be shooting targets at point-blank range?"

"No, you're practicing the right things: the Modern Weaver, or FBI stance, proper breathing and trigger-pull techniques. But you won't be thinking about any of that when a thug throws you out of the car and tries to drive off before your wife and kids get out. Right or wrong, your reactions will be automatic."

He had my attention. The image of some gang-banger driving off with my wife flashed through my mind.

"So let's concentrate on the basics, and hopefully your training will kick in, if God forbid, something like that ever happens to you or yours."

"Sounds great."

I'd been using the FBI stance—two-hand grip, legs set about shoulder-width apart—as I'd been taught in my initial training. But I was still pulling most of my shots slightly low and left. During past classes, I'd wanted to ask Sandy for advice, but I hadn't yet. With fifteen students in the class, it was unrealistic to expect much personal attention.

"Let's go to the firing line and get to it," Parker said, snatching the bullhorn from under the bench.

Chapter 6

The first time I saw him with that bullhorn he reminded me of Sergeant Carter—the drill instructor on *Gomer Pyle U.S.M.C.*, one of my favorite shows growing up. Luckily, I had previously bestowed that nickname to someone else, or I would have likely shared with the other classmates he intimidated, and Parker would have probably kicked me out of the class if he got wind of it. That happened to me once before—in grade school.

There were a couple of occasions during my classes with Sandy when someone continued to shoot following the command to cease. He could have used a megaphone, if he'd wanted to, but he must have felt it was over the top too. For all I knew, Parker was the only instructor who used one.

Parker stood beside me, put on his muffs and nodded. I drew my weapon and held it low-ready, pointed down range. When he gave the command to commence fire, I pulled the slide back on my autoloader and chambered a round.

"Taylor! Holster your weapon," Parker boomed, sliding off one side of his hearing protection.

I wasn't sure what I'd done to upset him, but I was seconds away from finding out. I holstered the gun and removed my headset, trying unsuccessfully to steady my trembling hands.

"Is that how you carry your weapon?" Parker bellowed unassisted.

I wasn't sure what he was referring to, but I learned long ago that it's easier to just tell the truth and take my punishment.

"That gun has been in my bag since the last class. No wait, I carried last weekend .when I took my wife shopping in Nashville." Nashville was a fairly safe place, but I carried whenever I took Suzy to any big city.

Parker stared at me for a long moment and then smiled, slightly, tilting his head sideways.

"Steve, how would you have reacted last weekend if someone had pushed your wife to the ground and stuck a gun in your face as you were opening the car door for her? Would you have drawn your weapon and said: Mr. Carjacker, I need a moment to get my own gun in order," Parker said, letting the smile fade.

"I'd take his gun away and beat him with it," I said, enraged at the idea of someone trying to harm my delicate Suzy. His scenario was my worst nightmare.

Parker sighed, "You make that sound easy. Why bother with all this training if you won't use your weapon to protect your family?"

I looked at him sheepishly.

"You have noble intentions, but drawing a weapon that isn't hot will get you, your family, or a six-year-old kid a block away killed, when the meth addict trying to take your car starts shooting."

"Won't happen again. I figured it was safer." What he said made sense. I just wanted to be cautious.

"Steve, I'm being a little hard on you today. In my permit class, I've had a couple of students who didn't know how to load their weapon. They don't pass until I feel they're competent, even if it means coming back for additional lessons on the house. I'd never mention it in that environment. You handle your weapon with care, and you're intent on improving your skills. I'm treating you like I treat my officers who depend on their sidearm to get home to their families. I'll chew your butts out when I see something that'll get you in trouble," Parker said, adjusting his headgear and stepping back, signaling he was ready to start fresh.

I ignored the drips of sweat running down my glasses and pulled my muffs over my ears, unholstered my weapon, and responded to his command to begin firing.

When I shot the last round in the magazine, Parker said, "Not too awful. I remember you shooting low-left, qualifying for your permit. Sandy should've broke you of that by now."

"I go to the Saturday class because it doesn't interfere with my job," I blurted out. "I'm going out of town this Saturday," I added, wishing I'd kept my mouth shut.

"Yeah, you told me that on the phone. Sandy's a skilled instructor and a great guy. I'm glad you're making the effort. Spread your feet a bit. That will make you more stable. And, please . . . *don't* jerk the trigger," he said as I swapped an empty magazine for a full one.

I experimented with the wider stance. It was awkward at first, but my shots were closer to the bulls-eye.

"Don't worry about shooting perfect patterns out here, Steve. Remember what I told you: the typical shot in the real world is up close. All it takes is a cool head and a weapon that is good to go."

Parker gave lengthy advice between my reloading and firing six more magazines, then he lowered the bullhorn and removed his muffs.

"Steve, you've gotten better since the last time we met. I think you've made some progress today as well."

"That last set was probably my best ever," I said, beaming.

"Let me show you how I do it," Parker said, reaching for my autoloader.

I took a magazine out of my pocket, loaded with my last ten rounds of ammunition. I handed it and the weapon over to him. Even though the slide was locked back, the gun visibly unable to fire, I was careful not to "laser" my instructor as I passed it to him. I learned from my father to treat every firearm as though it were loaded and ready to fire. In recent training, I learned to imagine the muzzle was a laser, destroying whatever it shined on.

The moment Parker took control of the gun, I detected something unique about the way he handled it. I'd never seen him with a real weapon. He used an orange rubber version of a large-frame *Glock* to demonstrate in the carry class. He held the weapon the same way anyone would, but somehow it looked more professional.

I had to admit, my gun appeared almost tiny in his hands. The smaller size was the reason I chose that model. The larger handguns seemed too bulky to hide under summer-weight clothes. I now understood that choosing an appropriate weapon and concealing it was the primary consideration; comfort was secondary. My gun was better suited for an ankle holster.

Parker released the slide gradually, holding it back as he pressed the button. He then ejected the empty magazine and installed the full one. He pulled the slide back with authority and then released it with a loud crack. He methodically set his feet wide, much wider than I considered necessary, then extended his arms and lowered his head slightly in the direction of the target. He was a textbook example of the FBI stance. The Modern Weaver was the original name for the pose every TV detective used when aiming a gun. The FBI adopted it as their training model—something Parker had told us in the classroom at the clubhouse.

He fired off all ten rounds, making use of the undamaged space in the very center of my target. I was impressed.

"You ever shot a gun before?"

"First time," Parker replied too quickly, like he'd been expecting a smart remark from me.

"I wish I could shoot like that," I said, as he returned my weapon.

I released the slide and put the empty firearm back in my holster.

"I like your attitude, Steve. You take the responsibility of carrying a weapon seriously, and it shows."

"Thanks," I said, gushing on the inside.

Chapter 7

"Refresh my memory, Steve. What's your motive for carrying a handgun? Who exactly are you trying to protect?"

"I carry when my wife and I are going into the city—any city. I want to be able to stop a carjacker or someone trying to hurt my wife after we give them our money. I got my permit to protect her," I said, assuming this answer would satisfy him.

"That's fine, Steve. It's an awesome privilege to be able to defend your family with a firearm. Most people in the world don't have that luxury."

"Yeah, I was nervous about carrying a gun at first, but I'm glad I got my permit."

"You don't have children? Why I ask, that's what I hear the most. Men and women—they want to protect their babies."

"No, I got married late in life—I couldn't find a woman who would put up with me," I said, using one of my comedy lines.

"I can relate," Parker said, not cracking even a hint of a smile.

"The reason I got the permit is because my wife is extremely frail. It wouldn't take much to seriously injure her. She uses a wheelchair, but her . . . being so fragile is really her only disability. When she *isn't* with me—I'm not afraid of much—I can defend myself without a gun."

"That's great, but let me paint a picture. You walk into your local convenience store one Sunday morning—in your sweatpants and T-shirt to buy a newspaper—and some shaky high-on pulls a stickup. Then he sees *you*—big guy, short hair, solid build—he thinks maybe you're a cop and pulls the trigger. Who'll protect your wife now? I train a lot of people, veteran police officers for the most part. What they tell me is, the time you need your weapon most is when you least expect it."

"I never thought of it that way."

"You should carry your weapon whenever you leave the house. I'll get off my soapbox, but think about what I'm saying. It might save your life one day . . . so you *can* be there for your wife."

I pictured Suzy struggling through life without me.

"I will think about it. I hope I never have to use it."

"Well, our hour went quickly. Let's pack up. I have the rest of the day off unless the bad guys do something to get me brought in."

"I wish I was that lucky. I've got a ten-hour shift tonight, and I still have to take my stuff home. My company frowns at bringing guns onsite."

"Carry your weapon whenever possible. You may need it one day."

I stopped at the bench and took the empty magazines out of my pocket and placed them next to my bag. I took the Glock, still in the holster, off my belt and ejected the empty magazine. I was about to put everything in the bag when Parker gave me another sideways grin.

"What are you doing, Steve?"

"Stowing my gear."

"Why not load some ammo and put the gun on your hip?"

"You shot my last bullet."

Parker rolled his eyes.

"Wait here one second. I'll be right back," he said, sprinting to his car.

I checked my watch and found my lesson going into overtime. I had about five extra minutes built in. I was hoping to stop at a drive-thru and indulge in something healthy-ish.

Parker returned with his hands cupped together.

"I owe you ten rounds. Try out these hollow points I had in my bag. I've got enough for one of your spares too. I don't have much use for 9mm ammunition anymore. I mostly work with .45 caliber weapons these days," he said, loading both clips as smoothly as he fired the gun.

"Thanks, I've always wanted to try those—and a more powerful weapon—but I figured the extra kick would cause me to yank shots even worse than I do already."

"You won't notice that in a live situation. It's okay to shoot practice rounds here, but I recommend you carry extra heft when you're out on the street," Parker said, racking the first round in the chamber, inserting the gun in the holster, then handing it to me.

"I appreciate your help today," I said earnestly as I put the gun on my belt.

I paid him the twenty-five dollars, which I thought was a bargain for the private lesson.

"Enjoy the holiday," Parker said sliding into his car.

"I will, thanks. I'm off tomorrow. My wife and I are driving to the mountains . . . once I get a little sleep."

"Sounds familiar, I'm picking up my girlfriend tomorrow. We're taking her folks to Gatlinburg this weekend. I just hope I don't get called in before we leave."

"Turn off your phone. That's what I would do," I said, opening the door of my truck.

"No can do. My luck, I'd miss something important."

I smiled and got into my truck. My mind labored to find a funny line to come back with but came up empty. Parker never showed any appreciation for my humor anyway. I wondered if maybe we'd gotten off on the wrong foot during the first class because of something I said. Parker never mentioned his role at the police department, but his comments about training officers led me to assume he was an instructor at the academy or firing range. I would make a point of asking Sandy when I saw him next.

Driving out, I saw Parker standing next to the gate, waiting to lock it behind me. I waited at the highway for a car to pass. Because of our chat, my schedule was busted beyond repair. No matter how fast I drove, I didn't have time to go home. Showing up late for work wasn't an option. At an auto assembly plant, you might as well stay home if you can't be on your job when the buzzer sounds. We were already down one person. If I blew in ten minutes late, my boss would have to jump in and take my place until management scrounged up another body. I wouldn't let Joe down like that. I turned left and headed into Columbia.

Chapter 8

After a few minutes with the air-conditioner in my truck blasting, my stomach began talking to me. I had skipped breakfast, and I usually ate a sandwich before heading into work. One of the salad bar restaurants in Columbia came to mind. I could eat a healthy meal and then take a short nap in the factory parking lot before my shift started.

As usual I overate, devouring a heaping plate of salad and a bowl of broccoli soup. I then went back for a large mound of cottage cheese and pineapple chunks. Even at a salad bar, quantity, not quality was my problem. My full stomach made me sleepy, as I knew it would. If not for the blackout provision of our contract, I might have called in sick.

Not likely though. For the first twenty plus years, I hadn't missed a single day of work, other than scheduled vacations. Not even during the years I battled my personal demons. My father and grandfather were both autoworkers, and Dad would have been disappointed if he knew I ever "laid out"—his words, not mine.

I busted my perfect attendance when I had to be in the hospital for almost a week to have surgery and a month to recuperate. A legitimate sick leave didn't count against me—technically. But in my own mind, the streak was broken and there would be an asterisk in the record book. It wasn't like the company would give me a new car when I retired to show their gratitude. My supervisor appreciated that I came to work every day, but even he didn't know how long that had been going on.

Before getting in the truck, I removed my jacket. I probably looked strange wearing it with shorts, but no one seemed to notice. The restaurant was hospital cold inside, and due to the blood thinners I was taking, I would have been shivering without it. I put the Glock in my bag and stowed it behind the center console. I then placed my gym bag on top and stuffed my jacket in to conceal the bags.

I'd never been stopped by security while passing through the gate, where a uniformed guard performed a cursory scan of each badge before waving the driver through. Everyone knew the company had the right to search any vehicle that came on the 2,000-acre site. Rumors had spread recently that several employees were stopped and their vehicles were inspected.

The rumor mill even suggested one of those cars had an empty adult beverage container under the seat, and the owner was punished with a short disciplinary layoff. I'd been vocally skeptical of the whole account, but as I neared the guard shack, my mind played out a scenario where I was told to pull my truck to the side.

Arriving forty minutes before the start of my shift, I noticed there wasn't the usual traffic backup at the security checkpoint. I grew anxious as the short, gray-haired lady came out. She brought me to a complete halt with her hand and walked over to my open window. *You've been selected for a random inspection,* were the words I expected to hear from the matronly guard. As she studied my badge, my mind flash forwarded to me explaining to my crying wife, how I lost my job.

After a tense moment, the guard I had smiled and waved at a thousand times, motioned me through. Putting myself in that position was stupid. My overactive imagination and bad poker face disqualified me for *any* type of shady activity. My hands trembled as I drove through the checkpoint—something that occurred whenever I got the least bit frazzled—likely due to my years of heavy drinking, when every morning was a tremor fest.

The day shift crowd had cleared out. My early arrival allowed me to get a front-row parking place. I would have the rare luxury of a short hike into the plant. If I hustled after my shift, I could also be the pace car leading the long procession out of the parking lot. One of the perks of working near the door.

I kept my truck's engine, air-conditioner, and radio turned on. I reclined the seat and shut my eyes. I reached across and turned the volume down to a barely audible level, and within minutes I dozed off. Fifteen minutes later, a car door slammed, jarring me awake. I shook off the fog, swapped out my regular glasses for the prescription safety glasses in my console, then went in before I fell back asleep and missed the start of my shift.

I was tired, but coffee would get me through the night. A cup to get started and another at lunch and each of my two breaks usually did the trick. The single thing my cardiologist chided me for was my admitted abuse of caffeine. I always promised to do better, knowing days like these called for liberal doses of my only remaining vice.

I just had to get through my ten hours—and a quick stop afterward to pick up the items on my wife's list—then my three-day weekend will officially begin. I promised myself I would run into the twenty-four-hour grocery store—the old fashioned kind, without a sporting goods department—grab only what I needed, and get out. Tomorrow, when I got out of bed—not the tomorrow at 3 a.m. when I got off work—would be a better day.

Chapter 9

As team leader, I was expected to arrive a few minutes early to ensure everything was ready to go. With the group of go-getters I worked with, that meant brewing the first pot of coffee in our team room. Door-fitters need only a rubber body hammer and a torque wrench in order to do their job. My teammates kept their tools in personal lockers and were quite capable of getting themselves ready.

"You're early," Joe Duncan, supervisor for my team and three others, remarked.

"If you feel like you owe me, I'd be willing to cut out early," I said as I poured water into the coffeemaker.

"That's funny. I wouldn't pay a cover charge, but that's a good one. Hey, put an extra scoop in there, Steve. I may need the extra kick tonight."

"Don't worry Joe, I'm way ahead of you on that."

"And don't let Janice make any coffee. The last time she brewed a pot, it looked like my wife's iced tea. I almost fell asleep driving home."

"I'll take that as a direct order," I said smiling. "Are you going out of town this weekend?"

"Yeah, we're making a quick trip to Michigan to visit our new grandson. My wife's picking me up after work. I had to get up early to take care of a few things."

"How old is he now?"

"Six weeks tomorrow. The wife said she's going with or without me. Truth is, I'm probably more excited than she is."

"Maybe we'll have a smooth night for a change."

"That's *really* funny. I'll be lucky if *I'm* not fitting doors across from you. *Everybody* wanted to make it a four-day weekend."

"I know I'll be on the line."

"Yeah, all my team leaders will be, whether they know it yet or not. I just hope nobody calls in sick. Cindy asked me for the day off last night, but Dave was already approved."

"Yeah, I heard."

"She said she was taking off anyway," Joe said, then watched for my reaction.

"I talked to her when we clocked out. I think she'll be here," I said, focusing on my task so Joe wouldn't feel obliged to respond.

"Tomorrow will be a better day," I yelled as he walked away. My usual response when someone was frustrated about something.

I remembered wanting to take the day off too. I could have lied and said I had an emergency and perhaps gotten off with a slap on the wrist. If it were anyone but Joe, I might have considered it. My perfect attendance was in the past. Loyalty to a boss who treated people well was probably something I picked up from my father.

Joe was one of the best supervisors on the line. If anyone in my team needed anything, he was always there to help out. I didn't know how old he was, but he had over forty years with the company. Most of the supervisors were young college graduates who were only concerned about hitting their numbers. That was the way to get on the career fast track at a car company.

Joe began his career spot-welding on an assembly line in Detroit and had probably risen as far as he ever would. The funny thing was, Joe's line outperformed most of the other supervisors, including the West Point graduate I had nicknamed *Sergeant Carter* and occasionally did impressions of for my teammates. He got in people's faces the same way Gomer's drill instructor did. The name had stuck, and even Joe used it occasionally—behind his back, of course, like everybody else.

Following the customary greetings to my teammates, I put in my earplugs—yellow foam bulbs connected with a red string—loosely enough to be able to hear someone yell for me. We had a good team, consisting of two women and two men, not counting myself—I was offline doing other tasks if everyone came to work. Our four jobs were all physically demanding and fast paced, but that helped the time go by.

I volunteered for one of the two less-appealing jobs: fitting the front and rear doors to the crossover SUV's body. Tonight I would be on the passenger side. Most people on my team preferred the less ergonomically stressful job of installing the hinges and then bolting the door to the car with the aid of an articulating arm.

When I first hired on, not everyone was physically capable of performing that task. The worker manually carried the door—which was much heavier back then—to the car. Big, strong, and usually young men were handpicked to do those jobs. Hanging doors was my first assignment when I hired on, only a week out of high school. I've been a door fitter for the last fifteen years—at two different plants. I was a spot welder in between, happily giving that job to the first robot willing to take my place.

But that night, as I worked the line, I daydreamed about my upcoming trip. Suzy discovered a deal online for a small cabin in a secluded area. I was certain the cabin had internet access so she could work. Suzy wouldn't let me spend the whole weekend fishing, but I would get several opportunities. I always managed to.

Chapter 10

Cindy showed signs of fatigue just before lunch.

"Stellllaaaa," I yelled in my best Marlon Brando impersonation. "You lost your groove again," I said, grabbing one of the small plastic caps I had on a table behind me so Joe wouldn't have to chase them down.

Recently added to our job, the part was to be inserted into the side of cars not getting the sunroof option. Cindy was required to check the manifest and put the caps where drain hoses for the sunroof would normally be sticking out. I was keeping an eye out for her.

"First one," Cindy replied.

"*Wrong again*, kimosabe" I said, switching to my Johnny Carson voice.

"Thanks, it's hard to teach a middle-aged dog new tricks," she said, stealing my corny line.

"That's okay, Cindy. Everyone's missed a few," I said, catching up my own job.

Everyone nearby got a kick out of my impersonations and wordplay. Most were surprised I didn't use that kind of material on the stage. Doing a cliché Carson impression would likely get a heckler's attention or possibly get me booed off the stage. Once a comic is labeled a hack, it's hard to get work in a comedy club. All my material came from personal experiences and twists on current events.

I lost a lot of material when I decided to work clean—not Disney clean but pretty tame by adult standards. In my younger days, I said a lot of things that would have killed on the stage. But while writing my first bits, I made up my mind to picture my mother sitting in the audience. My sense of humor and ability to turn a phrase came from her side of the family. Her brother, my favorite uncle, even gave me my best tagline.

I'm not going bald . . . hair won't grow on scar tissue.

I guess I was still trying to make them laugh, years since they both passed away.

At the beginning of my lunch break, I went outside and phoned my wife. After we discussed the trip, she suggested I should have called to let her know I wasn't coming home after the class. I used the restroom and then tried unsuccessfully to take a short nap in the team room—a large cubicle with enough tables and attached swivel chairs for the four teams in our area. Still full from the salad bar, I passed on making the trek to the cafeteria for the mystery-meat special. That was the name I made popular for the lunch plate, but the food wasn't terrible if you were hungry.

Walking back to the line with a fresh cup of coffee, I was more tired than before my longest break. An hour later, after completing her job cycle, Cindy ran over to me.

"Psssst—Steve—stalker alert. I was told to pass it on."

"Thanks Cindy, but don't get flustered and forget another drain plug."

I forced a smile to show her I wasn't mad. Everyone got a kick out of watching me squirm when Ella Thompson came by en route to use a bathroom too far from her job to be a coincidence. It didn't help that she was still somewhat hot for her age.

I didn't resent my co-workers' interest in the spectacle. Considering the monotonous environment, it was natural to delight in any drama that played out on the plant floor. My teammates, and everybody on our line, were often rejuvenated for hours after Ella paid me a visit. Her team appeared to have extra manpower to get her off the line. Or more likely, she sweet-talked her supervisor into doing her job while she gallivanted around the plant.

"Hello, Steve. Are you performing this weekend?" Ella asked as she approached, running fingers through blond strands to get them out of her face.

People were moving in as close as their jobs allowed, hoping to hear the conversation. I plucked out one of my earplugs and let it dangle.

"No, I'm not. How about you?" I said, giving my usual smart-aleck response.

"Gary and I are going to the river."

She'd once spent a few minutes telling me about the small cabin she and her husband purchased on Tennessee River backwater. Two paychecks and no kids gave them a decent lifestyle. Especially now that they were living in Tennessee, with its lower cost of living and no state income tax. Suzy and I were trying to live on my income and squirrel hers away. We hoped to start a small business so I could retire the minute I qualified for a pension. We didn't have a fortune saved, but we *were* debt-free and maxing out our retirement plans. I still hadn't figured out the most important thing: what I wanted to be when I grew up.

"Have fun," I said, sticking the earplug back in place and turning my attention to the next set of doors I would give a smooth fit—her cue that I thought now would be a good time for her to move along.

Ella stood there awkwardly for a moment after my brush-off—as usual.

"We will. Nice to see you again," she said before moving on.

"What did that woman do to you?" Cindy said. "It must have been awful."

I gave her my standard "no comment" grimace. I was just glad Gary's team was at the other end of the plant. Ella's husband seeing us together would have made this night one to truly remember. He'd once threatened me during a lunch break. Everyone on my line either saw or heard about it.

"Hey, Steve, what would MacGyver do with that?" Jerry, from the next team down yelled.

I ignored his reference to my favorite line when facing a challenge. Jerry was getting as close as he dared to making a sexually provocative remark, and I wasn't about to encourage him to cross the line by zinging him back. I wanted, as always, to let the incident die a natural death.

Jerry was just trying to get a laugh. He was one of several co-workers who came out regularly to watch me perform. I'd taken a lot more than Jerry dished out, especially from paying customers. Drawing a crowd is the best way to rise up the comedy food chain. Currently, I was equal to a funny amoeba.

Chapter 11

Thirty minutes before the end of shift, Joe came by, carrying a nearly full coffee carafe. "It may be a little strong cause I'm starting out in the driver's seat. You want one for the road?"

"Drive up in the morning, so you won't have to sleep twelve hours when you get there," I said, holding out my cup.

"I'm only driving the first couple of hours. My wife went to bed early; she'll take the wheel when I get tired. I'm stopping to buy my grandson a few toys, so we don't get there empty-handed. I'm going to spoil that kid rotten."

"What's his name, Joe? I never heard."

"I never said. They're christening him Joseph Duncan III on Sunday morning. That little man has been on my mind all night," he said, his weary face showing rare emotion.

"With that name to live up to, he's bound to do great things," I said, feeling my own emotions kick in.

Joe took a step closer and said in a low voice, "Thanks for that, Steve. Also, thanks for taking care of business tonight. I really appreciate it."

"My pleasure, Joe," I said, barely holding back a tear.

Since my surgery, I tended to be more sensitive. When taking in one of my wife's picks at a movie theater, I often needed to disguise the wiping of an eye to conceal my new weakness. That was the only side effect I was aware of. I was lucky I didn't have any of the others, like "night terrors"—jumping out of bed, dreaming my heart was blowing a gasket.

Joe turned to my teammates and said, "I appreciate your hard work tonight. Have a great weekend and be safe."

They responded in harmony, "You too, Joe."

"Be careful driving," I said as he walked back to his workstation.

Counting down the final minutes, I thought over my shopping options, missing the days when there were no twenty-four-hour grocery stores in the area. Since the new SaveMart opened, I did most of my shopping there. I seldom bought expensive items in the "not on my list" departments like sporting goods and electronics, but I always went by and admired them.

One of my biggest weaknesses was electronic gadgetry, none of it produced in the states. My watch was a recent example. A few weeks ago, I stopped at SaveMart, bent on buying a domestically manufactured wristwatch, whatever the cost. I went home with a foreign brand that showed temperature, altitude, and barometric pressure at the touch of a button. This was the kind of impulsive shopping that commonly drew dirty looks from my wife. We had a plan, and she was working it better than I was.

Between the coffee and excitement over my weekend plans, I felt more energetic than when I first entered the plant. I was feeling so peppy that I was considering the SaveMart option. I needed some new leader for my fly rod, and I could use fresh batteries for my flashlight.

That's how it always started. Once I got inside though, all bets were off.

The most persuasive factor on the SaveMart side of the ledger was my growing hunger. The only thing I'd eaten since I got to work was a granola bar from the vending machine. Suzy normally packed me a bag lunch, but I had waved her off, thinking I would buy a salad when I hit the drive-through. Thoughts of the sandwich display at SaveMart made me realize how famished I was.

"Have a great weekend," I told my teammates as I closed my locker and raced to the time clock. That last coffee would probably turn out to be a mistake, but right then it gave me a much-needed second wind. Running to my truck, I began visualizing the large turkey sandwiches at SaveMart, thus ending the debate over where I would do my shopping.

Chapter 12

3:15 a.m. Friday, July 3

I backed into the first parking space that didn't require a handicap placard, even though I had one hanging from my rearview mirror. The only activity in the parking lot was the slow trickle of vehicles following me from the plant and a street sweeper crisscrossing the nearly vacant parking lot.

It was still hot and humid. I left the motor and air-conditioner running while I took care of some preliminaries. I laid my wife's list on the center console and wrote the word leader below the last entry. That would remind me to stop by sporting goods, not that I was likely to forget. How much outdoor paraphernalia I ended up with was yet to be determined.

I studied the noisy sweeper as it passed in front of me. I pulled the notebook out of my back pocket and wrote a memo to research this business opportunity. I was analyzing anything that could supplement the small pension I would be eligible for when I reached thirty years of service. Retirement in my case would mean working somewhere other than an assembly line, preferably my own business. Cleaning parking lots would involve a hefty investment—unless I used a broom—but I would research the business model thoroughly before ruling it out.

As the sweeper headed for the exit, a white commercial van entered the parking lot. It occurred to me that the giant retailer must outsource a large number of services. I felt like I was on to something. The van made a wide arc across the back of the parking lot. It had a sign on the side that read: City Wide Pest Control. No need to write that one down. Before Suzy came along, I didn't set a trap until I had mice scurrying under my feet.

The van stopped in front of a small group of cars parked fifty yards out, those owned by the store's night shift crew, I supposed. The van's dome light came on, but if someone got out, it was from the opposite side of the vehicle. After two or three minutes of just sitting there, the van continued on, finally stopping in front of the far entrance, which was unlit and no doubt locked at this hour. I was expecting the exterminators to use a back door like the other vendors. I had never seen them in the store, but what better time than now? *At this hour, the only customers were "factory rats" like me.* I wrote some keywords in my notepad to remember the line for future reference.

For a second, I thought the van was some kind of police surveillance operation or a criminal enterprise. I had a reputation for thinking the mundane was something much more exciting, like an episode from one of my favorite television shows. My wife would be rolling her eyes if she were here listening inside my head right now.

A fifty-something woman from the plant parked across from me and got out, then hesitated when she spotted me. I waved. Her expression revealed the exact moment she recognized me. We didn't know each other by name, but we had chatted in the cafeteria line. The woman smiled and waved back. She seemed relieved to see a familiar face as she ventured across the parking lot alone. I guessed she too had once lived in a more crime-ridden part of the country.

I was adding items to my shopping list when a shimmering black crew-cab Chevy Silverado slow-rolled toward me; the driver seemed unable to choose a suitable parking spot out of the hundreds presently vacant. Definitely someone from the plant. Autoworkers love new vehicles more than most people do. We justified it with a long list of excuses: the employee discount, job security, yada yada yada. I suppose we became addicted to the new-car smell and needed a way to get our off-duty fix.

As the truck passed under the light, I could just make out the riders through the dark tinted windows. The passenger pointed for the driver to park in the open slot next to mine. I didn't recognize the occupants until the vehicle was right there.

The truck continued on, finally parking three spaces down. *Twilight Zone* music played in my head. There were only two people in the whole world who I would not want to run into at this moment, and here they were: Ella and her husband, Gary.

Ella jumped out first, with Gary a close second. She headed him off at the rear bumper where they commenced arguing. With my window open a smidge, I heard Ella tell Gary he should wait in the truck. I was trying to decide who I'd rather have win the debate, when I saw Gary get back in and slam the door. This occurred after Ella stuck her face in his ear, saying something I couldn't make out. As she approached, she flashed a big smile, as if everything were dandy in her world.

"Hey, Steve. Are you going in?"

I faked a smile and shook my head no. Not with her anyway. Ella was close to forty-five—I still remembered her birthday. And there was no denying it: She still looked good with her short Meg Ryan–style hair, faded skin-tight jeans, and a red polo. At twenty-five, Ella had been so attractive it hurt most men to look at her—or so I remembered one supervisor remarking to another. They were standing at the urinals while the line was running, unaware I was taking care of an urgent matter in one of the stalls behind them.

I resisted the urge to look at Gary but lost the battle. He'd lowered all four of his windows and was leaning over, staring directly at me. He seemed to be daring me to provoke him now that we were off company property. I would do no such thing, regardless of the time or place. My only reaction was to engage the power lock on my five-year-old truck. Gary was jealous of every man who came near Ella, but especially me. And she didn't help matters.

Once I was reasonably sure Gary wasn't planning to vent his anger on me, I turned on the radio to catch the headlines and weather forecast, while I mentally calculated how much lead time to give Ella.

Chapter 13

The newscast, originating locally, reported on an initiative by local churches to repeal the city's liquor-by-the-glass ordinance. When I first relocated to the plant, there were few chain restaurants in the area. They came later, when liquor-by-the glass became law. I didn't have a strong opinion on the subject. I didn't drink liquor now—or any alcohol. And back when I used to drink, it was rarely from a glass.

The weather report indicated a chance of heavy rain over the weekend. I had rain gear to wear fishing so that wasn't terrible news. In the here and now, lightning flashes and the rumble of thunder made me think I should put on my jacket before I went in the store.

I looked across the parking lot at the pest control van and observed the occupants—a fairly large group—walk toward the darkened entrance. It seemed like more manpower than necessary to do the job, though there was a vast area to cover.

A pearl white Cadillac stopped in the yellow-lined space commonly used for short-term parking. The sedan was either brand-new or had recently visited a detail shop. The chrome wheels reflected the bright lights nearby. This seemed suspicious as well. I could barely see the two occupants in the front with the light reflecting off the glass. I imagined they could be the kingpin and maybe an enforcer, in cahoots with the exterminators transporting drugs through the SaveMart supply chain.

The passenger-side front door of the Caddy slowly opened. When the light hit the man's black ripple-soled shoes, white socks, and brown polyester pant legs, I could "name that tune" in three notes. My boss, Joe Duncan, emerged from what I now realized was his wife's new car. I was glad to see he had changed his mind about starting out in the driver's seat. He entered the store as his wife waited.

Joe had told me his wife was driving a new car, but failed to mention it was the flagship model of our company. That was just like Joe to feel awkward about telling me it was an expensive luxury model. Joe drove an old S-10 pickup to work. He told me recently the odometer was about to roll over for the second time. Suspecting Joe was some drug dealer allowed me to momentarily dismiss my other conspiracy theories as well.

Once again the bug van drew my attention. Parked in front of the yellow barrier poles, its interior lights came on and the workers climbed back into the vehicle. I told myself that City Wide must be a new vendor, and tried to focus on real problems. Ella was probably deep in the store by now, trying to decide which brand of moisturizer to buy, knowing her. I quit procrastinating and got out of the truck, my legs and back already stiffening.

I pulled my jacket out from behind the seat, and my gym and gun bags both rolled out onto the console. My tired brain engaged, and I remembered my gun was in the truck. I needed to either stuff the bags out of sight or take the gun with me. On the street, an autoloader like my Glock was the same as money in the bank. I checked to see if Gary was still eyeballing me. He faced straight ahead, leaning back against the headrest. I assumed he was fuming, knowing him.

I reached into the bag, took out the holstered pistol, and hooked it on my belt. I felt around for the heavier spare magazine and stuck it in my pocket. I cracked a smile, recalling Parker's lecture from earlier in the day, as I put on my jacket. He'd be pleased to see me carrying the weapon I trained so hard with.

I had to admit, it felt right, pressed tightly to my side, not that it would be required here. I would let the armed security guard deal with any problems that might arise inside the store. Outside, my only danger was in the truck thirty feet away. And I would take a beating from Gary without even thinking about drawing a weapon.

Heading toward the automatic doors, I noticed the van's headlights illuminate. I figured the exterminators had called to inquire which door to use. They were probably on their way to use a service entrance. *Eradicating pests in the middle of the night made sense, though. Nobody cared what a bunch of factory rats saw*, I said to myself, test-driving my latest bright idea. I tried to think of some context I could work the line into a comedic bit to use onstage.

A minute ago, I was dreaming up all kinds of devious scenarios for the exterminators' presence. Now they were inspiring me with new material for my comedy act.

I smiled and nodded at Joe's wife as I passed in front of her car. She didn't smile back, and then I heard the power locks activate—rightfully so. We'd never met. As I was about to go in, the van rolled toward me. It appeared we were using the same entrance; perhaps the only one available to them at this hour. A touch of anxiety hit me as the automatic doors opened and I entered the store.

I've got to get some sleep, I told myself. *I'm definitely losing it.*
I blamed Parker's earlier forecast of gloom and doom for my paranoia.

Chapter 14

The carts weren't jammed together any tighter than normal. I just couldn't get one unstuck, which only happened when I was this tired. The electric scooter with a basket attached to the handlebars tempted me. I always preferred to drive something if given a choice. If those were available when I was a kid, I would have gotten in trouble flying around, running into things.

At forty-six, I was more likely to do it to get laughs from people who recognized me. My wife would tell me they weren't intended to play on and that I should leave it for someone who couldn't access the store otherwise. In the six years Suzy and I had been together, I'd learned a lot about the issues mobility-impaired people dealt with on a daily basis.

The cart finally released after a few violent jerks. I glimpsed the connecting end of a child seat strap go flying, reminding me what generally caused the problem. I turned and saw the bug van pull up in front of the entrance. The interior lights came on, and I took a long look at the man with a shaved head in the front passenger seat. He was staring straight at me. The hair on the back of my neck would have been standing up, but my barber had recently shaved that area with a straight razor.

The group filed out of the van. I told myself that nothing out of the ordinary was occurring. Whenever I encountered a blinking light in the sky, I wondered if it was a spaceship about to invade the planet. I pushed the buggy through the archway, focusing my mind on the sandwich case between the deli and the produce aisle. I was salivating like Pavlov's dog.

The old-timer who welcomes customers during the day was absent at this late hour. I'd recently stopped doing my impersonation of the greeter after hearing that all of them were veterans wounded in wars fought long ago. I'd only done that gag at work, thank goodness. I never made fun of anyone except myself on stage, and I rarely got heckled.

I smiled and nodded to the sentry posted at his usual perch. He nodded in return, a stern look stuck on his face. He was probably next in line for the greeter job. From previous excursions, I knew he had a serious limp. I figured him for a retired police officer who'd been hurt in the line of duty.

Seeing the sandwich cooler distracted me from any possible criminal plots brewing in my mind. Panic hit me, though, as I approached. There was no sign of the large sandwiches wrapped in thick plastic. When I got there, I found two ham-and-cheese croissants in a compartment intended for fifty larger sandwiches. I removed each one individually and inspected them. The first was open at one end, and the other appeared to have been used to play hacky-sack.

I continued on, trying to decide whether to create my own masterpiece in the truck after I finished shopping. The raw materials were already on my list. Then I remembered the disappointment on my wife's face the last time I brought home a bag of half-eaten groceries.

I returned to the wide aisle I used entering the store. A pallet of Gatorade in all the colors of the rainbow caught my eye. As I scanned the chest-high top layer for my flavor preference, the City Wide Pest Control employees came through the automatic doors sporting blue lab coats. None were carrying bug sprayers. *Maybe they were strapped on their backs*, I told myself as I pushed the cart ahead and got behind the display.

I grabbed hold of the plastic handle of a fruit punch–flavored eight-pack while peering around the corner. I'd drink a warm one on my long ride home. The sports drink would have to take the place of both food and beverage. Caffeine was only making me crazy, and I could bank the calories for the weekend.

I froze as the crew neared the threshold. I counted nine total. I stared at the group, certain there was something "not quite right" about these City Wide exterminators.

I was sure I was dreaming. After the group of men passed by the shopping carts and through the archway, they opened their lab coats and pulled out weapons. Most carried a shotgun, which appeared to have a shorter barrel than my father's Browning Sweet Sixteen. My legs got rubbery as I watched the mayhem unfold.

Chapter 15

I stood twenty yards away as the armed men startled the security guard. Two of the gunmen carried a different type of weapon; a rifle with a handle on top. I supposed it was an M-16 like the military used, but I couldn't tell them apart from various civilian versions. The bigger of the two men—the one with a shaved head—pointed his weapon at the guard. I couldn't make out what he was saying, but it was obvious he wasn't asking directions to the bug spray aisle.

As an afterthought, the security guard reached for his sidearm. The bald guy conked him on the noggin with the butt-end of his rifle. The guard fell hard on the concrete floor. His revolver skittered across the concrete without discharging.

I could hear people down by the checkout react as they became aware something was amiss. The registers normally in use, twenty-one and twenty-three, were at the other end of the store, a little farther from the action than I was. There was a murmur, but not the sound of full panic. Like me earlier, the people up front likely believed there was a logical explanation for whatever was happening.

The two big guys—obviously in charge—ordered the rest of their gang to spread out. The same man who had knocked the security guard down rushed toward the active checkout lanes while his partner went back to the entrance and appeared to be disabling the automatic doors. I saw the bald leader slap a cell phone out of the hand of a lady who was trying to get past him. He smashed it with his foot and pushed her to the floor.

Two of the shotgun-wielding gunmen came toward me but hung a quick left down the produce aisle. The second leader, who was similar to the first, except for his flat-top style haircut, came back carrying a duffle bag. He strode past the optometrist's office and nail boutique, which were both barricaded with a steel gate. When he arrived at the fortified two-teller branch of the local bank, he knelt down and started removing items from his bag.

Some words of wisdom that Parker dispensed at my permit class came to mind: "On television, they give the impression everyone is calm and cool when things go haywire, but that's not true. Everyone is terrified and wishes they were somewhere else. With proper training it's possible to force the butterflies in your stomach to fly in formation."

My butterflies were having mid-air collisions—making me nauseous. I had to do something quick. The two thugs would soon be at the end of the produce aisle, and the only way they could turn was right. This would put them in the meat aisle, looking directly at me if the opposite of luck should have it. Before I was able to unstick my feet, I saw the lady who had parked across from me running down the meat aisle. Seconds later, I witnessed the two exterminators giving chase.

The store suddenly erupted with sound. Calamity came from every direction. Apparently, the small army was now dealing with customers and employees who were discovering what all the commotion was about. I snatched a bottle out of the eight-pack and ran into the men's clothing department. I cut straight across, running unnoticed along the tall shelves that held bundles of socks and underwear.

I jammed the bottle into my jacket pocket and slid my right hand under the jacket and placed it on my weapon, which I feared may be useless to me, with the amount of firepower I was up against. I kept the gun in the holster. I would rather be captured like everyone else than get into a battle with so many armed men. I worried that being spotted with the gun would get me killed. I envisioned them at their murder trial, claiming they acted in self-defense.

I wasn't ready to surrender. Not until I knew it was wise to do so. So far, they had only injured the guard. If no one else got hurt, I would ditch the gun and raise my hands. I stood beside a tall rolling step ladder with an Employees Only placard. It was the kind used to reach the top shelves.

One of the men shouted from what sounded like the electronics department, or possibly sporting goods. Then a sound shook me to the core: a gunshot reverberating through the building. I guessed it was a shotgun, but I'd never heard *any* gun fired indoors. The shot was followed by an anguished moan that soon faded. The robbers weren't just using their weapons to frighten people into submission. Surrender was no longer an option.

Searching for a place to hide, I spotted a circular rack with nylon running jackets hanging from the top bar and matching pants on the lower. It was tall enough to hide me, but I decided to try for something more bulletproof, or at least something that would not show my feet sticking out the bottom. It was just a matter of time before someone came through to flush the stragglers.

I turned the corner into the big and tall section and spotted a fitting room. It was in a corner, just beyond a red I-beam holding up the roof, just like in the building I worked in. I tried to turn the knob, but it was locked, possibly off-limits to shoppers at this late hour. I wouldn't know. My approach to buying clothes was to make my best guess on size and return anything unwearable. But this wasn't an ideal location anyway. The room, with a flimsy slatted door, would leave me cornered. But I might've ducked in for a quick minute to contact the police—a brilliant idea that just came to me.

I hid behind the I-beam to sort things out before I sent the call. I couldn't stop thinking there was a logical explanation for all of this. Like they were filming a movie, and I was the only unsuspecting person with live ammunition. I knew it wasn't true, but thanks to boatloads of previous experience, I had a fear of doing something stupid. This definitely wasn't some kind of undercover bust. The police wouldn't assault the old guy in uniform. The logical explanation was either robbery or terrorism. And these guys didn't look like jihadists.

I put my back against the beam and slid down until I was sitting on the floor. I wasn't sure if it was hunger or fear making my hands tremble as I twisted off the Gatorade cap. I took a long swig, unaware until now that my throat was parched, like when I used to wake up from a weekend bender.

I flipped open my phone and powered it on. I always kept it powered down at work; a fully charged battery would have been dead in a couple of hours, searching for a signal. I should have called the police when the people in the van were acting suspiciously, yet I hesitated even now. I worried I would somehow embarrass myself enough to get on one of those shows where people do something dumb, and the whole country finds out. Not exactly the funny persona I was going for.

I couldn't remember when I'd last charged my phone. It definitely wasn't plugged in this morning when I grabbed it. I recalled talking to Suzy at lunch. If the battery were run down then, I would have heard the chirp. I rarely charged it until it reminded me to. I wrapped my fingers around the phone, unsuccessfully trying to muffle the default ditty that played when it booted up. I studied the screen, expecting to see the low battery message. Instead, I saw the device's typically green light, blinking red.

I raised my head to view the tiny screen through the bottom of my bifocals. The "No Service" message was on the display. But that didn't make sense because I'd phoned Suzy from inside this store the previous week. I had the bright idea to wake her when I realized I lost my shopping list. That was the reason she'd started putting the list in my wallet.

I must be standing in a dead spot. I fought the urge to think the criminals were jamming the cell towers in the area. I had to keep reality and television separate in my mind. Something I often had a problem with, according to my wife. I clicked the phone's side volume button until it buzzed in vibrate mode. I noted the charge level at 20 percent, then powered it down. I was pleasantly surprised when the phone vibrated at shutdown, instead of playing the usual xylophone music.

Suzy told me she planned to get up at six o'clock to work a few hours before leaving for our trip. If I weren't lying in bed next to her by then, her first response would be to call me. She wouldn't panic yet.

In the past, I'd volunteered to stay over at work—even when I had plans the next day. She *would* panic when she turned on the TV and saw news-chopper video, likely to be broadcast by then, with my truck in the parking lot.

I put the bottle in my coat pocket and stood. My knees were stiff from exercising and keeping up with the assembly line all night. I peeked out from the I-beam. Shelves filled with husky-sized jeans blocked most of my view. I could see the tops of several heads moving along the aisle on the other side. According to my watch, I entered the store less than fifteen minutes earlier. Time was running even slower than it did at work.

I knelt down again, the backs of my legs cramping from the leg presses. Thank goodness I hadn't gone downstairs to do squats with a couple of hundred pounds on my back. I put the phone in my pocket and listened as someone in the aisle gathered his posse.

"You two—get over here—*now*."

I then heard what sounded like cheap plastic gym shoes clapping on the floor. I was reminded of the cool kids in P.E. class who wore Converse, calling my discount-store sneakers "slippery slides," which gave an accurate description of what I did on the basketball court.

"How much do we have secured?" the same voice barked. I guessed it was one of the big guys I'd seen earlier.

A different voice jumped in nervously, almost stuttering, "We cleared the whole store, Bear. We rounded up everybody and copped their cell phones."

"I haven't seen the guy who walked in ahead of us. Looked like a cop. Go find him—now."

"Yes sir," both replied, clip-clapping away.

I stood and drew my weapon. I tugged the slide back far enough to see brass reflect the overhead light. I was glad Parker returned my weapon with a round chambered. Impossible to fire unintentionally, Glock designs their triggers without a traditional safety mechanism. The sound of my own breathing seemed loud to me. Racking a bullet into the tube would have been like yelling, "Here I am, and I have a gun."

It wouldn't be long until the exterminators searched my area of the store. I needed to hide in a department they had already cleared. There had to be a place in sporting goods or automotive where I could safely wait for the police to figure out something was wrong. I pictured myself crouched down inside a stack of tires, with a half-dozen people shooting into them. I would be the proverbial fish in a barrel.

Chapter 16

I limped a few steps until my knees began working properly again. I raised my weapon in the two-handed FBI stance, with my trigger finger running alongside the trigger guard. I recalled being schooled on that. Parker gave us our instructions, and we pointed our weapons toward the targets, waiting for the order to begin firing. Speaking through the bullhorn, he blared, "Taylor, get your finger off that trigger until I give permission to fire." I wanted to protest that it was okay to do so with the gun pointed down range. But instead I replied, "Yes, sir" and shifted my finger to the side of the trigger, as we were instructed an hour earlier in the classroom.

I stayed low, ducking behind display racks as I cut diagonally across the store in the general direction of the sporting goods department. That section of the store was calling out to me, but I couldn't think of any particular place to hide. I changed course, turning toward the rear wall. I thought it would be a less-dangerous route than traversing across wide-open spaces. I stopped short of the aisle bordering the clothing department. Hiding behind a rack of women's bathrobes, I couldn't work up the nerve to cross the aisle. Walking around with a gun in my hands made me think it wouldn't be long until I was forced to use it.

I considered holstering the Glock, but the voice of Parker was telling me to keep my weapon out and defend myself. Not that he or Sandy ever instructed what to do in this type of situation. I figured the robbers were through taking prisoners. They had already wounded, likely killed, one person. Two, if you count the assault on the security guard. I doubted they would be civil if I dropped the gun and surrendered.

Only on television, I reminded myself.

I aimed the weapon low and took long, quick strides across the aisle—like the "Keep on Truckin" guy with a gun in his hands. I proceeded down a narrow aisle, lined on both sides with women's dress shoes. Reaching the back wall, I sat down in the fitting chair and listened for clues that someone had seen me. I realized I was in plain view of anyone gazing from either side of me. I had to consciously defend against believing the situation was hopeless.

I visualized the police notifying Suzy I had been killed while attempting to fill her shopping list. Action seemed better than dwelling on worst-case outcomes. I continued along the back wall in the direction of that rubber fish barrel. Approaching the merchandise return counter and restrooms, recessed midway down the wall, I thought I'd discovered the perfect location to take cover but quickly nixed the idea. Seeking relief one night, I came there drawn by the large restroom sign. I was disappointed to find a handwritten note on each of the metal doors, indicating the facilities were closed after 10:00 p.m. The padlock hanging below each hasp had told me it was more than a suggestion.

I considered hiding behind the return counter, but that would be one place they would expect me to go. Also there would be nowhere to run, and the plywood construction wouldn't stop a bullet. I stalled, building up the courage to pass by. Moving on, I gazed to the right to ensure no one was in the aisle that dead-ended there. I raised the pistol and swiveled left, suddenly aware that someone could already be in there hunting for me.

I gave the area a quick examination as I went by. I was looking for an exit or a storage room I could lock from the inside. There was nothing. From my angle I could see one of the bathroom doors and the lock I expected but hoped someone had forgotten tonight.

I spooked when someone began shouting. The sound of my running shoes against the concrete floor seemed as loud as stampeding elephants to my ears. As I approached the first row of electronic merchandise, I noticed a display with cell phone accessories. I remembered stopping in to buy a charger for my phone. The one that came with it only functioned correctly if I held the plug at a certain angle. Unable to locate the one I needed, I asked someone stocking shelves for assistance. She looked at my phone and told me they no longer carried accessories for that model. I was peeved, but went home and performed surgery on the connector, and it has worked fine since. With my battery nearly toast, I was mad all over again.

I turned on my phone to check for service. If I could tell the police what was happening, maybe they could end the confrontation before I made a fatal mistake. The phone indicated a weak signal. I was grateful but thought it strange my phone didn't have better service. Not only had I once completed a call from the store, I remembered seeing people use their phones on those rare occasions when I stopped in before work.

After my heart surgery, Suzy insisted I get a phone, and I went with the cheapest deal—refusing to pay extra for call waiting, voice mail, or text messaging. Most of my co-workers got better reception than I did at the plant. This huge structure was just like the factory, except that it was filled with products mostly manufactured in China and did not roll out American cars at a rate of one per minute.

I decided to notify the police before moving on. My hands started shaking as I relived the events I was about to report. A concept I remembered from my training came to mind; be a reliable witness. You don't draw your weapon to make a citizen's arrest because someone jaywalks. Observe, and if the situation warrants, pass your concerns on to the authorities. Doing so is much safer and less likely to cause legal problems for you. I could hear activity: loud voices, banging and clanging up front. But I could only guess what the criminals were up to.

Holding the phone in one hand and the gun in the other, I recalled something else taught in my permit class. The scenario Parker called "talking on the gun while aiming the phone." I laid my Glock on the shelf. He lived by the same motto that hung over the entrance to my plant: All accidents are preventable.

I punched in 9-1-1 and hit send, rehearsing my lines as the call went through. My anxiety level was high. It felt like the stage fright I experienced before going on stage. The call was slow to connect, likely due to the weak signal. The ring sounded like a rotary phone from my childhood.

"9-1-1 operator; please state the nature of your emergency," the female voice crackled.

"I'm in the Columbia SaveMart. There is a robbery in progress by nine men armed with shotguns and military rifles. They have taken everyone else hostage and may be attempting to break into the bank."

"Standby," she responded without emotion, like she heard this stuff all the time. After a few long moments, she came back, "I have notified the police. Please give me your name, address, and home telephone number."

I gave her the information, instead of arguing about the importance of where I lived, when I was currently forty miles away. I guessed this was the drill used on callers they deemed crackpots. I worried somebody would dial my house. I wanted to be the one to break the news to my wife after I was safely outside.

The operator was in the process of asking me where exactly in the store I was situated when something exploded. It felt like I'd jumped three feet in the air, before cowering to the floor. I convinced myself the blast came from the bank. I was in a daze, broken by the chatter coming out of my phone. Before the phone was halfway to my ear, I heard the operator yelling for me to respond.

"Hello, can you hear me now?" I smarted off, remembering the commercial.

"Are you okay? What happened? Was that an explosion?" The operator shouted, going off script.

"Someone just blew open the bank vault. I'll call you back," I said, then powered down the phone.

I'd be on a "don't call me, I'll call you" basis until further notice. I slid the phone into my pocket, snatched my gun, and ran all the way to sporting goods. Knowing that law enforcement was on their way gave me confidence things would turn out well, for me at least. I had no idea what the police would do, but I planned to be hunkered down when they did it.

I probably knew this department better than most of the employees. I was either familiar with, or the proud owner of most of the products sold. I needed to get out of sight, preferably behind something that could stop bullets. *A large, well-concealed rock to crawl under would suit me just fine right now.*

I doubted any such place existed. There were only a half dozen aisles until I reached the block wall at the far side of automotive. I advanced, stopping at the end of each aisle to take cover. I expected the police to bust in and apprehend the robbers, but I feared the explosion would force a more tactical operation. I hoped this didn't turn into a SaveMart version of *Dog Day Afternoon*.

Chapter 17

Three rows into sporting goods, I gazed past the department's checkout station, watching for movement in the aisle beyond it. I noted the tall vertical cabinet where six or seven long guns and some archery equipment were showcased. I preferred the old-school gun displays, with long guns lined along a wall behind the counter. The SaveMart version was a glass pillar that held half as many firearms. The thing I did like was my ability to get close enough to fog up the glass. Something I had done early one morning, straining to read the fine print on an over-under shotgun I was jonesing for.

The sight of the firearms was alluring this morning as well. I could almost hear them calling my name. I resisted the temptation. Even if I had all those guns loaded with ammunition, I couldn't possibly take on the small army robbing the store. I had one weapon already that I wasn't in a hurry to use. I'd stick with my strategy and look for a hole to crawl in.

During late-night shopping forays, I typically perused the high-end products in the gun cabinet and the glass case below the counter. I never bought any of those items, because none, I was told, were available to purchase before 8 a.m. Good thing too, my wife would likely get agitated if I stopped for groceries and came home with milk, bread, and a five-hundred–dollar shotgun.

I was about to move on when something caught my eye. Between me and the counter, there was a wooden pallet loaded with stock waiting to be put away. Sticking out from the corner of the pallet was a shoe. My first instinct was to think someone was hiding there. I studied for clues. The shoe definitely wasn't a product sold here. I could see some mileage on the sole. Also, it wasn't a hunting boot, which was the only type of footwear sold in this department.

This was the kind of shoe my father had worn. Service Oxford was the name used in catalogs. Like Joe wore, without the rippled sole. They were built for standing on concrete for long periods. This was a workingman's shoe—most likely an older workingman. I had recently tried on a pair but couldn't get past the looks. I knew one day the comfort, durability, and protection would win me over.

True to my nature, I became curious. I would have to solve this puzzle, and *then* hightail it to automotive. I raised my gun and impressed myself with the quality of the Modern Weaver stance I found myself in. I then advanced in perfect Jack Bauer style.

I swept my gun across the aisle in front of the sales counter as I inched forward, expecting a gunman to pass by any second. I swung wide as I approached the pallet and saw part of a white sock and then a blue polyester pant leg. Moving forward, I noticed blood on the floor and a SaveMart nametag pinned to the chest of a man wearing a blue smock. I was about to put the pieces together when something made me scream.

Actually, it was more of a yelp. This explosion wasn't as loud as the first one. This one sounded smaller, or farther away. I figured the police were blasting through the door, and I knelt down behind the gun cabinet. Seconds later, one of the exterminators ran past, coming from the automotive department. I assumed all of them were now heading up front to deal with the police.

I studied the dead employee. Ed had been hit in the chest at close range. I stood and noticed a large ring of keys dangling below the key in the lock. I now understood why he got killed. In the middle of an armed robbery, he attempted to grab a weapon and make war with them.

Not a great idea for a lot of reasons. The biggest one in my mind, none of the firearms were loaded. The ammunition was in a separate locked case behind the counter. I appropriated the keys, like the lock would stop anyone who needed additional weapons, and ran to the back wall. I promised myself I wouldn't commit the same blunder Ed had. I would stay out of sight until the police took control of the situation. And if I found a way to leave the building, even better.

For now, I just needed to get out of sight. Surveying the immediate area, I saw no prospects. Walking on, a singing deer nearly gave me a coronary: the motion-activated trophy buck began a chorus of "On the Road Again." On another night, I had fallen in love with this novelty item. The fake deer head had startled me then as well, but I had almost convinced myself Suzy would think the $300 item was well worth the money.

Looking down the back wall, I noticed a black plastic toolbox like the one I had in the bed of my truck. It was large enough to curl up in, but the resemblance to a coffin was a deal breaker. I heard someone running and hid behind flotation devices stacked on an end-of-aisle shelf. This sounded like one of the jackbooted leaders—the big hombres carrying the automatic weapons. The pounding footsteps came closer, down the aisle in front of the sales counter.

I was afraid the gunman would turn left and spot me cowering there. Along the back wall behind me, there was a two-tier display of camouflage clothing on hangers. The top rod held out-of-season insulated coveralls; the lower tier held matching jackets. I spread the garments apart to discover more space behind the clothing than I expected. I climbed over the lower bar and peeked down the row of merchandise in front of me. I saw the guy with a flattop run by, heading toward automotive. He had a milk crate in one hand and a rifle in the other. Metallic gizmos swung from his bulletproof vest as he ran.

I pulled the clothing together like drapes, and felt well concealed when I ducked down a bit. I had the perfect back-row seat to watch the excitement unfold. I didn't plan to come out until uniformed police hollered my name.

After a few minutes my adrenaline boost died. I felt tired and hungry. I holstered my weapon and took a long drink from the bottle that had been sloshing around my jacket pocket. That caused the crooning deer to go into his rendition of Rawhide. My whole body jerked and a few drops of red liquid spilled down my chin. His life support was plugged into an outlet on the wall behind me, so I pulled the plug. I tossed the empty bottle in the far corner, wishing I had grabbed the ham-and-cheese croissants.

Since the second explosion, I hadn't heard anything that sounded like the police were storming the doors. I needed to know what they were doing to rescue us. I turned on my phone and noted the time.

Suzy would be rolling into her office in a couple of hours—unless the police had already given her a wake-up call.

My phone indicated a weak signal. The bad news was, the charge indicator showed only 15 percent remaining. I wasn't surprised. This phone was old and didn't hold a charge long under any circumstances. I punched in 9-1-1 and hoped I wouldn't have to repeat my entire personal history to a different operator.

One ring later, a gruff male voice answered, "Standby for transfer."

Finally, someone is taking me seriously, I thought, my hands trembling again. Three rings later, a different voice came on.

"Captain Lewis here. Who I am I speaking with?"

"Steve Taylor," I whispered, looking out to see if anyone was within earshot.

"Are you inside the store?"

"Yes, I called earlier," I replied with a tremor in my voice that sounded like I was talking into a fan.

"Where do you live?"

"Centerville," I said after clearing my throat. I didn't know if he was verifying I was the person who called before, or testing to see if I kept my story straight.

"I was just about to call your house," the captain said, lightening his tone.

"Feel free. I'd rather my wife got it from you, then seeing it on TV."

"She knew you'd be in the store?"

"Yeah, but she wasn't expecting me to take all night."

"Where are you right now?" the captain asked, unfazed by my sarcasm.

"I'm hiding in sporting goods, but I'm going to find a way out of here. The leaders are two big guys. One has a shaved head, and the other has a flattop," I said, my voice straining again.

"Has anyone been hurt as far as you know?"

"Two, the security guard was knocked out, and a guy named Ed was shot and killed when he tried to arm himself. My phone's battery is near dead. When are you guys gonna come in and rescue us?"

"It may take a while. Whoever is robbing the store set off Fourth of July fireworks a day early as we rolled in. They blew up several cars in the parking lot."

I understood now why the van stopped by the cars in the parking lot. The criminals were putting some kind of explosive device under the parked vehicles as a diversion, in the event police came before they could escape. Like that would make them turn around and return to the station.

"I saw them out there, but I had no idea what they were up to."

"I requested assistance from Nashville PD after your first call—and a second call from someone in the parking lot. They're dispatching a SWAT team and bomb squad. They'll take command of the scene when they arrive."

"I've got to go. My phone is dying."

"All right, but stay put. If you're able, call 9-1-1. They'll patch you through to whoever is in charge."

"Don't forget to call my wife and tell her I'm fine."

"You want me to lie to her."

"No, make it the truth."

Chapter 18

I squatted down on my haunches with my back against the wall. I was tired, and my legs ached. My hamstrings soon began cramping again. I stood and peered over the top bar. The first things to catch my eye were the buoyant marine cushions I'd taken cover behind. I was tempted to grab one but decided to stick it out for now. I was finally out of sight and even one of those so-called lifesavers couldn't inspire me to move.

Looking down the aisle to the left of the cushions, I spotted an item that would function much better; an ingenious device I purchased months earlier. Necessity apparently inspired someone to fasten a pad—probably a boat cushion—on top of a five-gallon bucket. Realizing the potential, the individual marketed this simple product and probably made a fortune. Painted green, these ordinary five-gallon buckets had a padded swivel lid that snapped on top.

I needed the seat. I was exhausted, and the thin metal floor underneath my feet buckled loudly whenever I shifted my weight. Sitting down, I could wait patiently for as long as it took the police to resolve this. If I was risking my life to grab the seat, I might as well snag a few additional items while I was out there. I didn't intend to make a grocery run, but if there was anything useful between that bucket and my new home, I would be taking it. I finally had the hiding place I was searching for, and now I was going out to do a little shopping.

The lids and buckets were in separate stacks. The pails were compressed together in space-saving fashion. I holstered the Glock and pulled at the top one, but they were stuck together like the shopping carts had been earlier. I wanted to shake the stack until the one I clenched broke free, but I calmed myself and flipped the pile, allowing me to slide one off without effort.

A camo head stocking caught my eye as I turned back. These were designed for turkey hunters, and I thought it might be useful if I continued to peek over the top bar. I recognized this was impulsive, like the lip balm and gum I tended to snatch at the checkout line, but I threw it in the bucket and headed back.

I parted the longer garments using the bucket and set it beside the metal divider to my right. I grabbed one of the boat cushions and tossed the plastic wrapper into one of the twelve-pack coolers on a shelf next door, then positioned the cushion on the seat. Once I was in, I shut the curtains and unholstered my weapon. I slid my back down the divider and sat down. The recliner Suzy bought me for Christmas never felt so comfortable.

I heard loud voices coming from the exterminators at the front of the building. It appeared they had bigger concerns than locating me. I gently laid the pistol at my feet and savored my first moment of relaxation in many hours. I leaned against the divider and closed my eyes, knowing what would happen next.

Chapter 19

4:00 a.m. Friday

"What time is it?" Lieutenant Tom Parker answered the landline beside his bed without opening his eyes, already sure who was calling and what she wanted.

"Sun will be up in a couple of hours. How's your day going so far?" the night shift captain, Jennifer Sanders said.

Parker turned on his bedside lamp and forced his eyes open. "Stayed up late watching an old movie. I planned to sleep in so we'd be on the same schedule,"

"Officially your—our—vacation already started, and Sanchez is on call, but I thought you'd want this one."

"I always knew you'd be the one to get cold feet."

"Oh, we're still picking up my folks *and* doing the deed. But first, I need you to go take care of a problem just south of here."

"Give me the details," Parker said, awake enough now to hear why his SWAT team was activated.

"We got a request from Columbia PD. Seems a crew went in to rob the SaveMart and possibly a bank this morning."

"They're still in there?" Parker asked, trying to step into his jumpsuit one-handed.

"Yeah, a nine-man crew and I'm guessing fifteen to twenty civilians they've taken hostage," she replied.

"How bad did it get before they requested assistance?" Parker asked.

"It's Columbia, Tom, not Mayberry. Captain Lewis knew right off they weren't dealing with amateurs."

"Yeah, kinda sounds like somebody we know. Hit my cell in five minutes. You can fill in the rest on my way in."

Chapter 20

The walk from Jennifer's office to SWAT headquarters took exactly four minutes. She made this walk several times a week at the end of her shift in order to visit Parker. Being on different shifts made their relationship difficult, but both were intent on making it work. She stepped out through the exit nearest his office, took out her phone, and called him.

"How's your breakfast, Parker? I've heard it's the most important meal of the day." She stood on the sidewalk in front of the parking lot and pictured him trying to wash down a week-old donut with yesterday's coffee.

"Great. Eggs Benedict with a little garnish on the side of the plate. But not as tasty as what you'll be making every morning."

She rolled her eyes. "Yeah, right. Listen, someone inside called 9-1-1 shortly after the store was hit. The operator was suspicious until something exploded in the background. A minute later, another man—hysterical as all get-out—called from the parking lot."

"And now they believe."

"Local PD and sheriff's deputies will secure the area until you arrive."

"Any bodies yet?" Parker asked.

"Yeah, it appears one of the employees got in the way, according to the caller."

"What kind of weapons?"

"Shotguns and maybe M-16s," Jennifer said, knowing he'd be thinking what she was thinking.

"So, we do know who it is."

"Probably. The caller described two of them. If it *is* Clarence Jenkins, he's shaving his head now. And it looks like his brother isn't merely setting up the explosives. Someone fitting his description is in there as well," she said, pacing a ten-foot section of the sidewalk in front of the parking lot.

"He was a Navy guy, wasn't he?"

"Leave it alone, Parker," Jennifer said, clenching her jaw. "He washed out of the Navy, remember. He'd be a general by now if he'd been in the Corp." Jennifer was proud to have been an officer in the Navy, and she wasn't letting him get to her today. Then and now, they were on the same side.

He sighed. "I'm a couple of blocks out. Anybody there yet?"

"Everyone on duty tonight. The rest were sleeping, but they know the drill. I suppose this *does* change our plans for the weekend." She stood next to his assigned parking space in wait of his arrival.

"Meet me in Columbia. We'll get one of your judge friends to stop by and say the magic words. I've always wondered how you'd look in a SWAT jumpsuit."

"I was saving that for the honeymoon," she said. "And you know I only come out for the victory speech after you save the day . . . and what about my parents?"

"Bring them along. We'll have the reception on the bus," Parker said through his open car window as he parked beside her.

"Thanks, but no." Soon as she hung up the phone, it rang. "Sanders," she said.

She listened as the Captain on duty in Columbia updated her on the situation there.

"Thanks," she told him, deeply concerned that this was turning out to be a lot more serious than a robbery. She turned to Parker. "They blew up some cars in the parking lot as the police arrived . . . apparently with a remote control."

Jennifer watched Parker digest this new information.

"Sounds kind of showy for our guys."

That's how he describes someone blowing up cars? Jennifer thought, as she headed into the building, all but jogging at this point. "Maybe it's the Mafia, Tom; they've been blowing up cars since the first one rolled off the assembly line. I checked with the Feds. They're still watching his mother's house in Nashville and haven't seen anything to indicate he's back in town."

"Did you speak to Powell?" Parker said, keeping pace.

"Not yet. I hear that Special Agent Powell has been spending time in Virginia teaching classes since you last worked with him. I'm sure he'll want to be involved once we verify who's in there. I failed to mention to the Feds that 'number seven' on their most-wanted list might be involved, but the bank is enough to bring them in. You should have command unless they decide to pull rank on you."

"I'm thinking they won't be so eager this go round—unlike you, my darling."

"Not for much longer, Lieutenant."

"Yeah, I got the memo, Captain. I wonder who'll wear the pants in this family when you don't outrank me," he said.

She swiped her identification and held the door for him. "You will, dear—I insist," she said with a laugh.

They entered the locker room. The men were there, some milling about, others suiting up.

"Listen up. We've got a tough assignment this morning—botched robbery with hostages," Parker told them.

Jennifer stood beside him, feeling proud that they didn't bat an eye at the female captain's presence.

"As soon as everyone gets here, we'll shove off. I'll brief on the way. I estimate departure in fifteen," he said, and they headed for his office.

"Did you notify our bomb squad?" he asked, opening the door.

"Yes," Jennifer said. "Most of their personnel and equipment ought to arrive shortly after you get there. Some of the larger pieces are on standby." She leaned on his desk, pretending not to be nervous that her fiancé was going into battle with a psycho killer.

"Good, what else?" Parker said, opening his locker and pulling out his headset and radio, then putting in new batteries.

"There's a van parked in front—most likely the perps'—probably stolen. Columbia police tried to get back to the person who called from inside, but his phone is either dead or turned off. I texted the number, but it came back undeliverable. I'll send the number to your phone."

"Can we access the security cameras?" Parker asked.

"No, I talked to the company's security chief. The manager on duty has control."

"I hope the locals stay calm until I get there," Parker said.

"You're pretty sure *it is* Clarence Jenkins, aren't you?" she said, rising from the desk and walking over to him.

"Fits his M.O. for the most part. And he was bound to resurface. Clarence was raised here, has a lot of connections, most of them ex-cons. I need to stop him before he kills anyone else," Parker said, studying her reaction.

"Don't you get hurt over there, Lieutenant. That's an order." She looked him in the eye, lingering for a serious moment.

"Ma'am, yes Ma'am," he said.

She left the room, walking at a brisk pace to her section of the building.

Chapter 21

8:00 a.m. Friday

Loud snoring woke me—my own. Several moments passed before I knew where I was and how I got there. My mouth was parched, and I now craved whatever kind of soda was stocked in the small refrigerator beside the gun display. Something else was troubling me, but I tried to ignore the last thing that would come to mind if I had to list everything that could possibly give me grief. I checked my watch. The urge was hours ahead of schedule, but it felt like my morning ritual couldn't tell time.

The situation soon became quite urgent. This was something you didn't see on television. All the tight jams MacGyver and Jack Bauer found themselves in, I couldn't remember either needing to discreetly take a dump. I stood, hoping to silence the call of nature. I was reminded of the gun by the weight of it against my foot. I reached down and retrieved it. I feared moving too quickly would lead to an accident—not in any way involving the gun.

I powered up my phone, planning to call Lewis for any suggestions he might have on how to deal with this predicament. The charge meter on my phone showed what I expected: 10 percent and the low battery message. I thought for a second, then pressed the button until the phone went dark. Even with a full charge, I'm not sure I would have bothered the Columbia Police Department for guidance.

The logical decision would be to use my new bucket. I was almost certain it wasn't airtight, even with the lid snapped on. My intuition told me this wouldn't be one of those days I could get away with that. Someone walking by would surely notice.

The urge became intense. I would have to do something soon— real soon. I decided to use the bucket and then exchange it for a new one. I needed something to take care of the paperwork. I thought about the RV toilet paper in the camping section, but I searched my pockets first to check for anything useful. My shopping list wasn't enough for the task. I certainly wasn't using my notepad, even if there were enough empty pages to do the job. One of the sets of keys gave me an idea for another, if not better, way to deal with my predicament.

Ed's keys made me think of a solution my television hero, Angus MacGyver, would have considered too easy. Or maybe he wouldn't have been stupid and taken such unnecessary risk—assuming he ever had this kind of real-life problems to deal with. I opted to retrace my previous steps and see if any of the keys would unlock the restroom.

This was not unprecedented for me. I used this approach once, in a somewhat similar circumstance. While camping in the woods with my buddies during a deer-hunting trip in Michigan, I got in my truck one day and drove five miles into town to use the indoor facilities at the gas station. I climbed out of my tree stand and walked past my friends, most of them already in camp because their deer were hanging on the big oak tree. If I had pulled that stunt on opening morning, someone would have likely shot and tagged me. That night at the campfire, my hunting companions rode me hard.

I figured there was a fifty-fifty chance one of the keys would fit the padlock. As a backup plan, I would use the not-so-private facilities behind the merchandise return counter. I would let the robbers take credit for the untidiness—assuming the police didn't find my bullet-riddled body with my pants down.

As I hurried along the back wall, I was hit by the stupidity of my strategy. I kept moving forward because it was farther to go back. I had an eerie feeling I was being watched. *Too much television*, I reassured myself. Common sense told me these weren't the kind of people who would sit back and watch. I would know when someone spotted me.

I held the Glock with two hands as I neared the alcove. I stuck my head out from behind a rack of ladies purses and scanned for any sign of the gunmen. Passing through the archway, my legs shook so hard I could barely walk. I wasn't crazy about my strategy, but I was committed to it. My options were to either take care of business here or shop for new clothes.

I holstered my weapon to locate the correct key and remove the padlock. I inspected the bottom of the lock to determine which of the keys would get me out of sight the quickest. My instincts told me it was one of the thick and short keys, like the one for my locker at work. I chose the most likely and it fit perfectly, but wouldn't turn, not even when I wiggled it furiously.

I gave up on my theory, trying every key, holding the keys that had failed to one side with my trembling fingers. The next-to-last key turned, and the lock popped open. I was on the verge of a panic attack, which was the least of my problems at the moment.

The door unstuck when I nudged it with my shoulder. The hinges needed lubrication, but slow movements kept the screech to a minimum. The men's room was pitch dark, and my first swipe on the wall found nothing. I'm not usually afraid of the dark, but my imagination painted images far worse than the monsters in my childhood closet.

I opened the door wide and used outside light to locate the switch on the opposite wall, glad it wasn't the kind you needed a key to operate. I flipped on the light and headed for the sink. I scooped water into my mouth and then entered the first of two stalls, leaving the handicap stall for one of the criminals who might have been maimed or dismembered during a previous heist.

The truth was, since meeting Suzy I became enlightened about disability issues. Suzy told me how frustrating it was to enter a public lavatory and find an able-bodied person using the only stall she could get her wheelchair into. I was now in the habit of leaving the larger stall vacant, sometimes waiting a few minutes—even at work—where I'd never seen anyone using a wheelchair.

I entered the stall and removed the holstered gun. I laid it down on the floor because there was nothing else flat. The industrial-style toilet had no tank, which would have made a perfect temporary place to lay my weapon. The toilet paper dispenser wasn't big enough and had rounded corners. I yanked my shorts down, and thanks to the urgency and my high-fiber diet, completed the job in under a minute—including the paperwork. I rose to my feet, relieved in more ways than one to have *that* task completed. I hitched up my shorts, and cinched my belt, debating whether to flush or to simply leave.

I heard noises outside the door. It was the clink that guns and ammunition make when you walk with them. There was a pause, and then the door began to squeak. I jammed the holster on my belt and raised the toilet seat. I stood on the porcelain and peeked over the partition. I thought most people would look under the stall dividers to see which, if any, were occupied. I doubted they would suspect it was me.

What kind of fool corners himself in a bathroom when nine armed men are searching for him?

I drew my gun as the muzzle cleared the doorway. I ducked down before I could observe who was carrying the weapon, but I didn't think whoever it was expected me to be in there, since the barrel was pointed at the floor. I thought over my options: stand and surrender, hoping the startled gunman didn't blast a hole in the metal partition in front of me, or lock the door and pray he went to the other stall without attempting conversation. Neither played out well in my mind.

When I heard the door close, I rose quickly, swinging my weapon across the top of the stall and pointing it at him. My years of television-viewing experience told me I must order the man to drop his weapon. Parker and Sandy both taught this as well. I didn't think it was in my best interest to yell something that would make him think I was the police. Instead, I kept silent, aiming at the middle of his chest. The criminal looked up and wheeled his weapon at me.

I fired five rounds, all landing center mass—as Parker had referred to it on a silhouette target. His gun went off as he fell backward, blowing a hole in the ceiling tile directly above him. Seemingly in slow motion, the exterminator sprawled out on the floor. The gun fell toward me, the end of the barrel pointing in my direction as gravity brought it down, but I was more concerned about his comrades coming to investigate.

I hopped off the commode, my ears ringing, and tore out of the stall. I aimed my weapon at the intruder in case he still had some fight left in him. I watched him for signs of movement and decided only cowboys in a Western recovered from such wounds. This real-life outlaw was dead. I holstered my gun and took a deep breath before I confiscated the shotgun, ejected the spent shell, and slammed a fresh one into the chamber. I was well acquainted with this type of firearm. I'd hunted pheasant and rabbits with a pump gun when I was a teenager. My parents gave me a similar model on my sixteenth birthday.

I verified the weapon was hot, then clicked the button to make it safe. I tilted the shotgun until I saw brass, telling me there was at least one shell remaining. I assumed there were four, but I would have to pump all the shells out and count them to know for sure.

I ran back down the aisle as quickly as my wobbly legs would allow. As I reached electronics, I ducked out of sight when I heard a small stampede behind me. I looked back and saw several men run toward the restrooms. After they passed by, I got back in the aisle and ran. Standing next to the singing deer, I slipped the shotgun through the curtain and leaned it in the corner. I wanted to climb in but remembered I used five of the twenty 9mm rounds I brought with me, and I had one less round in the scattergun than it could hold. I needed ammunition and twelve-gauge shells were just around the corner.

It was risky, with all the commotion, but I backtracked one aisle and studied the various brands and sizes of shotgun shells—the only ammunition not under lock and key. I grabbed four boxes of twelve-gauge and lined them down my arm.

On impulse, seeing the two small refrigerators and knowing one contained liquid refreshment, I went over to get one. I stepped across Ed to shorten the distance and reached into the refrigerator—the one that didn't contain glow-in-the-dark night crawlers from Canada—and removed a diet soda.

Chapter 22

Satisfied I had everything I needed for the moment, I stepped into my hideout, lined the ammunition against the wall, and sat down. My heart was pounding. I could hear the clicks loud enough to count. In a quiet environment, I could easily calculate the rate my "bionic" heart—as I liked to call it—was beating.

I exchanged the half-empty magazine in my Glock for a full one. I took a long hit off the soda, then another, draining the twenty-ounce bottle, reminding me of the way I had guzzled beer before I discovered hard liquor. I heard the exterminators yelling as they ran through the store searching for me. I was now a giant blip on their radar. And that worried me. A lot. I did what I always do when I lose hope: I rediscovered my religion. My first spiritual quest came when I realized I was drinking myself to death. You don't come back from where I was on your own. But a few months of sobriety later, after the daily cravings dissipated, I lost that close relationship with my maker.

When I went into the hospital to have my defective aorta valve replaced with a mechanical one, I reestablished communication—no lukewarm Christians in a foxhole. I was on a first-name basis with God for a while after I got out of the hospital. Probably didn't hurt that a nurse, who my wife still met with occasionally for lunch, told Suzy that I'd acted strangely coming out of surgery. I was mumbling about how I needed to get back to the light. I couldn't remember having a near-death experience, but my heart had been on a table while doctors rebuilt it like a carburetor and a heart-lung machine kept me alive and breathing. That qualified as a close call in my book.

Every night since, lying in bed listening to the device in my chest, I remembered to say a prayer for my wife and I. Hiding behind a cloth wall, while dangerous criminals hunted me, stirred me to request help from above. The angels protecting me since I entered the store no longer felt sufficient. I asked their boss—Jesus Christ—to help out personally.

The search party was closing in. They began to holler threats—when we find you, we're going to kill you etc.—from across the aisle in housewares, hoping to spook me out of hiding. Peeking between garments, I considered making a run for it, before someone yanked my curtain open and blasted me. A scared pheasant flushes, leaving safe cover—the last thing they ever do. There was no better place to go anyway, so I sat there holding the Glock and waited for them.

I figured the police heard the shots and knew something had gone wrong. I doubted they could do anything to assist me, but I was mistaken. Before I got a glimpse of my pursuers the lights went out. There was total darkness for several seconds and then emergency backup lights kicked on throughout the building. The store lit up to about one-third the previous level, reminding me of camping at night when I was a kid. If you were close to the lantern, you were drowned in light, but any danger that lurked ten feet away was impossible to see.

Luckily, my hideout was in the shadows. I listened for clues as to what the police would do next. Perhaps something tactical. I heard no helicopters nor people running on the roof, not that I expected such a dramatic response. I wanted to let them know I was still alive, but chose to conserve my phone's remaining battery life. I thought about my wife, wondering if she was watching the news and had learned shots were fired. I wanted to call her and let her know I was okay, but I couldn't. In my current state, calling Suzy would only upset her and leave me without a lifeline.

If I had known the lights were going out, I would have picked up a flashlight. *I'm in a SaveMart for goodness sakes.* I had everything right here, just out of reach. I spread the top row of hangers open enough to let a glimmer of light in. I couldn't see any flashlight beams from the enemy. Maybe they didn't bring any. I took out my wife's shopping list to create a new one on the blank section at the bottom. I saw my wife's message on the back. She wouldn't have to worry about me getting a new DVD set.

Unless I came across a small TV/DVD combo in electronics.

There wasn't enough room on the paper for all the merchandise that came to mind. I pulled out my notepad and folded the top pages back to expose a clean sheet. I started making a list of every item I could possibly use. This was a brainstorming session. No idea was a bad idea.

The first thing on my list was a portable toilet. I added the quick-dissolving toilet paper and a jug of liquid sanitizer, while I was in the neighborhood. Then I scribbled down everything Rambo would have taken in the first movie if he were acquiring survival gear in a SaveMart instead of a small gun shop.

These items included a rifle, ammunition, knives, and the mono-vision night optics I knew to be located in the showcase below the cash register. No doubt I would not be able to get everything I wanted, but I could try. The ten feet of space I occupied would hold a lot of merchandise. I wouldn't require the toilet for anything solid for a while, but I underlined it. My pail could hold items not needed right away or often, like the extra ammo for my *Glock*, also underlined halfway down my list.

The things I might need in a hurry I could keep in a knapsack. I could grab it and run if I had to. I felt my eyelids get heavy, and I added five boat cushions to my list. With the one I already had, that would be enough to spread out on the floor and lay down.

I wish I had them right now. I drew the curtain together and leaned back.

I was about to doze off when I heard the cavalry shouting through a bullhorn. I assumed the police were demanding immediate surrender, though the blaring message was garbled where I sat. The reverberating communication reminded me of the voice of Charlie Brown's parents in the television specials of my youth. I expected a SWAT team to enter any moment. I kept the Glock ready in case any of the exterminators came seeking refuge.

Chapter 23

The police never crashed the doors. Hours later I heard screams and shouts from the front of the store, and I speculated the hostages now had guns pointed at their heads. Then I remembered that Joe, Ella, and no telling how many more of my co-workers were among those in jeopardy. I figured after a short time holding Ella captive, they would kick her loose, or at least tape her mouth shut. I knew I would.

Luckily, I wasn't one of the unfortunate ones in immediate danger. I was a captive, but I still had some freedoms. I also had better odds of surviving a police invasion than the hostages near the doors. I would have to play it smart if I wanted to see my wife again. She needed me, and I was determined to survive this nightmare.

The lights had begun to dim. This was perhaps more noticeable for me, behind the curtain, trying to open my phone. I needed information. The police had stopped blaring their demands, and the criminals had settled down as well. I wanted to know if it was the calm before the storm. The battery meter showed 8 percent. I called 9-1-1, and the operator told me to remain on the line. I waited anxiously, hoping for good news.

"Lieutenant Parker here—who is this?" the voice on the other end of the line barked.

Confused by the familiar voice and name, which I hadn't yet put a face to, I whispered, "Steve Taylor—is Captain Lewis there?"

"Steve, I told Lewis I recognized your name," Parker said, softening his growl. "I've been waiting for your call. What took so long?"

"It's complicated," I responded, finally figuring out who I was speaking to. "When are you guys gonna break down the door and arrest these thugs?" I asked.

"What happened in there? I wasn't sure you were still alive."

I hated to confess anything without a lawyer present, though I knew from Parker's classroom I was within my rights to protect myself.

"Just using those self-defense skills *you* taught me," I said, carefully choosing my words.

"I'm glad you were paying attention."

"My phone's about dead. The store doesn't sell a charger that fits my phone. I'm going to look for a way out of here," I said, throwing it out there again.

"Hang tight. The doors we can see through have what appears to be C-4 taped to them and some kind of motion sensor device wired to it. If they move, we think they'll blow. The perpetrators are threatening to kill all the hostages if we even *try* to come in. They're watching the exits to make sure we don't."

"I'll bet I can find a door that isn't booby-trapped. I'll leave it open, so you'll know which one to use."

"Those gunshots sounded like a 9mm. You wore your Glock in there?"

I thought about the scenario he described yesterday and got a déjà vu chill; something I seemed to experience more than most people.

"Yeah, I've got it. And you were right about those hollow points. They pack a punch."

"Glad I could be of service. I need *your* assistance now. You're the only hostage who doesn't have a gun in his face. That you are someone I know and trust is, well, you have no idea how valuable you are to me right now. You'd rather be home with that sweet wife you told me about, I get it. But I'd like you to help me out, be my eyes and ears in there."

I'm a sucker for someone in authority who asks for help. I couldn't say no, especially now that I had a relatively secure location to see and hear from.

"Yeah, I'll stick around, but I need you to do something for me."

"What's that, Steve?"

"Call my wife and tell her I'll be late. She's gotta be scared out of her mind."

"Lewis called her and explained things. I'll update her periodically when I have time. She sounds like quite a lady from what you told me yesterday."

"She really is. I have to get out of here in one piece . . . for her sake," I said, trying not to let my voice crack. Parker would likely tell me to man up if he heard me crying—even a little.

"I just got off the phone with their leader. He thinks he has *us* by the short hairs, so this could take a while."

"I heard them call somebody Bear. Sounded like he was the leader," I said, wanting to be helpful.

"Clarence Jenkins is what his mother named him. We believe his brother, Marvin, joined the team since I dealt with him last. Marvin likes to watch things explode. He got a Section Eight out of the Navy when they evaluated him for SEAL school. They picked an excellent night to hit the bank. The branch was scheduled to be open, cashing paychecks and doling out cash withdrawals. An armored car delivered nearly a million dollars just before it closed. They were expecting a heavy day with the holiday this weekend.

We suspect Clarence had inside information. From what we can see through the door, the rest of his gang look like a bunch of ex-cons who got suckered in, thinking they could make some easy money. We recognize a couple of them."

"With names like Clarence and Marvin, it's no wonder they turned out wrong. I changed my mind; I'm going to sweet-talk them into letting me slip out the back door. They've got enough hostages."

"Not gonna happen. Clarence wanted to know if you placed the initial call to the police. He saw you walk in . . . considered you a threat even then."

"Yeah, I wish I'd pulled an Elvis and left the building."

"So far he believes we aren't communicating, but if he finds out different, he'll want me to give you up."

"Those guys would kill me."

"I said he'd want me to, not that I would. If they see you with a phone though, Clarence will start killing innocent people to force my hand. I'd have to crash the doors. I don't want to do that . . . not when I know where those hostages are located."

"Can they see me on the security cameras?"

"No, they haven't attempted to access them."

"What are they asking for?" I said as my phone chirped.

"The usual: planes, trains, and automobiles."

"Will you give it to them?"

"Not likely, Steve. We'll settle this right here. Let me say this quickly: I heard from the FBI negotiator based in the Nashville field office. He's out of town, booked on the next flight. We've dealt with Clarence. He's a bad boy."

"How bad?"

"I'm getting you—all of you—out of there before we find out. I'll turn the power back on after the sun goes down. Clarence is demanding we do it immediately, but I'll make him wait. I cut the lights when I saw them through the door . . . hunting for you.

"Thanks for that."

"And don't use any of the column phones. You won't get an outside line, and we think they'll light up the phone Clarence is using. Call this number if you're able." Parker gave the digits as I wrote them down.

"Is there anything else?" Parker asked.

"Yeah, I'm puzzled about something. Why are *you* here?"

"I'm the comm—" was all I caught before my phone beeped, and the call dropped.

The phone was still illuminated, but the battery meter showed zero. I put his number into speed dial #2 and powered down. I had a better chance of making another call if the phone wasn't completely dead.

I gazed into the darkness, sifting through the new information Parker had just given me. I imagined there must be a lot of cops out there if he was called to a town thirty miles away from his employer.

And why did Parker answer the phone? Had Captain Lewis found out somehow that we were acquainted?

I enjoy a good game of Six Degrees of Separation, but this weekend was turning into a *Twilight Zone* episode starring Kevin Bacon.

I took out my notepad and wrote down the line. Who knew, I might get some exposure out of this. One of the local comedians at my level started getting paid gigs after bombing horribly on *Last Comic Standing*. Maybe this would become my fifteen minutes of fame. I wondered how that would turn out.

Chapter 24

6:00 p.m. Friday

Sitting in the dark for many hours watching flashlight beams shine across the ceiling, I had one of my bright ideas and pulled out my notepad. I parted the curtain to let in some light and added a portable radio to the list. I didn't think the store carried the one I wanted, but any type would allow me to get news updates. And I would need headphones so I could listen without giving away my location. *As long as I was strolling around electronics, I may as well acquire any other items I deemed useful, like the TV, or better yet a laptop computer with a DVD slot.* The thought made me crack my first smile since the criminals had entered the building.

If I wasn't worried about getting killed, I would have felt like a kid locked in a toy store. I looked at the items on my list. Parker said the lights were coming back on at some point. If I was serious about venturing out, now was the time. I got my autoloader and rose to a standing position. My aching joints cried out for me to sit down, but I holstered the Glock and stepped out.

I pushed the coveralls to one side because I would definitely be carrying a toilet when I came back. The backup lights were much dimmer now. I could see the way but not well. I listened for any signs that the exterminators were nearby. Both sides of the aisle contained products you would require to spend a few days in the great outdoors. Or inside a giant store, if you don't have sense enough to split when you think it's about to be robbed. I should have trusted my intuition on that one.

I removed the portable toilet from the box. I flipped open the lid and placed deodorizer, and a two-pack of the special toilet paper in the bowl. I couldn't carry much else, so I returned and placed it a couple of feet across from the bucket. I removed the merchandise in the toilet while I still remembered it was there.

I went back, familiar enough with this area that I could find my next acquisition without any light. I grabbed a plastic tray hanging on a rod that contained the smallest version of the kind of flashlight I preferred. It came with a pair of AA batteries. I owned one of almost every size and appreciated they were all manufactured here in America. Today I was upgrading to the LED version—brighter, and easier on batteries.

I cut open the theft-resistant package, careful not to slip with the knife. According to my lab results, my blood wasn't scary thin, but I would still bleed more than most people. Slicing my hand open would be life-threatening, and 9-1-1 wouldn't be any help, if I *could* make the call.

I installed the batteries and held the flashlight under the Glock, as Sandy once demonstrated in class. I remembered feeling foolish when we practiced this on a bright sunny day. Feeling foolish again, I put away the gun and proceeded to the next item on my list. I selected one of the knapsacks, cut the tags off, and removed the wad of tissue paper stuffed inside.

I went back to the flashlight section. The LED version was a little brighter than I needed, but I would be converting my flashlights as soon as I got home. I took the largest flashlight, a four-cell that could also double as a billy club if I needed one. I cut it out of the tray and slid it into the knapsack. I spotted a column display of batteries and grabbed a four-pack of the D size, then exchanged it for an eight-pack. I then procured the largest container of each size battery in stock. I wasn't sure what kind of gadgets I would come across, but I didn't want to return for batteries.

I got paranoid, thinking about the two gorillas with M-16s. I told myself it was better to get this out of my system while the lights were out. I certainly needed more 9mm ammunition. I used five rounds on one easy guy, and there were eight more not-so-easy guys remaining. I would get hollow points if they were in stock. Parker was right. They had tremendous stopping power. I think my first shot put the guy in the bathroom down. I fired four additional rounds before I bothered to notice. He was the first person I ever killed. Hopefully the last.

I glanced at the buoyant cushions as I passed by but decided to get them last if I still thought they were needed. *No room for impulse shopping*, I scolded myself.

I turned left at the next corner. At the end of this short row, I passed Ed, trying not to look at his face. I proceeded through the gate on the service island and removed the keys from my pocket. I knelt down to get out of the faint light shining down from the backup light mounted directly overhead. I inserted the first key I came to, and the key turned.

Things are finally starting to go my way, I thought, cracking myself up.

I slid the door open and studied my choices. There were six boxes of 9mm Luger rounds—the kind my weapon used. One was a larger hundred-count box of loose practice rounds. Four boxes contained fifty practice rounds in a Styrofoam divider. The box I'd never purchased held fifty hollow point rounds. I took all six and opened the box of hollow points. I plucked half the bullets out of the Styrofoam and put them in my pocket, then refilled my magazine.

I scanned the ammunition for anything useful. Two boxes of .270 caliber ammunition and one box of .223 caught my attention. I set the ammo in my backpack and relocked the case. I had no use for the .223 ammo, but I remembered reading an article about the M-16 and was sure it was the civilian variation of the bullet the gun fired. I didn't want the criminals using them against me.

As I was about to walk around to the gun cabinet, I heard something. Those clip-clapping shoes again. I pulled my weapon and got down on the floor. Sounded like those same two exterminators I'd heard earlier, were approaching on the aisle in front of me. I was hoping they kept on going. But if they stopped for ammo, I was prepared to defend myself.

I didn't like my chances. In the movies, a trained killer could double tap two guys before they could raise their weapons. The way my hands were shaking, I could empty my gun and not hit anything. A moment later, they passed by heading toward automotive. I stuck my head up and saw them stalking the aisle like Elmer Fudd, pointing their shotguns in every direction. They looked as scared as I was.

I stepped through the gate and noticed a rack of camo sweatshirts nearby. I grabbed an XL, not intending to wear it. Since the power went out, the temperature in the building had risen to the point that I was sweating. I had a different application for the garment in mind. I made my way past Ed, speculating how long until his body started to smell. I hoped I was home with my wife before that happened.

Standing in front of the gun display, I set the pack down and studied the rifle I intended to purchase before the next deer season. I had already begun the process by tossing hints to my wife. In its current state, I considered it almost useless. There was a chance the rifle was bore sighted when the scope was mounted, but I figured Ed or someone else just slapped it on as a package deal. I needed a way to verify the accuracy of the weapon, but I assumed Clarence wouldn't agree to a truce while I dialed it in.

I inserted the one key I was sure about. I remembered it resembled the one to my wife's jewelry box, the key I saw every day on the dresser next to her jewelry. I removed the rifle and locked the door. I topped off the knapsack with a half-dozen bottles from the fridge and snatched two bags of beef jerky off the adjacent rack. Out of habit, I started reading the nutrition label, then stuffed them in the pack and secured the flap. Cholesterol and sodium wasn't the biggest threat to my life at the moment. I thanked God for my new lavatory facilities, as I climbed back into my hideout.

Chapter 25

My limited space was getting cluttered, even by my standards. I placed the rifle in the corner next to the shotgun and lined the food and beverages against the block wall. The boxes of ammo and batteries remained in the knapsack. I still had six feet of floor space left of the original ten that were empty when I moved in. My accommodations weren't very wide, but I probably had enough room to lie down.

My caffeine and adrenalin levels were both winding down. I still had one item I had to get before the lights came on. A way to communicate with Parker was essential. The walkie-talkies sold here probably worked fine in the forest, but with all the concrete and steel surrounding me, I doubted they would transmit beyond the block walls. I stepped out and spotted the boat cushions. I needed them as much as I needed anything else, so I grabbed five of them and removed the plastic, temporarily stacking them on top of the toilet. I wanted to climb back in and go to sleep, but I closed the opening to my hideout and headed to the electronics department.

I didn't believe the store carried what I was looking for, or I would already own one, but I had to check. I'd seen this particular device on an electronic gadget website while surfing for a present to give my wife. I almost whipped out my credit card and bought it right away, but instead I took a cold mental shower and waited for the urge to pass. I had a rule that I rarely broke: don't buy presents for myself when Christmas shopping for others. And even if I had bought it back then, I would not have had it with me now.

The backup lights were becoming as dim as my solar patio lights after three days of steady rain. I would need the small flashlight to illuminate the area when I got close. For now, I opted to feel my way along. As I entered the electronics department, I could hear muffled voices up front. The murmurs soon became obvious signs of unrest—screaming and yelling from male and female voices. I wasn't able to make out the words, but I didn't like the sound of it. I figured the exterminators were threatening to kill the hostages.

I was within twenty feet of my destination, so I pressed on. I turned on my small flashlight, covering it with my hand, as I approached a variety of boom boxes and small portables displayed on the shelf. There was no sign of the multiband radio I came for.

A flashlight beam sliced through the darkness. Then I sighted a woman who was really throwing a fit. This was not just any woman. I was able to identify the approaching storm. A man with a flashlight in one hand and a long gun in the other was steering Hurricane Ella straight toward me.

Some daylight sneaked through the far-off entryway behind them. It was only nighttime inside the store. Beyond uncooperative, Ella was being prodded along with the business end of the shotgun. The electronics sales counter was between the two of them and where I stood. As they drew near, he shined his light on the service island and nudged Ella along with more urgency.

I crept forward, stopping behind an I-beam. I wasn't sure what the gunman had in mind for Ella, but I doubted he sought her opinion on a CD selection. Ella was in no way responsible for what was happening to her, but I already wasn't a fan of hers. Drawing me into this predicament didn't help. She continued to struggle as they neared the kiosk. Unwanted and repressed feelings for her emerged, as I was likely about to witness her sexual assault unless I stopped him.

I would come to the aid of any woman—or man for that matter—in the same situation, I reminded myself. That was true, but I could only have been more compelled if it was my wife in danger. When the light beam moved away, I scurried over, got down on my knees, and hid behind the counter.

I intended to keep out of sight and surprise this degenerate—like I did when I attacked the first gunslinger who crossed my path. But I was concerned that Ella would be in the line of fire. The best-case scenario bothered me as well: I kill this piece of garbage and take Ella back to my hideout. Picturing that in my mind made me think that whoever's guardian angel put this chance encounter together had a warped sense of humor.

Chapter 26

I peeked over the counter. They were about thirty feet away and still tracking toward me. The guy looked like a player, though well past his prime. Like a fifty-year-old Fabio, who hadn't aged well. He had long greasy hair he kept slinging out of his eyes because his hands were full. He was bigger than some of his pals, though, and broad shouldered. I reminded myself that he was also armed with a shotgun and probably knew how to use it.

I couldn't stand by while he assaulted her, no matter what she had done to me in the past or how she continued to bother me in the present. I pondered whether getting us *both* killed was the right thing to do. I dropped down to my knees and pressed up against the glass showcase in front of me. The backup light above me was dim, but the glow through the display was enough that I worried he would see me.

As Ella and her attacker crashed through the swinging gate, I thought about the best way to stop the assault. I couldn't focus because directly in front of me were a dozen portable electronic devices: voice-activated digital voice recorders, mp3 players, and a radio with a crank handle on the side. The exact model I'd hoped to acquire.

I crawled on all fours until I reached the spring-loaded half door they just went through. I got up and drew my weapon. His flashlight was laying on the counter, and I could see both of them plain as day. He pinned Ella against the showcase, then stood his shotgun in the corner. She kicked at him, but her hands were tied behind her back and she was unable to stop him.

He faced away from me, and she was screaming at the top of her lungs. Also, the police began blasting something over the bullhorn. There was not, however, enough noise to drown out the awkward sound of my autoloader firing a bullet into the back of his skull. I pictured one of the machine gun–toting brothers running out to investigate.

His body and lab coat blocked my view, but I was sure the sound I heard next was Ella's shirt ripping. I stood tall and raised my pistol with both hands. Rage at what this animal was doing motivated me to action. Ella once meant a great deal to me, and it took many years to get over her. I pushed through the gate, taking one hand off the gun for a second to make sure it didn't snap back. I was surprised my hands weren't trembling as I held the gun straight out in front of me.

The rapist's body and long hair blocked Ella from seeing my approach. With her hands tied, removing her clothes was proving difficult so he pulled a knife out of a scabbard on his belt and cut her top off, discarding the red polo and bra onto the floor. Ella's cries morphed into a shrill scream.

He set the knife down and pushed Ella back on the counter. Her head was hanging over the far side. I now had my shot but seeing the knife gave me what I prayed was a better idea.

Why shoot him and draw all that attention?

I didn't know if I was worried about his buddies hearing the shot or I had watched too many episodes of *24*, but I removed my small, razor-honed knife and struggled to open the blade with a gun in my hand. I somehow managed it without dropping the knife or shooting myself.

I wanted to yank this guy's head back and cut his throat like some Special Forces operator in a jungle scene, but I wasn't willing to put the gun down. Circumstances could turn against me in a multitude of ways. I took a few cautious steps with the knife grasped, the sharp edge facing me as I held it at arm's length. He gave no indication he knew I was standing behind him as he unbuttoned her jeans.

With the gun in my right hand and the knife poised in my left—definitely not something I had seen on television or learned from Parker or Sandy—I advanced close enough to tap him on the shoulder if I wanted to. As Old Fabio took a second to sling the hair out of his eyes, I reached around and slid the blade across his throat—deeper than I needed to.

I moved aside as he fell backward, crashing to the floor as I held my gun on him. The only sound coming from him was blood gurgling out the gash in his neck. Ella, on the other hand, was making plenty of noise as she flailed, unable to sit up.

Given the lighting and obvious distractions, he never saw it coming. I was glad because the alternate strategy was the gun pointed at his ear. And my knife hand would have been in the line of fire. I knelt down to verify he was no longer a threat, then wiped my blade clean on his lab coat and put it in my pocket. I checked to see if anyone was approaching before I holstered the Glock. I intended to go with the dead guy's shotgun if trouble showed up. I shined the light on me—trying not to make a ghoul face.

"Ella it's me, Steve," I whispered.

She lifted her head, and I saw the surprise on her face when she recognized me. She was still hysterical but brought it down a notch or two. I reached behind her neck and brought her into a sitting position on the countertop. I picked up the dead guy's knife and whispered for Ella to let me cut the rope. She turned at the waist, and I sawed the rope with the toothed section of the blade. As soon as she was free, she wrapped her arms around my neck and sobbed.

"I was praying you would help me . . . but I didn't think it was possible."

"We aren't out of the woods yet," I whispered, wishing she would let go of me.

I helped Ella to her feet and emptied my jacket pockets, transferring everything into the large pockets of my carpenter shorts. I removed my jacket and offered it to her.

"Thank you. I can't believe you're here . . . that you stopped him from—" Ella said, unable to speak when the tears started.

"I'm glad I got here in time," I said, my own emotions starting to unravel.

"I assumed you went home . . . when you saw me go in the store. I wouldn't have blamed you," she said as she put on the jacket.

I had no choice but to take her back with me to my hideout. I thought we had a few minutes before anyone would come to investigate why the screaming stopped.

"Ella, do you know how to work this?" I said, holding up the shotgun, wondering if I should unload it before I let her carry it.

"Oh, yes. Gary and I . . . we shoot skeet," she replied, regaining her composure.

"This is a pump gun. You have to rack in a new shell each time you fire. The safety is here next to the trigger," I told her, not taking any chances she knew how to safely handle the weapon. "Do you want to carry it?"

"Yes, I'd like that a lot," she whispered, transferring the weapon with the muzzle pointed away from me.

Clutching the gun seemed to have a calming effect on her. I was more shaken up than she appeared to be, my hands trembling again—not that I would let her see.

"I've carried one like this on pheasant hunts with Gary, back in Michigan. This one looks shorter, though," Ella said, inspecting the gun.

I was surprised at her knowledge and experience with firearms. She wouldn't even let me keep a BB gun in the house when we were together.

I picked up the dead guy's flashlight. "Hold this, I need to get something," I said, searching through my pockets for the keys.

I doubted Ed had a key for every lock in the building. I was surprised he had one for the bathroom door. Maybe every person on the late shift had a key to use the facilities. The radio was a must-have, and I would break into the case if I had to. Luckily, one of the keys opened the lock. Ed must have been a trustworthy employee. It was probably the same key I used for the ammo, but I wasn't sure. His willingness to fight for his life seemed more honorable now that I had to do it myself a couple of times.

Ella held the light as I pushed a few items out of the way and took the radio still in the box. I needed all the accessories. I wanted one more item I had seen, but Ella was getting impatient, shining the beam every direction except where it was needed. Somehow I located the premium set of earphones—the kind that inserted snugly into the ear canal.

"When did you decide to get all that?" It was a loaded question. Years in the making. I knew what she meant. She'd never liked my compulsive ways or my penchant for gadgetry.

"Right before I came and saved your ungratef—" I replied, shutting up before I let the horse completely out of the barn.

All these years apart and we're still having the same conversations, I thought, as I watched her march off.

Chapter 27

Ella proceeded a few steps in the wrong direction and stopped. I wasn't looking for a fight. I just wanted to get out of sight before someone discovered us. I wasn't sure if there was indeed an angel guiding me, or I was being punished for transgressions in another life—the one Ella had been a part of. Captive in the same store, then coming along at the precise moment to liberate Ella, seemed far beyond coincidence. I hoped this attempt at cohabitation worked out better than the last one.

"I have to pee," Ella said as we crossed into the sporting goods department and officially ended her first silent treatment, with me anyway, since we had broken up. It was also by far the shortest.

"I promise that where we're going you'll have all the comforts of home."

As we approached the now-silent crooning deer, I explained that I had my phone and was communicating with the police. I failed to mention the incident in the men's room. Going there was a bad idea, and I didn't need her to point that out, now that she was speaking to me again.

I pushed open a gap in the clothing, took the shotgun from her, and propped it beside the other long guns. Ella stood behind me, shining the light inside, probably checking to see how clean it was, knowing her. I divided the flotation devices evenly between the two seats and stepped aside. Ella climbed in, repositioned the cushions on the pail, and sat down. After I was sitting opposite her, she watched me rip open the cardboard box the radio was in.

"Nice place you got here," Ella said, but looked as though touching something might give her cooties.

"I've lived in worse."

Her comment, which was innocent enough, ripped the scab off an old wound. After Ella ended our relationship, I'd lived in places homeless people would have passed on. We were laid off for nearly a year following our split, and I spent my unemployment checks on liquor instead of rent somewhere decent. None of that was her fault, but being in the same part of the country as me right now *was* her decision.

She held the light as I took the device out of the Styrofoam shell. I searched for the accessories, which would determine if my acquisition was invaluable or just a device to play with. Ella could think whatever she wanted either way. The product's manual and attachments were both in the same plastic bag. I tore it open and set the booklet aside.

"You won't be needing that," Ella said, grinning so hard I couldn't take offense.

"I've never seen MacGyver read the instructions."

"Who's MacGyver?"

"Television show I like . . . it's nothing. Point the light over here."

"What's all that stuff?" Ella asked, as I examined the contents of the bag.

I ignored her question because I had no clue what most of it was.

I took out a cable and set it on my lap. The adaptors were in a small resealable bag. I dumped them out in my palm and sifted for the one I needed. I wasn't optimistic. My phone was so outdated the store no longer carried hardware for it. Descriptive text on the side of the box stated any adapter not provided would be mailed free of charge. As I was about to lose hope, I recognized the prongs that matched my charger at home.

Ella waited patiently as I plugged the adapter into the end of the cable. If we weren't to some extent back in the "polite stage" of relationship dynamics, I was sure Ella would have pestered me until I told her what I was doing.

"It's a generator," I said, plugging the adapter into my phone.

Ella grabbed the manual and studied it until she was satisfied I was telling the truth. She didn't know me to be *that* kind of a liar, but she'd witnessed some of my wild ideas get proven wrong. I gave her the benefit of the doubt—this time. I attempted to plug the radio end of the cable into a couple of incorrect ports, then studied the connector to get a match.

"It goes right there," Ella said, pointing to the slot I was attempting to plug the cable into, reminding me how often she was spot-on that way in the past.

"Must use a lot of batteries," she said, setting down the manual.

"Wrong again, kimosabe," I replied, not bothering to change my voice. I guessed from her expression that she was still tired of that line. I uncoiled the cable and handed her the phone.

"If you would kindly assist me, Mr. Watson," I said stalling, trying to move the crank handle into position.

"Whatever you say, Sherlock."

"That's 'Doctor' Watson—never mind."

I finally managed to flip the recessed handle out of the radio and began turning it at a fast clip. A moment later, Ella smiled.

"Your phone's lighting up."

That's what I expected. When I plugged the powered-off phone into my charger at home, the light came on first, then indicated it was charging the battery.

"Charging . . . it says so," Ella said, sounding as delighted as if we *had* actually invented the device, instead of just learned how to operate it.

I lost interest after a few minutes and stopped.

"Keep going, it turned off again," Ella said, showing me the display.

I passed her the radio. "This will be a good job for you."

She laid the still-illuminated flashlight on the floor and said, "I'll do it—until my hands start hurting."

Every person in our line of work had some degree of Carpal Tunnel Syndrome. I had once dropped a fork at the dinner table when the wiring in my wrist short-circuited. This occurred at Thanksgiving when I was meeting Suzy's parents for the first time. I covered by joking that it was part of my new weight-loss program. Suzy was the only one who laughed—a somewhat nervous chuckle.

While Ella charged the phone, I went through the knapsack, checking out the merchandise I acquired earlier. Ten minutes later, I held up a bottle of orange juice to see if she was interested.

"Thanks, but I'll wet my pants if I drink anything."

"Sorry, I forgot."

Safety would have to come before modesty. I wasn't sure Ella would go along with my plan, with all she'd been through.

"Stand up," I whispered, then rose to my feet and took out my flashlight, partially blocking the beam with my hand. Ella set the radio on the floor, turned off her light and stood, unsure what to do next. Apparently, Ella hadn't noticed our hideout was fully equipped—minus the bathroom door.

I looked over the rail to see if anyone was nearby. There was nothing but darkness. I put the cushions under my arm and shined the light on the camp toilet. Ella practically shoved me through the curtain as she squeezed by. I gazed out into the void as she got in position.

"Have you got the toilet paper?" I whispered, hearing the lid open and the sound of her jeans unzipping.

"No, shine the light over here."

I pointed the light at the two-pack next to her, and Ella put them in her lap. I turned off the light and listened to the sound of rain hitting a tin roof.

"I haven't gone since I visited you at work," Ella said minutes later, as the sound of her relief slowed.

I wanted to lay into her about the visits at work, but she was in easy reach of a weapon.

Chapter 28

Ella bounced into her one-size-too-small jeans, buckling the metal floor with each effort.

"Turn on the light, so I can pour in some of that blue stuff."

"Yellow is mellow, brown you drown," I said, remembering the line one of my buddies used on a camping trip.

After a long silence, I turned on the light and watched her open the deodorizer. She gave me the same frown she used when she had to remind me to flush the toilet. Ella then proceeded to pour in half the bottle.

"All finished. . . . Now where's that OJ?" Ella said, taking the cushions and sitting back down.

I pointed the light at our refreshment assortment against the wall.

"I'm starving," she whispered, eyeing the bag of jerky.

"Make yourself at home," I whispered, recalling Ella utter those exact words. I had just moved in with her and asked for permission to get something out of the refrigerator.

Ella opened the bag of jerky with her teeth. "You don't have any hand sanitizer in that pack by any chance?"

"No, I didn't think of it."

She gave me the frown again but didn't say anything.

She plucked a piece with her fingernails and devoured it.

I assumed Ella was no longer a vegetarian.

I uncapped a mocha coffee drink and took a sip as Ella opened her orange juice.

"You good?" I asked.

"Yes, you were right: all the comforts of home," Ella said, with a hint of sadness.

I remained silent, bracing for the stroll down memory lane I was dreading.

"What's it been Taylor? Fifteen years since we spent time alone together?"

I didn't know what to say, so I turned off the light, hoping darkness would silence her.

"You still hate me, don't you?"

"Let's focus on getting out of here alive. Gary's probably scared sick," I said, wishing I could see her face when I reminded her who moved on first.

"How could I know you'd get your act together?"

"I got worse before I got better, Ella. You did the right thing."

"Did I?" she whispered.

A long silence passed, then a loud pop triggered a squeal from both of us. Seconds later, the lights came on. I stood and looked over the curtain, my hand on the Glock. Ella sensed we were in danger and grabbed one of the shotguns.

There was no one in sight, and my heart rate quickly returned to normal—not that I was counting. Since my surgery, I was hyperaware of what my repaired organ was doing, even though my cardiologist assured me that my heart was strong and reliable. Daily intake of caffeine was the one thing he scolded me for at my annual checkup. I would have laid off the caffeine on a normal day—but this was anything but normal.

"What do we do now?" Ella asked.

"Hang loose. I'll call the police after you finish charging the phone," I said, looking at the radio and phone lying between us.

"You do it," she said, shaking out her wrist,

I avoided eye contact as I turned the handle. I intended to crank for an hour and call Parker. I wanted to check on my wife, but I doubted I'd be able to do both. Ten minutes later, I grew restless again. I pinned the radio between my knees, so I could turn the crank and empty the knapsack with my other hand. Loud voices came from the direction of electronics. The exterminators discovered another one of their cronies had gone down. I had now killed two of them. They were going to be looking for me again. I was sure of that.

"Going somewhere?" Ella whispered when she noticed I was piling things beside the shotgun ammunition and putting the rest into the pack.

"I'm just sorting stuff out."

"You're leaving me, aren't you?" she asked, clearly still able to hear what I was thinking over the sound of what I was saying—even after so many years without practice.

"I'm not *planning* to go anywhere," I sort of lied.

I hadn't devised a plan yet. But I wanted to leave as soon as possible. This was the safest location, so I'd give it to her. I felt guilty, but the thought of being cooped up with her got me over it.

"How about charging the phone for me Ella, so I can organize our stuff?"

"Fine, but switch seats with me. I want to lean against the wall. I'm bone tired."

Ella slid by, still clutching her weapon.

"I get the feeling you wish I wasn't here," she said, apparently hurt by the way I avoided contact as we passed.

"C'mon Ella, that's not true. I wish both of us weren't here."

Ella shot me a scowl as she sat down.

"Crank for twenty minutes, and I'll see if I can make a call," I said in my best non-confrontational voice, the one I used whenever one of my teammates was upset about something. She gave no reply but situated the shotgun in the corner and went to work. I slid the knapsack in front of me and continued separating the provisions I wished to take, from the ones I intended to leave behind. Fifteen minutes later I shut the flap. Ella took this as her cue.

"I quit. Keep cranking if you want."

"That should be enough. Thanks."

"You're welcome. Sorry I got upset."

If we had people skills like this back in the day, Ella and I might still be together.

I powered up the phone. The battery meter showed 20 percent. I was a little disappointed the generator wasn't more efficient, but I was thankful to have a way to charge the phone. At 20 percent, I was able to call my wife but could expect the battery reminder if we chatted long. I had some work to do before I could see how she was holding up. I was just happy she was safe at home, and I was the one in danger. If the situation were reversed, I would have already driven my truck through the door to get her out—bombs or no bombs. As I thought about my wife sitting at home, worried sick, my thumb hovered above my speed-dial options. I selected the first one and hit the green button.

It rang once before she picked up.

"Babe, are you okay? You must be so scared," Suzy said.

"I'm fine sweetheart," I said with my soft voice, watching Ella's reaction. Her smirk indicated she knew I wasn't talking to someone in law enforcement. "Did the police contact you this morning?"

"Yes, Captain Lewis was very nice. He told me the bank robbers captured everyone but you."

"That's true, darling. I found a place to hide before they could get to me."

"When are you coming home?" Suzy asked, her voice cracking.

"I don't know yet, sweetheart. I'm in a real safe place, so don't worry about me, okay?"

"I can't stop worrying. I've been watching the news all day. Promise that you'll come back to me, babe. Please promise me," she said, weeping now.

"I promise," I said, choking up. I couldn't stand to hear her cry. "The police will get us out. But I have to go. I need to save my battery. I'll call again when I get a chance."

"Please be careful—don't do anything foolish."

"I'll see you soon. Love you, darling," I said, ending the call.

My wife knew me well. The biggest danger I faced was myself. I gazed at Ella for any snide remarks as I highlighted Parker's number. I thought I had enough juice to at least tell him I found a charger.

"You can call Gary, later, after you charge the phone," I whispered, as I waited for the connection to go through.

"I'm sure he doesn't want to speak to me," Ella said, averting her eyes.

Chapter 29

I still couldn't believe, with all my other problems, I was now stuck with the last person on earth I would choose to be with.

"I'm glad you called, Steve. You need to go find a slimeball holding a pretty blonde."

"Already found the blonde. She's here with me, but the slimeball isn't doing too good."

"Nice work. We were concerned about her. We'd been watching the hostages through the door. That horn-dog pestered her for hours. The hostages threw a fit when he stood her up. One of his associates wasn't happy about it either. He tried to stop him from taking her, but got cold-cocked. My people will be relieved to hear she's okay."

"Is Clarence upset with me?" I joked, my voice breaking like a kid going through puberty.

"Yeah, he would definitely like to have a few words with you. I just got off the phone with him. And he still believes we aren't able to communicate. I told him we found a cell phone in your truck."

"And he's buying it?"

"Yeah, until he sees you with it."

"Can't you slip in here and just take them out?"

"I'm not even considering it. They'd start killing hostages before we could get close."

"So what's the plan then?"

"I'm working on one, but I need your help. Can I count on you?" Parker said.

"Yeah, but I'm not doing anything that will get me killed."

"There will be *some* risk. No worse than you've already encountered."

"I hope my luck isn't running out."

"I think you've created your own luck, but I won't sugarcoat it. I wish it *were* me or one of my men in there. The next best thing is someone I've worked with. I know your strengths and limitations. With my guidance, *you will* stop Clarence before he can hurt anyone else."

"I hate to bring this up, but I remember you informing the class about legal liabilities. Are you deputizing me or something?"

"These guys are a threat to your well-being and the well-being of other hostages. They can't sue you—and I for sure won't charge you with anything. But deputize you? No, that only happens in old Westerns."

"Just thought I'd ask."

"Steve, I've got someone's life in my hands more days than not. You have to trust me *and* do what I tell you."

"Okay, but I have to survive this and get home to my wife. I promised her I would," I said, my phone chirping midsentence.

"Believe me, I understand your desire to stay out of danger. Without your help, I'd have to drive an armored vehicle through the door and shoot until no one was shooting back. We'd probably kill all the bad guys and every hostage except you and the lady."

"Clear something up for me Parker: why is a Nashville Police officer—a firearms instructor involved in this?" I asked, trying not to sound disrespectful.

He laughed. "I never reveal the full skinny on my police duties to the students at the range. I lead the Nashville SWAT unit. We respond throughout the area when we get a request. The only *official* weapons training I do is with my team. I like to make sure guys like you are capable out there. The money I earn at the range pays for equipment at the boxing gym where I coach."

"I get it. I'm an idiot," I said, a little embarrassed. As usual, I get my biggest laughs when I'm trying to be serious. Of course he had to be with some kind of tactical unit to be on the phone with me. Lewis even told me they were coming.

"I'll call back in an hour or so. I'm assuming you've found a way to charge your phone."

"Yeah, even when you turn off the—" That's when the call dropped.

I powered down my phone and commenced turning the handle at a frenzied pace.

"What was all that about?" Ella asked.

"Everything's going to be okay," I said. "You ever watch *SWAT* on television?"

"Gary and I don't own a television. But I'm not stupid, special weapons and tactics."

"If you *did* own a television, you'd know having a SWAT team here means this thing is about over—case closed."

I wondered how she convinced Gary to give up the tube. He and I used to binge on old movies when we were roommates sharing his two-bedroom single wide—until Ella came along.

"So what do we do now?" Ella asked.

"Lean back and shut your eyes," I said, hoping she would take the hint and be quiet.

"I'm too scared to sleep. I don't think we're meant to get out of here alive. It's like we were put here to reconcile our differences. And then we'll die," Ella said, tearing up.

I passed her the roll of RV toilet paper.

"Quite a coincidence," I said, like I hadn't reflected on this myself.

"All I've hoped for since you got sober . . . was to get you alone and talk it out. I feel bad how things ended . . . and that you hated me so much," Ella said, as the wet paper disintegrated in her fingers.

She waited a moment for me to respond, but I didn't.

"Having you cornered in here is not the way I imagined it," she added.

Again, I said nothing. I wasn't comfortable listening to this. I couldn't discuss our past. The anger from that time in my life was still bottled up inside me, and I was afraid to uncork here or anywhere else. I sat still, contemplating what Parker was planning while Ella glared at me. He needed my help and that meant I was in a world of trouble.

I pay my taxes; you handle it. That's what I should have told him. But no, I had to reply with an answer that would please him. On top of that, Ella was forecasting the outcome. My surroundings reminded me I was already more involved than I wanted to be. Killing two of the criminals probably meant I was a big part of why the negotiations weren't going well. Parker seemed pleased I was taking a proactive approach, especially when it came to Ella. But I wondered if this whole situation might be settled by now if I hadn't been able to call the police. Clarence and his gang would have got what they came for and left.

Parker had kept his position in the police department quiet. Not a huge surprise. If he'd told the students at the range he led a SWAT team, it would have changed things. The young studs would have been pleased. I'm sure they would have bragged to their friends and brought in additional business. He could have bought a lot more boxing gloves that way. Me, I would have been more intimidated of Parker than I was already.

Ella sat there with her mouth shut, just studying her nails. She may not have known it, but I honestly believed she made the right decision when she threw me out. I just wished she wasn't here to remind me why she did it. It had been close to an hour since Parker and I talked. I turned my phone on, awaiting his call. It vibrated a few minutes later.

Chapter 30

12:15 a.m. Saturday the 4th of July

"Steve, I've got a little job for you," Parker said.

"How little?"

"They haven't given me a deadline yet, but Clarence is threatening to kill every hostage, one by one, if I don't provide them with a clear path to freedom. Steve, that's not happening. You and me—we'll have to find another way. I've got high regard for your—"

"I said I'd help you," I interrupted. "Stop playing me and tell me what I have to do to get home to my wife."

"Tiptoe up close and shoot their leader—both, if you're able."

"That's . . . crazy talk. I thought you wanted me to go scout 'em out or something."

"No. I want you to take them out. Both Heckle and Jeckle, and then you'll be home with your wife in a few hours because the rest will lay down their weapons."

"No way. There is no way I can do that without getting killed."

"Relax, Steve, I've been studying them. They're all standing out in the open by the front wall. You'll be able to get off a couple of shots before anyone spots you. Don't be too concerned with those dried-up ex-cons hovering in the middle. They're only here as bullet bait."

"Yeah, but the ones you want me to kill have automatic weapons. When they start shooting, I won't even know what hit me."

"We'll create a diversion so you can get into position. One of my guys will slip a tiny camera through the roof that I'll be able to access remotely—video and sound."

"Why not drop your guy in here and let him kill them?"

"I would if I could Steve. There's no way to get someone in there without making a lot of noise. I wish there were."

"Parker, how am I going to pull that off? You've seen me shoot."

"You can do this, Steve," he said. "You ever do any boxing? You gotta stick and move. Take a good rest, fire a couple of shots, and then get out before your opponent can touch you."

"Touch me? Blow me away is more like it. When you ding the bell, will they stop shooting and let me sit down for a minute to catch my breath?" Fear and anger had taken control of my mouth.

"Then I'll ding it again, and you'll get back in the fight," Parker said.

I'd done some boxing growing up. My friends and I built a ring out of trash cans and a garden hose. My reputation for leading with my head was well deserved. Being able to take a punch was the only compliment my fellow teenage ruffians ever gave me.

"Do you think I can do this without getting killed?" I asked.

"I know you can. You've already earned the criminals' respect and mine as well."

After a brief pause, Parker said, "Okay Steve, I won't blow smoke. With Clarence in there, more good people will die before this is over. The quicker you take him out, the lower the number of fatalities."

"I won't get in trouble if I kill someone—unprovoked—not in self-defense," I asked, wanting to understand the ground rules.

"That's what I would do. Knock them off one by one until they give up."

"Don't you have to make an effort to negotiate a peaceful settlement first? Don't they have rights?"

"They already committed a dozen crimes today, including murder. And they could surrender and walk out anytime they like, but they won't. Clarence will kill everyone, including you and Ella, if *you* don't stop him."

"I'm not as good as you seem to think I am. I got lucky with those first two guys. You ever play baseball—three strikes you're out."

"Will you to do this for me, Steve?" Parker asked, sounding like a used car salesman throwing out his final close.

I knew that the first one to speak loses, but I replied, "I'll do whatever you think will get me back home to my wife."

"That's what I was hoping you'd say. What do you have for weapons and ammo? Your Glock and what . . . fifteen rounds left?" Parker asked.

"Hold on," I said, taking inventory of my cache. Ella stared in disbelief. I guess she was getting the gist from only one side of the conversation.

"I have my Glock with about 200 rounds . . . and a sawed-off pump gun with as many shells as I want. I also have a bolt action .270 rifle and forty cartridges. It has a nice scope, but I doubt it's zeroed in."

"Man! I knew I had the right guy for the job. Most people aren't that resourceful." Ella was trying to tell me something, so it was hard to focus on what Parker was saying. "I assumed you'd have to get close and use those hollow points. The rifle will make this much easier."

"Make that two pump guns. Ella's holding one. I could get some rifled slugs for the shotgun. I've used them deer hunting; they're accurate under a hundred yards," I said.

"Probably not in a sawed-off."

"Yeah. I didn't think about that."

"Get a charge on that phone. We'll turn off the power in about two hours. They'll make some noise about that, and we'll make some noise back. During that diversion we'll set up the camera. I'll be able to observe you and give direction. Check the rifle. Can you see the steel sights under the scope?"

"It has see-through mounts," I said, studying it. I'd heard of this type of base, but I was told they were inferior because they positioned the optics too high above the barrel.

"Take a steady rest, and then line something up in the crosshairs—as far away as possible."

I set the rifle on the top bar and put the phone back to my ear. "Okay, now what?"

"Look under the scope. What do you see?"

I did what I was told, tucking the phone against my shoulder.

"I see both front and rear sights. I'm aiming at a light on the ceiling about thirty yards away."

"Good, keep the weapon steady and switch between the open sights and the scope. Are they both on target?"

It hit me like a brick. I wouldn't trust untested open sights either. But if they both pointed at the same thing, the rifle was likely accurate.

"They're in full agreement," I said, alternating several times to be sure.

"It'll be good enough for the shots you're taking. Most likely the scope was lasered in like you thought."

"I think so too. Hey, I'd pay a lot of money for a sniper lesson before deer season," I kidded, not that I couldn't use it.

"Pay attention here, Steve. I'll be giving you stuff money can't buy."

"Where do I set up?" I asked, starting to feel better about the whole thing.

"All I've got is a general layout of the building and what I see through the front door. Anywhere front and center of the checkout lanes."

"That sounds like my first hiding place—men's clothing."

"The hired hands are congregating in front of the restrooms like a bunch of junior high kids. Don't worry too much about them. Their leaders are standing against the block wall next to each entrance. They're wearing body armor, but they're out in the open. A head shot or a femoral artery will do the trick."

"Then what?"

"Take off running if they come after you. Anything else, you'll have to think up on the fly."

"Where is everybody? I haven't seen or heard anyone for a while."

"They're tired. Most have been up since this began, and we'll make certain they don't get any rest. How about you, Steve?"

"I slept a few hours, and I've got enough caffeine to keep me awake for days," I replied, giving him the answer I figured he was looking for.

"When the lights go out, move into position, but be careful. They've no doubt still got someone looking for you. The FBI negotiator is boarding a plane as we speak. I'd like to be walking you all out when he arrives."

"Okay, Parker, I think I know where I can take some shots. I'm not too sure about the rifle or my abilities, but I'll see what I can do."

"One last thing, and I can't stress this enough. Do not harm even one of the short hairs on the head of his little brother until you are sure Clarence is dead. You got me, Steve? This is important."

"I hear you, but what's so special about Flattop?" I asked.

"Let's just say that he's their mommy's favorite. They called him Bubba when he was a kid; his mother still does. Sounds crazy, but please don't aim a weapon at Marvin until you take care of Clarence. If Marvin were to die, or even get shot, Clarence would likely kill all the hostages. If you get both brothers and wish to knock off some of the others, that'll be icing on the cake. But, and I'll say it again, take Clarence out first, then his brother. The rest will probably lay down and play possum."

"Got it, I'll go for Clarence first."

"Okay, so, move into position when the lights go out. I should have eyes inside when you get there. I'm figuring out a way to give you signals. Call me just before you set up. I'll have it worked out by then. Are you good to go?"

"Will you bust down the door if you see they have me pinned down?" I asked, assuming he wouldn't have a choice.

"Not if the hostages are in danger, and they would be in that case."

"Yeah, that makes sense," I said, feeling stupid for thinking I was less expendable than the other hostages. "Okay, Parker, I'll do what you say, but I need this to turn out well."

"Take Ella if you want, but she's safer where she is," he said, ending the call.

"I agree. Ella should wait here," I said loud and clear.

Chapter 31

Ella jumped right in, busting my chops, after I ended the call. "How's it going with that SWAT team? Are they still coming to save the day?"

"Sort of. Parker wants me to see what the criminals are up to."

"Don't lie to me. I heard what you said."

She was right. I'd held back the more dangerous aspect of the assignment. But that was because she was scared enough already.

"Parker thinks I can take out a couple of the leaders and maybe the rest will give up. Please don't argue with me. I don't want to do this, but I have to."

"Steve, I've seen those two in action. They're out of your league, no offense."

"Parker has a plan," I said, not even *trying* to sell it.

"What about me? What was that about?"

"He definitely wants you to stay here."

Ella was silent for a moment, seething. I'd seen her seethe before so I knew the look well. "Okay, but you come right back here when you're done playing cops and robbers," she finally said.

I wasn't asking for Ella's permission, but I had to admit, she wasn't as difficult as I remembered. In the old days, she would have kept arguing until either she won or I stomped out looking for a bar to get drunk in. She was pouting now, with her arms folded across her chest. The last time I witnessed that pose, I'd just told her I didn't have a drinking problem, and she'd kicked me out the next morning.

I hoped her patience continued. The odds were good that I had a key to the lock on the beer coolers. This would be a bad time to go off the wagon. I was glad the store didn't sell liquor. Graduating to the hard stuff after Ella kicked me out had been my downfall.

"Ella, I have to get ready. Will you charge the phone, please?"

My phone still had some life when I shut it down, but who knew when I'd get a chance to charge it.

"Alright, but I think you should let the police do *their* job. You're gonna get killed," Ella muttered as she connected the phone and took her frustration out on the crank handle.

I wanted to argue, but for the first time in a long time we were in complete agreement. I sat down and dumped out the contents of the knapsack. I needed a total repack. I had a mission to prepare for.

I installed four batteries in the larger flashlight, then reviewed the other items before putting them in my pack. It was mostly ammunition and caffeine. I intended to grab some jerky on the way out and leave Ella what we had. She had enough food and liquids to last a day or two. This was my chance to separate myself from Ella. I didn't plan on returning—even if I were able. She would follow me like a puppy on a leash if I told her.

I stuffed the sweatshirt into the knapsack to dampen the noise; the reason I took the shirt. I'd seen enough war movies to know it was always the grunt with a noisy pack who got killed.

Chapter 32

3:00 a.m. Saturday

Ella charged the phone and watched me pretend not to be nervous. I didn't want my last words with her to be an argument, so I kept quiet as well. My religious reawakening was approaching unseen territory. I made promises to God both of us knew I wouldn't keep. The central theme of my prayer was that Suzy would be okay—whatever happened.

I stood, picked up the rifle, and put a cartridge in the firing chamber. Then I slid the full magazine into the receiver. One in the tube, and four in the mag. Five shots wasn't a lot, but I doubted I would empty the gun before someone started shooting at me. I considered putting a few extra cartridges in my front pocket, but I planned to go with the Glock if things got ugly. I wouldn't exchange fire with the rifle. It's not that kind of weapon. A shotgun might come in handy, but I preferred to travel light in case I had to make a run for it.

"Can I get you something while I'm out?" I asked when I was finished.

"Yeah, I'll make you a shopping list—dear."

"Seriously, I'll be in the clothing department. I can get you a new top or something."

I was aware how dumb this sounded, especially since I had no intention of coming back. I hoped to leave on a happy note, and I couldn't think of a better line.

"A bra and T-shirt would be nice."

"What size?"

"If you're serious . . . I wear a 36D and a men's small."

"Really . . . I used to date a 36D?" I said, trying to be funny.

"First of all, what you and I did was not dating. I was grooming you for marriage. Second, I had some work done. Gary wasn't too happy about it, either."

"I thought my memory was playing tricks on me," I said before I could stop myself.

"I noticed your surprise," Ella laughed, making me blush. "Be careful out there, Steve, I've missed you," she said, gazing into my eyes.

"Maybe we can all be friends again when this is over," I said, feeling guilty for planning to find another place to hide after I finished my mission.

"If you're including Gary, I don't see that happening. He's still mad about the way you treated him back then—among other things," Ella said, studying my reaction.

There was a long silence and then the lights went out. Time to go, and I didn't mind nearly as much as I should have.

Getting up to leave I said, "Stay here until I get back. You'll hear some commotion, but you'll be safe here."

"Don't get yourself killed. Promise me."

I ignored her request. I'd already made that promise to my wife. I didn't want to break it to yet another person.

"Spread out the cushions and get some rest. Hopefully, we'll be out of here before our next shift."

"You're going out to shoot at monsters, and you're worried about missing a day of work. You need help, Taylor."

"Monday's a blackout day Ella. We *have to* be there," I said, trying to look serious.

"Good luck with that. I'll probably take a month off to let my nerves recover."

I put my leg over the bar, mindful not to jar the rifle. I remembered my father making me remove the ammunition and reminding me not to bump the scope whenever we crossed a fence. I questioned the accuracy of the rifle already. No need to complicate matters. I would have unloaded the rifle too, but this was a war zone. No one in a combat movie unloaded their weapon for any reason.

Chapter 33

4:00 a.m. Saturday

As I was making a pit stop for jerky and Gatorade, I noticed a nice pair of binoculars in the display case. It was compulsive, but I went around and grabbed them, thinking they might come in handy when deciding which brother to shoot first. The police started making noise on the bullhorn as I was sliding the door shut. Parker's plan was in motion.

The reality of what I was about to do hit me. I adjusted the straps on the knapsack and put it on, then cradled the rifle in my arm and forced myself to push on. The disorder at the front of the store intensified. I wasn't able to comprehend the shouting or the short squawks from the bullhorn, but the danger I was approaching made my whole body tremble. I hadn't had the shakes this bad since I quit drinking.

I focused on getting to my destination; the rolling ladder parked next to an I-beam. I crossed the aisle and turned right at one of the narrower intersecting corridors. I advanced shadow to shadow through the store. I could see red-and-blue flashing light coming through the front doors now. At the rear of the building, it was easy to feel no one was trying to help us. But now I could tell there was a well-choreographed circus outside.

I moved on, staying low as I entered the killers' base of operation. I had blood on my hands too, but I felt no guilt or remorse. Not after what they intended to do to Ella. I still had unresolved issues with her, that was true, but I had once loved her deeply. Giving up the booze was nothing compared to getting over her.

The clamor from the robbers began fading, but the voice on the bullhorn was still going strong. I could understand the repeated words clearer now: "Lay down your weapons and come out with your hands up."

A minute later I marched back into the aisle, hoping the gunmen were focused on their own problems. The last thing I needed now was for someone to come up behind me on their way back to headquarters. I passed through housewares and crossed into the women's clothing department. I went a little farther, then stepped into a shadow. I was standing in the women's sleepwear section, my legs visibly shaking. I had no choice but to stop until I could get it together.

I was about to press on when something caught my eye. The emergency light closest to me was secured to an I-beam twenty feet away. There were two racks of brassieres directly underneath. These were not the "cross your heart" kind I remembered seeing on commercials when I was a kid going through puberty. This collection wouldn't have been flattering on the full-figured actress in the commercial. I thought they *would* look great on Ella, not that I would tell her. I was stalling, afraid I was about to get killed, but I wanted to do something nice for her. She had sounded sincere when she asked for it. When we were a couple, she didn't own a bra.

Like a moth about to be incinerated by a flame, I went to the light. It took me a minute to figure out how the sizes ran, then track down until I got into her range. I felt foolish; I would obviously rather do just about anything other than stick my head up like a prairie dog so the exterminators could shoot at me.

I found the correct size and chose the least provocative one available. I knew my wife would find it "interesting" that I got a woman I once had a relationship with a black lacy bra on my way to shoot our captors. She wouldn't hear it from me. I removed the pack and stuck the bra deep into the canvas bag. I figured I could use my last dying breaths to launch it away from me if need be.

I continued to my objective, promising myself there would be no more stalling. I moved into the menswear section. I could see the I-beam where I was expected to demonstrate my sniper skills. Luckily, there was no backup light attached. The enemy was silent, but the bullhorn chant continued just outside the doors. It seemed staged—because it was. I prayed the enemy didn't figure that out.

I hoped the police had the camera set up so they could warn me if someone were bearing down. Then I remembered my phone was turned off. I walked the remaining distance like a man with rubber legs. I leaned the rifle against the girder and held my hand out to see how bad I was shaking. Physically, I was in position, but mentally I wasn't even close. Seconds later, the bullhorn went quiet. I was sure the police were now viewing activity inside the store. Everything was happening the way Parker said it would. That gave me hope. Maybe he *could* get me through this, and I could go home to my adorable wife.

I called Parker. He answered on the first ring.

"You picked a great location, Steve. I see you on my monitor, so just shake your head yes or no when I ask a question."

I nodded, and Parker responded. "Excellent, Steve, we can do this. The camera is infrared; I see fine in low light. Any questions?"

I paused for a moment and then signaled with my thumb that I was good.

"Great, I like communicating this way. It cuts out the hilarious sarcasm."

I tilted my head back and smirked. I was sure he got the message—even through my head stocking.

"Okay Steve, let's get down to business. We have a system. When you get up the ladder, you'll be able to see either a green or red light shining through the door to your left. They're xenon flashlights with colored lenses. They'll be distinct from the other lights out here. We'll use them to warn you if there is a problem."

He didn't speak again until I nodded.

"We'll keep it simple. Green indicates everything is good; take your shots. We'll shine a steady red if we want you to wait. Blinking red means you need to run. Do you understand these directions?"

I gave a nod.

"One last thing. Your face isn't visible on the infrared. Are you wearing something on your head?"

I lifted the mask and smiled like somebody said cheese.

"You never cease to amaze me, Taylor. Good luck and happy hunting," Parker said, hanging up.

Chapter 34

I readjusted my head cover. Parker may not have been impressed, but I still felt it would make me less noticeable. I climbed two rungs up the ladder and placed the rifle on the top shelf, just to the right of the beam. The police blasted their demands on the bullhorn again to drown out any noise I made. The volume-level at this distance startled me. I stood there for a moment, my whole body shaking.

I cleared bags of athletic socks out of the way and hoisted the knapsack onto the top shelf. Surveying the landscape reminded me of the panoramic view from my deer stand. I could definitely see through the exit to my left. It was dark outside, and the blue-and-red strobe lights reminded me of Christmas. Despite all the other lights, I could see a bright red light that seemed to be pointed directly at me. I gave another thumbs-up. Then I turned my attention to the action at center stage. The sight made my knees weak again, and I held onto the I-beam for a moment in case they buckled.

Like sitting in my deer stand, I had a good view of the unsuspecting targets below. Using the binoculars, I observed the four still wearing their lab coats standing in front of the entrance to the restrooms. They looked like junior-high delinquents all right, smoking and joking. All four were facing the exit to my left, where the police were now broadcasting their message continuously.

The two M-16-wielding bandits were posted as Parker said, one at each end of the block wall, standing next to an exit. The family resemblance was obvious. The one to my right was the muscular guy with a flattop I had seen run past me. He looked like a cross between a commando and a bar bouncer. Bear, standing at the far left, scared me the most. He had thirty pounds more hard muscle than his brother. Bear had a build that came only from spending hours a day inside a gym—or a prison exercise yard. He was bigger in the arms and chest than any of the guys at the fitness center.

Dialing in the glasses, I could see every flaw on Bear's face. His pockmarked cheeks reminded me of some of the power lifters, the ones rumored to be "juiced" when training for a competition. The tattoos that covered every inch of his exposed arms appeared to be homemade, rather than the professional quality of the cartoon wolf depicted on my own arm.

Both brothers wore black tactical pants and tight black T-shirts covered by their bulletproof vests. They were the only members of their crew not wearing lab coats. I examined both from top to bottom, convinced I was no match for either in a fair fight. Seeing the impressive display of police and emergency personnel outside reminded me the situation was not hopeless. Which was how it felt where I was standing.

I pointed the binoculars at the fifteen or so hostages and refocused. They were restrained: wrists tied behind their back, legs bound at the ankles. They were spread out on the floor in front of the checkout lanes. They weren't directly under a backup light, but the powerful binoculars allowed me to see their faces clearly. I recognized most of them but knew the names of just a few. I studied Clara, the cashier I had chatted with whenever I was the only person in her line. She appeared tired but unharmed.

Joe was with another male hostage, the manager I spoke to one night when I needed assistance. He seemed like a nice guy, though I wasn't exactly thrilled with him at the time. They were at the end of the center checkout. Joe was closest to me, leaning against the bagging station. He was the only hostage sitting up, probably rebelling against his captors I guessed, knowing Joe. Other males included a couple of employees and the security guard, who didn't look well, stretched out flat on his back with his eyes shut. I focused on his face but couldn't tell if he was dead, unconscious, or somehow sleeping through all the noise.

I quit stalling and put the rifle to my shoulder. Within seconds the signal light turned green. Getting the go-ahead made me feel a little better about doing this. I killed twice now in life-and-death situations, but I was hesitant to kill someone who stood unsuspecting. I always preferred to shoot ducks in flight, instead of those bobbing on the water.

Sanctioned by the police, I considered what I was about to do necessary and in the best interest of all the *good* people involved. These murdering thieves needed to be stopped before they killed anyone else, including me. I almost had myself convinced.

Far from the nearest light and in the shadow of the I-beam, I was almost in complete darkness. I didn't think anyone would notice me until I began shooting. I centered the knapsack in front of me and laid the rifle on top, imitating the snipers I saw in movies who used beanbags to support their weapons.

I panned the scope across the congregated lab coats. Most of them had bony frames protruding through the garment, making it unlikely they had Kevlar underneath—neither of the other two I killed wore a vest. I swiveled the rifle until my primary target's body came into view. I levered it upward and Clarence's head filled the scope. His bald skull never moved, but I couldn't keep it in the crosshairs. My shaky hands were affecting my aim despite the stable rest.

I put the crosshairs on his chest. I didn't intend to waste a bullet putting a dent in his armor; I just wanted to see if I could hold on the larger target. Somewhat satisfied, I raised my aim until his face came back into view. He turned, facing me directly now, but not looking upward as if he detected my presence. Still, seeing him glance in my general direction frightened me. I remained in place, believing he couldn't make me out.

I placed the crosshairs on his nose, or at least I tried to. It was more like I was circling his head, occasionally seeing an eye or ear. I had five tries until I ran out of bullets, but the element of surprise only existed for the first shot. Parker suggested the femoral artery as an alternative kill shot. I'm an autoworker, not a doctor. I *did* know Suzy had a stress fracture in her thigh six months ago. I remembered her surgeon referring to the bone as a femur. I knew there was a sizeable vein running down my own leg. I figured that was good enough for government work.

I wanted to follow my father's advice: don't start trouble and there won't be trouble, but I shook it off. If I blew Bear's leg off with the first shot, I would assume he was cooked. And then I would see if I could take out his brother. I'd put myself in a lot of danger to just stand there and observe. The signal light was now blinking. Flashing green was not discussed; I was almost positive. This must be Parker's way of telling me he was growing impatient.

I pushed bags of socks out of my way to clear space to cycle the bolt. I would have preferred a semiautomatic rifle since the accuracy of the weapon and shooter were in question. Bolt action is the best choice when the gun is dialed in. One shot taken by a skilled shooter and the target is dead, whether it's a deer, wild boar, or dangerous criminal.

I aimed at Clarence's upper leg, but my hands were shaking so hard I couldn't even hold that target. The crosshairs were circling his midsection. I had to do something before Parker picked up a bullhorn and started yelling at *me*.

I adjusted my aim to the center, below the vest. The target I was now circling was definitely a vital organ—to him anyway. I hit the trigger before I could talk myself out of it. I watched through the scope as the bullet tore through the leader's right leg, inches above his knee. I had pulled the shot down and to the left—by a lot. Not a big shock to anyone who'd seen me yank on a trigger.

I then remembered too late, my father's instruction about taking a deep breath and squeezing the trigger halfway through the exhale. Let the bang surprise you. I always remembered that bit of information just after the shot—when I was following the bloodless trail of a gut-shot animal. I didn't hear the bang, but my ears were ringing like a church bell. I wasn't surprised. I'd never heard the first report out of my deer rifle when shooting a buck either.

I ejected the smoking shell casing, then cycled the next cartridge home. Bear leaned against the wall, still clinging to his rifle. The lab coats remained huddled outside the bathrooms. I suppose that since their leaders weren't running for cover, they felt no need to exit the danger zone. Over the buzzing in my ears, I could hear Clarence groaning. Flattop shouldered his weapon, but his eyes focused on his brother.

Bear still had both lower extremities, so he was still my target. He pressed one hand to the front of his leg, which was bleeding profusely. I aimed for the other one, but he was bent over too far. The top of his bald head was pointing at me. I tried to match his swaying skull with the circular motion I was making with the scope as I squeezed the trigger. I heard the report this time, and saw the hole I made in the block wall about six inches left of his head. Another pulled shot.

I slid in the next round. My hands no longer shook. I had something to keep them busy. Spooked, Clarence raised his rifle, but he wasn't stable enough to seek out a target. I put his nose in my crosshairs and pulled the trigger. His body recoiled, and he clutched at his chest like he was having a heart attack. I hit him center mass—sending a swatch of cloth flying off his vest.

I glimpsed the green light as I ejected the spent casing and bolted in number four. Everyone who wasn't a hostage ran for cover, except the two I feared most. Flattop swept the rifle back and forth, looking for me. Clarence was down on his good knee raising his weapon, but he had too many other problems to be a threat. He *was* successful, considering his hunched over stance, in denying me a target large enough to aim for.

This wasn't going well, but I still had two more rounds. Parker advised trying to get a few of the ex-cons hovering outside the restrooms when I was finished with my priority targets. Since I couldn't shoot at baby brother, I was through. I wanted to see if I could fire into the exterminators retreating behind the block wall where the men's room door was located, without missing all of them. I wasn't pleased with my marksmanship, but I never told anyone I was a great shot with a rifle or any weapon.

I lined up on the chest of the first one who came into view. He was turned around facing me, probably expecting to see an army of police officers approaching. I fired the shot, and this time I remembered to exhale as I squeezed the trigger. It was down and out a couple of inches, but he crumpled to the floor. I sent the empty cartridge flying and rammed the last bullet into the firing chamber.

The area was clear. The criminals were probably lighting cigarettes by now. Then one of them stuck his head out. I put the crosshairs on his outside arm, then moved my aim slightly left as I squeezed the trigger. I watched the bullet hit the corner of his chest, and he fell to the floor. I looked over the scope; the light had turned red, and then started flashing. Flattop was sidestepping along the wall toward his brother, his weapon pointed directly at *me*. I grabbed my rifle and knapsack, then jumped off the ladder. A stream of bullets blew sock debris all around me.

Chapter 35

I ran straight back for twenty yards before I checked to see if anyone was chasing me. I saw no one. Flattop must have taken a minute to check out his brother. I figured I could get back to Ella without being seen, but I turned in the opposite direction and ran like I'd stolen something.

I crossed the corridor and ran down the potato chip and soda aisle. I waited at the end, afraid to venture across the wide expanse, divided by a long row of open-top refrigerated cases. I stood still and listened for Flattop—nothing. I looked for the double doors I remembered seeing stockers banging through with pallet trucks. I couldn't see my escape route in the dim light but knew it was located in the dark hole between the lunch meat and cheese coolers against the wall. More afraid to stand still than move forward, I unholstered the Glock and pressed on.

As I approached, the large gray doors became visible. I cradled the rifle across my arm, took out my small flashlight, and shined light through one of the windows. The rectangular porthole was scratched and greasy, making it impossible to see much. I hesitated before going in, remembering how Parker told me that someone was probably searching for me. I figured there was a chance one of the gunmen was waiting beyond the swinging doors. They would be on high alert after hearing the recent gunfire. But then someone behind me was shouting, and I liked my odds better through the door.

Whatever greased up the windows didn't touch the spring-loaded hinges. The slower I advanced the door with my foot, the louder the squeal. I pushed my way through with my flashlight hand, then tried to catch the door and missed. The light hit the floor and the door snapped back and forth several times. The light never flickered, shining brightly across the floor. I stood there hyperventilating for a second before I snatched up the flashlight and turned it off.

The employee-only section was much darker, but there was a dim backup light on a far wall. Something was stacked to my left, blocking most of the light. I was afraid to move for fear of knocking over a bread rack or whatever was next to me. I imagined someone standing there, eyes adjusted to the darkness, watching my every move. I turned the light back on.

My breathing returned to normal, but my hands shook. I set the rifle next to the door and removed the knapsack. I held the light under the Glock and swept the area. Milk crates, I soon discovered, were warehoused in this section. I holstered my weapon and instantly missed the security of having it in my hands.

I shined the light along the wall next to the door. A concrete ledge ran about knee-high along the wall beside the milk crates. A shiny gray wall reflected my light beyond the plastic boxes. The ledge was only a foot wide—not the luxury accommodations I was used to in sporting goods—but it looked like an oasis compared to the situation on the ladder. I picked up my gear and got on the ledge. Holding the light in my teeth, I held to the wall, inching my way toward the corner.

Two feet of space separated the milk crates from the metallic wall. I pointed the light down the glimmering partition. Beyond the milk crates, stood a door with a big lever similar to the ones old child-killing refrigerators sported back in the days of my youth.

I assumed the room was cold storage for meat sold in the store. I wondered if butchers processed pigs and cows in that room, or if they performed the slicing and dicing at a different facility. I hopped off the ledge at the corner and made camp, liking my ability to see in both directions. I lowered two of the crates and sat down, wishing I had a boat cushion to lay on top.

Sitting in the dark for a while, my sense of impending doom returned. The block wall obstructed any clues to whatever occurred on the other side. The silence was deafening. I tried not to, but I began reliving the ordeal. My last shot, the one I took my time on, was right on the money. I was definitely the weak link in the process. Even with the perfect opportunity, I'd failed to kill Clarence and his brother.

I put the pistol between my feet and laid the rifle across my lap. I fished inside the pack for the cartridges and took five out of the box. With the rifle fully loaded and propped against the wall, I had only one thing left to do—call Parker. No doubt he'd already tried to call me, but my phone was off. I wasn't sure which of my concerns were greater: having him send me back out there to finish the job or ordering me to go back and wait with Ella.

I don't want to leave here until I am free to go home to my wife, I thought as I turned on my phone.

"Are you okay in there? You did great by the way," Parker said when he answered.

"I'm hiding behind some milk crates," I told him, wishing I'd made the location sound more suitable for long-term housing.

"Hold tight for now. I've got another location for you to set up. I'll call back with specifics when things calm down."

"I'm not budging. I like it fine right here."

"Hey, man, I know that wasn't easy. And when I said you did well, that was an understatement. They were running like headless chickens after you bailed. We were able to winch their van out. That will make it easier for us to come in and get you."

"So, how's Clarence doing?" I asked.

"He's alive but seriously wounded. You did good . . . *real* good. Excellent shots on those two scarecrows. You looked like a real pro out there."

That seemed like a little too much praise. And I wondered why he was buttering me up.

"Great, what would you have me do next, I mean, if I *was* to go back out there?" I said.

"More of the same."

"How many do I have to kill before I can go home?"

"I won't say all of them, Steve, but it may come to that. Keep your phone on. I'll call you back shortly." Parker said, ending the call.

I didn't like the idea of risking my life again, but sitting there twiddling my thumbs wouldn't get me home. Maybe I'd get lucky and kill Clarence the next opportunity I got. I needed something to do besides worry, so I pulled out the radio, hooked up my phone, and started cranking.

I got fidgety a short time later, sitting on the uncomfortable seat. I decided to pass the time by listening to the radio. I wasn't sure if I could do that and charge simultaneously. That led to a low-level brainstorm. The device was also battery-powered. I popped off the cover to determine the size and then dug in my pack for the batteries.

I was disappointed when the phone didn't light up. I was hoping the multifaceted radio, now powered by fresh batteries, would allow me to charge the phone as if it were plugged into a wall charger. I'd seen products that charged phones from batteries. The ongoing expense was a deterrent. The store likely carried them, but the cable holding the connector for my phone probably wouldn't fit the device.

I *was* pleased to discover that I could listen to it while charging the phone. I plugged in the earphones and the speaker went silent. I inserted one of the buds into my ear, turned up the volume a little, and dialed in the local station. The next newscast was coming on shortly. I could crank for hours this way without losing interest—I might even surf the TV band if I moved to an area with better reception. The outdoor patio department came to mind, but I assumed there had to be an armed sentry posted there.

I raised the antenna, and the reception got much better. At a minute before the hour, a commercial came on that made driving a big rig sound like the opportunity of a lifetime. If I were still single, I would have jotted the number down. Suzy wouldn't be willing to live and work out of a truck. She was too fragile for that lifestyle anyway. And I didn't want to be away from my wife for extended periods. This was the first time we'd spent a night apart since we got married, and I wasn't enjoying it so far.

"This is *WKOM* breaking news," the deejay said. "Reporting live outside the Columbia SaveMart, here's Bart Thompson."

"Recent disturbances leave many worried innocent lives may have been lost in the standoff, now entering the second day," the reporter stated.

He continued, not telling me anything I didn't already know. My mind wandered to Suzy sitting at home, most likely watching the talking heads on television speculate on what happened and what would happen. I needed to call her. Parker promised to keep her informed, but he was probably occupied with more urgent matters. Suzy wouldn't be shy about asking the police for information. Her business savvy gave her special powers to get information from people without them realizing it—a knack she occasionally practiced on me. She would call anyone who might provide information.

I didn't think she would call me. She didn't know I had a charger and would also assume I'd have the phone turned off. After the news segment ended, I began missing my wife in earnest and called our house.

"I can't talk now. Someone's at the front door," Suzy said when she answered.

"Don't open it."

"It's probably the police. They're outside keeping the reporters away. Chief Simmons came to the door a half hour ago to ask if I needed anything. I have to see what they want. Call me back," she said before hanging up.

I was upset about the media trying to hassle my wife, but it sounded like the Centerville Police were handling the situation. I wasn't surprised they would help out. I knew most of the officers by name, and Suzy regularly dropped homemade goodies off at the police station after one of the young officers changed a flat tire for her. My wife was getting a taste of the chaos without having to leave the house.

Chapter 36

10:00 a.m. Saturday

I was listening to Elvis Presley's "Suspicious Minds" when my phone buzzed. "Steve, I need you to move now. Go back out there and take some more shots," Parker said, skipping formalities.

"Reporters are at my house, Parker. Suzy's got enough problems to worry about."

"Television crews are camped out at some of the hostages' homes. We won't let anyone bother the family members on the scene, so they're trying to get interviews that way. The reporters probably have a source that ran the license plates in the parking lot, but they don't know you're actively involved. Suzy will let the police handle it. I spoke to her personally."

"Does my wife have to come down here to get away from reporters?"

"Steve, you need to focus on what's going on in *your* world right now. I persuaded Suzy to invite a friend to stay with her. She should be arriving soon."

Doris Jones was probably knocking on the door. She would be an excellent source of moral support for my wife. I pictured them sitting in our living room praying for my well-being. Parker was doing all he could to help Suzy. It was my fault this was happening. We would be in the mountains now if I weren't such an idiot.

"It drives me crazy that my wife is getting drawn in and I can't do anything to help her."

"She's fine, Steve. I've got my friends from Centerville PD watching out for her. Just a heads-up: two gunmen are wandering around. It's not Marvin, or Flattop, as you call him."

"Are they looking for *me*?" I asked, realizing how ignorant that sounded.

"I think they were ordered to search for you, yes. They're not trying too hard to find you, though. Probably scared you're set up in another sniper's nest somewhere. They got close to Ella a few minutes ago, but they moved on."

"How close?"

"I doubt she even noticed."

I wouldn't bet on that, I thought. "Maybe I should lay low until they give up the hunt."

"You need to finish Clarence off. He's getting angrier by the minute."

"What about that roving band of murderers?"

"Just keep your eyes open," Parker said, raising his voice.

"I guess I'll do whatever you tell me. Why should I worry about vicious criminals trying to kill me?"

"My sense of humor is always the first thing to go when I don't sleep for a day or two," Parker said, lowering his volume.

I didn't like the level of sarcasm coming out of my mouth either. I wanted a small amount, but I sounded like a bratty, teenaged version of myself.

"Where do you want me to go?"

"Set up in the deli. I know a good place in there where you can take some shots. You have two options: cut through the meat locker, or go back out in the aisle and enter through the next set of service doors."

"I'll take the shortcut. I don't like my chances out there," I said.

"That's definitely safest, but the aisle is clear if you have a problem with whatever's hanging on hooks in there."

I got a mental image of killing hogs at my uncle's farm but got past it the only way I knew how: "You gotta kill it before you can grill it," I said, stealing a line from Ted Nugent, my favorite philosopher on sportsman's issues.

"Get moving. I'll call if there's a problem."

"What do you want me to do when I get to the rendezvous point?" I asked, wishing I didn't watch so many war movies.

"Whack 'em and stack 'em," Parker said, surprising me with his own passage from the Motor City Madman.

"Roger that."

"Call me after you exit the meat locker," Parker said.

I collected my stuff and left for hog heaven. There was just enough light to see the way. I pulled on the latch. Definitely the kind responsible for the deaths of many a young hide-and-seekers of my generation. I remember when my suburban town outlawed them. My father had to take the door off the old refrigerator in our basement—

the one he kept adult beverages in for their annual New Year's Eve party.

I opened the door, and a cool, dank wave hit me. The smell wasn't of rotting meat—not yet anyway. It smelled coincidentally like our basement refrigerator when left unplugged. I shined my light around the room. SaveMart definitely cut meat in the store. There were whole pigs and cows split down the middle, all swinging from hooks. Their hide was removed, giving them a human resemblance, which made me ponder my own mortality.

I managed to reach the other side without having a stroke. I rushed through the doorway without regard for what might be out there. Within seconds, my phone buzzed. A moment later the lights came on.

"What's up," I whispered.

"Bad news. Ella flew the coop, and Flattop is nearby—real close," Parker replied.

"What should I do?" I asked.

"If it were me, I'd go find her."

Chapter 37

"Where is she? Why'd she leave?" I asked.

"She just stepped out a minute ago, got scared with all the commotion around her. Flattop is the only one out there. He ordered the other two home. They're walking through the cashier lanes as we speak. I turned the lights back on before he could see the beam from her flashlight."

"Where is Flattop now?"

"He was poking his rifle barrel in stacks of tires in automotive, but now he's moving straight toward her like he heard something. Keep your phone on and go find her before *he* does," Parker said, then hung up.

I wished Parker had given me some pointers. I had no idea how to go about rescuing her. I put the rifle and knapsack down, and looked out through a different set of swinging doors with greasy windows.

I leave her in the best possible location, and she decides to go for a stroll.

What mattered now was to locate her without getting both of us killed. I couldn't stop thinking about her earlier predicament. The leaders must have permitted their subordinate to cut Ella from the herd, fully aware what he was up to. I tried not to think what Flattop would do if he captured her.

I didn't want the extra weight of the rifle, but I now preferred killing exterminators from far away, rather than the 25 feet I was consistent with the handgun. I threw the pack on my shoulders and grabbed the rifle, then set off to find Ella. I prayed to God I could do this. I had come too far to die now.

I cut across the store, taking the most direct route. I proceeded as quickly as I could without running because running would make too much noise. I paralleled the edge of the clothing section to avoid the main aisle, but otherwise I did nothing to mask my approach. A deep voice called out, "Give it up, Sniperman. I'll find you eventually."

Evidently I had achieved superhero status, but I didn't like the name. It would never sell comic books. Flattop was acting like a bird dog working the brush, and he succeeded in spooking Ella out of hiding. I passed the electronics department and entered sporting goods, continuing out in the open far too long.

Ella was in the neighborhood; I could sense it. I peered around each corner, hoping to find her and not the psycho killer. I went by the checkout station, creeping toward the aisle I'd acquired the bucket from. The singing deer and our hideout were at the far end. Leading with the rifle, I stepped past a steel girder located at the end of the corridor.

My phone buzzed about the same time I heard the shot. I jumped back before I could see who pulled the trigger. The squeal that came from the same direction as the bang, led me to believe it was Ella who just shot me.

Chapter 38

Ella's first screams were probably in recognition of who she'd fired at. There was no discernable pause in between, but her cries abruptly became shrill. I awaited the sound of her pump gun cycling another shell into the chamber. Instead, I heard the grunts of a man who sounded like he was fighting a wildcat.

"Drop the gun, or I'll snap your neck," he demanded.

I retreated a few steps, listening for clues regarding Flattop's next move. The pain in my shoulder, chest, and neck smarted, but I was afraid to look at my wounds. Ella's high-pitched banshee screech arrived just before what I thought must be her shotgun clattering to the floor. I wanted to rush in and save her, but fear and possibly wisdom kept me from venturing down that road—aisle. I suspected Flattop was looking to see if he still needed to kill what Ella was shooting at.

Judging by the sound of Ella's screams, they were moving toward me. Sticky moisture soaked my shirt. The damage couldn't be too serious, or I wouldn't be standing like I was, shaking like a cold, wet dog. If she had been patient enough to wait for a good shot, she would have also been able to identify her target. She was like a dangerous hunter shooting at noises and rustling bushes. But considering the circumstances, I doubted I would have done any better.

While Ella attempted to fight off her attacker, I inched past clearance-priced golf towels displayed at the end of the aisle and peeked around the I-beam. I showed just enough skin to validate what my ears were telling me. Flattop was facing me as he moved forward, holding Ella a foot above the floor in the crook of his right arm. He held his automatic weapon like a pistol. I hoped he wasn't a lefty, but he didn't appear to have any trouble controlling either the gun or Ella.

She was pedaling air as I swung the rifle around and took rest on the steel girder that possibly saved my life—the jury was still out. Holding Ella as a shield, Flattop aimed his weapon at me. I jumped back as several rounds thumped into the I-beam. Knowing he could do that in spite of Ella's kicking and thrashing scared me nearly as much as the bullets themselves.

I backed up a few aisles and knelt down, resting my rifle on the shelf at the end. I aimed to the right of the I-beam and took some deep breaths. A paper bag to breathe into might have helped. It sounded like Flattop had Ella under control. He stopped yelling at her and began barking at me.

"Let me pass by, or I'll shoot her right here . . . then I'll kill you."

"No deal. You can go back after you turn her loose," I said, my voice breaking.

Flattop didn't respond.

"Let her go," I shouted.

The police were on the bullhorn now, but the words reverberating through the store sounded like gibberish. I feared it was a warning that someone was approaching. I heard Ella whimper as she and Flattop approached the aisle where I was waiting. I suddenly remembered Parker didn't want me to kill this guy until his brother was dead. He may already be dead—but the last report I got from Parker, he was still alive.

Surely Parker would shoot this maniac himself, given the situation. I made a vow to kill Flattop or die trying. I put my eye to the scope and waited for them to emerge. Ella was quieter now, but I could still hear her muffled whimpers, like he had his hand over her mouth. He was clearly a much braver man than I am. I pictured Bear hobbling up behind me as I waited to kill his brother. I chose to focus on one threat at a time.

First I saw the M-16's barrel come past the leading edge of the support beam, then Ella's red, tear-streaked face. They were in the same configuration I witnessed earlier, but now his thick arm was clenching Ella's throat. He seemed to be allowing her barely enough air to live—but not enough to struggle.

"Do you see him?" he barked. She looked at me and the weapon I had pointed at them.

"He's gone," she managed to choke out.

I admired her bravery, but I wondered if it would have been healthier for both of us to acknowledge my presence, possibly forcing the exterminator to retreat. Ella appeared ready to settle this now, rather than risk what might happen if he managed to get by me.

He came forward, holding Ella's face level with his, making it impossible to see more than the top of his head. The view through the scope was a little blurred at this close range, but I could distinguish the features on Ella's face.

He was unwilling to expose himself by turning in my direction. I had a couple of moments when his face swayed into view, but I knew a yanked shot could put a round into Ella's head. He sensed I was gunning for him and swung his weapon, then fired another short burst. The rounds whizzed over my head, his aim was too high to be a threat. And that was a good thing because I was frozen like a statue.

It was cooling off in the store since the power came back on, but sweat trickled down my face. I recalled seeing comedians dripping wet when they came off the stage, having performed their entire set without so much as a chuckle. Between my flop sweat and the way I was trembling, I was glad I selected the rifle as my weapon of choice. A handgun would be worthless to me right now.

Ella stared directly at me, begging with her eyes for me to take the shot. I didn't think she understood the risk involved, but I would seize any decent opportunity. Flattop was still holding Ella's face next to his. Her feet dangled limply now, trying to touch bottom with her toes. He was swaying a bit and seemed to be tiring, holding Ella that way now for a few minutes. At one point he turned toward me, but not far enough to put his face in my crosshairs. Ella winked at me. Something she'd always done to get my attention in a crowded room.

Seconds later, she hooked her feet behind her captor's legs and bent forward. This put the right side of his head in the crosshairs. I let out the breath I hadn't noticed I was holding and slowly applied trigger pressure.

A volcano of red and brown liquid erupted, but I couldn't tell through the scope exactly who I'd hit. Both Flattop and Ella fell to the floor. Only one was screaming loud enough to wake the dead. Apparently, she wasn't loud enough. I was close enough to see Marvin had a real flat top now. His head looked like something out of the *Zapruder* film. Ella, covered in blood and brains, climbed out from under the carcass. I ran to her, taking a quick glance behind to see if anyone was approaching.

Ella continued wailing as she reached for a golf towel. She used it to wipe the gray matter off her face. I seized the dead man's gun and then removed two banana clips attached to his vest. I thought about taking the body armor for Ella, but my arms were full, and the vest was covered in the same ooze she had in her hair.

My phone vibrated, reminding me how vulnerable we were standing in the open.

"Take cover! Clarence sent a guy to check on Marvin."

"No, I'm fine Parker. I've been shot, but thanks for your concern."

"I'll hug you later. Climb back in your hole—*now*." Parker said, ending the call.

"Ella, let's go," I ordered, taking her arm.

She yanked it away, then grabbed a stack of golf towels. She was a mess in every imaginable way.

"C'mon Ella, someone's coming," I said softly.

I led the way, back down the aisle Ella got ambushed, and she followed like a gun-shy beagle. I noticed the damage her shot did to the row of camping supplies, which most of the pellets had struck before glancing toward me. Thank goodness these guys were using birdshot. Getting hit with buckshot would have been vastly more serious. Reaching the back aisle where Flattop had captured her, I suggested she pick up the scattergun. She did, but would have shown more enthusiasm if it were a rattlesnake.

I looked both ways to make sure the coast was clear, then we quick-stepped to our hideout. Crossing the bar, Ella left a gut trail on the leaf-patterned garments even I could have followed. She sat on the toilet clutching the shotgun as I climbed in. I stood both rifles in the corner next to the bucket. I took off my backpack, noticing one side was a little shredded and colored with a red stain I trusted was from one of the bottles in there. I drew my Glock and gazed out, waiting for whoever wanted to mess with me next.

Chapter 39

Parker watched the skinny runt in a lab coat walk nervously toward Flattop's location, waving his shotgun around like he expected Steve to jump out from behind a clothing rack. Meanwhile Special Agent Michael Powell changed out of his suit and put on his tactical gear. He arrived in time to watch Clarence's little brother get his head splattered.

"He found Marvin. I thought maybe he'd chicken out and tell Clarence everything was good. That would have bought you a little time," Parker said.

"You should've told your boy to hide the body," Powell replied.

"I told you not to question my decisions."

"Like you did the last time?"

"Hey, there aren't a lot of places to hide a body in there. The mess on the floor would have been a dead giveaway—pun intended," Parker said.

"They would be safer if he took the woman back to the deli. Then he could have put Clarence down like you wanted him to . . . before he killed Marvin."

"I'll send them over when things calm down."

"Before or after Clarence kills all the hostages?"

"At least somebody will survive . . . unlike last time," Parker said, staring at him.

Following a long silence, Powell asked, "What are you going to do when Clarence finds out about his brother?"

"What am I going to do? You're the negotiator. My men are set to take down the doors if you drop the ball."

"Well, the good news is, the guy doing recon is in no hurry to get back," Powell said, studying the monitor.

"Yeah, maybe he's taking Marvin's wallet to identify the body."

Chapter 40

Jimmy Martin, the young sturdy-built manager, was trying to figure out what just happened at the back of his store. He'd heard gunfire, then screaming and shouts, and then a final shot was fired. He guessed the sniper was out of commission now. The big guy in charge ordered one of his flunkies to check it out, but he'd been gone a while.

He was sitting next to Joe Duncan, both leaning against the bagging station. The hostages were on edge since the mystery sniper had fired on the enemy—directly over their heads. Jimmy attempted to reassure them in whispers that the attack would help the police negotiate an end to the standoff.

The thin sentry with the scraggily beard returned from his assignment and went straight into the bank. The leader everyone called Bear had been hiding there since he took the bullet in the leg. Joe leaned over and whispered, "He seemed kind of happy when he passed by. Can't be good news for our side."

"I was expecting two people," Jimmy replied.

"You're right. That other gorilla should have come back with him. Unless—"

"Unless he couldn't," Jimmy said, smiling.

They sat back, studying the bank. Joe gestured to Jimmy and leaned in. "Maybe there was an off-duty cop in here already when those bank robbers came in," Joe whispered.

"I'm a part-time deputy and know most of the law-enforcement around here. I was working up front, keeping an eye on things, and I don't remember seeing anyone who carries a badge," Jimmy whispered back.

Jimmy watched the thin sentry run out of the bank and point his shotgun at the hostages. Seconds later, the phone on the customer service counter rang. He glanced at it but never took his shotgun off the people sitting in the floor. Bear limped out, looking like a man in pain, scanning for signs of a sniper and using his rifle to help him walk. He answered, with a grunt, on the tenth ring. He appeared less than overjoyed by the call and became more agitated the longer he stood there.

"Agent Powell," he said. "I've been wondering when I'd hear your voice. Figured you were pulling the strings in here. The least you could do is offer your condolences for killing my brother."

Clarence listened for a moment, then laid the phone down and limped toward a cluster of ladies, all donning the same blue smocks. He scanned their faces and stopped when he got to one of the more elderly hostages.

Holding the rifle by the grab handle, he clutched the rope binding her ankles with his free hand and dragged her, powering with his good leg. The woman screamed, as Bear pulled her toward the exit.

Standing two feet away from the automatic doors, he lifted the distraught woman to her feet and put the muzzle of his weapon to her temple. They stood facing the outside world as the elderly woman begged for her life. Without any attempt to use his wielded power to negotiate, Bear pulled the trigger. His weapon sounded like a jackhammer. He threw her near-headless body to the side and hobbled back to the telephone, using the rifle again to assist him once he turned the corner.

"That's in case you had something to do with my brother. If I find out for sure, I'll kill them all and as many of you are stupid enough to try and stop me," Bear said, slamming the phone down.

Jimmy watched in horror, not believing what he'd just seen. The hostages were hysterical, screaming at their captor, especially the ladies who had been sitting with the executed woman. One of the elderly women cursed him and told him what to expect in the afterlife. Bear rode his rifle back to the bank, in a hurry. Jimmy heard the volume go up on the flat-screen television he'd seen one of the men lug past earlier. He watched the killer adjusting a portable antenna positioned on one of the teller stations.

Jimmy whispered to Joe, "I've worked with Gertie since I got home from the desert. We need to figure a way to take him down. He's hurt bad. I'll finish him off with my bare hands if I get the chance."

Joe nodded. "This guy's going to kill us all if we don't."

"Tell me about it."

Jimmy wasn't sure, but he thought he recognized Bear from news reports and wanted posters he'd seen. The shaved head is not what he remembered, but he was convinced this was the felon who had been the subject of a nationwide manhunt.

"Maybe the sniper is one of your employees," Joe whispered.

"I thought about that earlier. But I've accounted for all of my people except for Big Ed. Sounds like he tried to stop them, but if what we heard is true, he can't help us now."

"Maybe Ed survived. Maybe he's the one making trouble."

Jimmy shook his head. "It's not him, not that he wouldn't if he was still alive. I heard one of them bragging to the boss about Ed getting shot in the chest at close range. He was a tough old coot. Fought in Vietnam three tours."

Joe nodded.

"That sweet woman over there has been with the company thirty years; since the first store opened, Jimmy said. "We go to the same church with her and her husband, Dickie. Their daughter had a baby girl two weeks ago—first grandchild. Gertie was driving to Memphis this weekend to see her for the first time. Dickie was coming by after her shift. She talked about it all night," Jimmy said, stopping when he noticed every word brought Joe closer to tears.

Chapter 41

Ella sat with the shotgun across her lap, wiping her face with a slimy towel. She was in a trance—unable to speak—which was far better than the spasms she was having before I told her somebody was approaching.

I felt I should be more traumatized. Within a span of about fifteen minutes, I had been shot and then I'd killed yet another exterminator. I wanted to believe I was getting better at this, or at least used to it. But I just felt numb, like I was shell-shocked or something. When we heard someone rummaging near Flattop's body, I stood waiting, maybe even hopeful, he would come looking for us.

After he moved on, I offered Ella a bottle of water and a fresh towel. She wet the cloth and began wiping her face. I was concerned she hadn't noticed the goop that remained in her hair.

I sat down and studied the new rifle. I thought about calling Parker for one of those "lessons money can't buy" he talked about. But every conversation we had lately ended with him conning me into doing something suicidal. I'd rather figure it out on my own.

I located the rifle's safety switch and found it was in the off position; an important detail I should have already attended to. The switch that allowed the user to toggle between "semi" and "burst" was in the rapid-fire mode. I put it in single-fire mode. I was confident I could operate this weapon, although I was clueless about the complex scope. I located the lever to release the magazine and ran a full one in, getting it on the first try. *Who says Rambo movies aren't educational?*

As I was about to put the rifle back in the corner and rest my head back against the wall, I heard what reminded me of a tommy gun from an old *Untouchables* episode. I assumed that was how an M-16 sounded from a distance. With a somewhat delayed reaction, Ella swung her shotgun around as she stood up, pushing the hunting suits aside with the end of her barrel.

"Relax, Ella, I've got this," I said, calmly patting the rifle.

She sat down, and we peeked through the opening.

"It's probably nothing," I said, thinking Bear had killed several hostages.

"You better call the police," Ella said when she saw me digging in my pocket.

I let it go, pleased to witness the first indicator of normal behavior. My cell phone vibrated as I took it out. I started quivering too as I comprehended the significance of a call from Parker at this moment. I assumed angry gunmen were either coming our way or he wanted me to go seek them out. I was relieved to see my wife's nickname in the display.

"Well, hello there Suzy-Q," I said, trying to sound like I didn't have a care in the world.

"They killed a hostage," Suzy said, weeping.

"What? How do you know?"

"They showed it on television. She was just a sweet old lady."

"Did they say who she was?"

"Not her name, but it was an employee. She wore the uniform. A reporter interviewed her husband a half hour earlier. He held up a framed picture of the woman."

I fought to reign in my emotions as I visualized my favorite cashier being gunned down. Though it didn't feel altogether right to do so, I regained control by telling myself the odds favored it being one of the other ladies, one who I never made a connection with. I always said hello to anyone who glanced in my direction, but Clara on lane twenty-three had shown me pictures of her grandchildren.

"I've got to go babe. Parker may be trying to contact me."

"You know how to work call waiting, right?"

"I don't have call waiting."

"Right, I forgot—you have the dinosaur."

My phone chirped.

"Sounds like low battery," Suzy offered.

"Gotta go. I'm in a safe place, so don't worry."

"Love you, sweetheart. Please be careful," Suzy said, then hung up.

Ella stared, waiting for me to update her.

"They killed one of the hostages."

"Ella gripped her shotgun and put her finger on the safety.

"Easy does it, Ella. How about you put that away and charge the phone. I'll keep an eye out for trouble."

Ella nodded but held onto the weapon.

I took the radio out of my pack and attached the phone. I eased the gun away and parked it in the corner, then laid the devices in her lap. Without a word of complaint, she began turning the lever. I wondered if I might have lasted longer than six months with this new *Stepford Wives* version of Ella.

Chapter 42

"Parker, can you come in here for a minute?" Powell yelled out the open door of the SWAT command center.

"It's my bus, so I guess I can," Parker muttered as he climbed the steps.

"You set me up there, didn't you?"

"How'd I do that?"

"You got your boy to kill Marvin less than thirty minutes after I got here. Now I'm the one who has to deal with Clarence. Is that why you asked for my help? So I would get the blame when he started killing hostages? I thought I knew you better than that," Powell said, scowling.

"Hey, *I* didn't ask for you. That was my boss's idea. You told me over the phone you wanted to good cop-bad cop, him. You should have told me you wanted to be the good cop."

"I guess I picked the wrong time to get here. I'm surprised he only killed one hostage," Powell said, rubbing his temples.

"Me too. I thought he was going to kill them all. My men were about to breach the doors."

"Maybe I shouldn't have called," Powell said. "I figured Clarence sent his lap dog out there to slaughter the hostages. Maybe he wouldn't have killed her if I left him alone."

"Quit second-guessing yourself. That's my job. He *would* have killed everyone if you let him stew. We lost one hostage, but we saved fifteen by making the call. That's what we do."

"Anyone with a zoom lens can get a shot of the dead hostage right now. Those pictures will go viral," Powell said.

"I spoke to Jennifer. A local affiliate showed the execution. They were doing live coverage and zoomed in when they observed movement at the door. They promised not to play the clip again," Parker said.

"Great, just what we needed."

"Don't sweat it. The next time you lure Clarence out to answer the phone, I'll get Steve to take him out. We both know he won't surrender."

"I don't understand how you've gotten away with it. Having the civilian shoot Clarence and killing his men. And until he killed Bubba, not a hint of retaliation," Powell said.

"That's what I've been telling you. As far as Clarence knows, it's Steve—the guy I supposedly have no contact with, who's doing all the damage. Clarence told me they watched him go in the store and saw him as a threat from the get-go."

"Now he thinks I'm the one ordering hits in there. That'll make it hard for me to work him," Powell said.

"I heard what Clarence said. If he truly believed we were pulling strings, he'd be setting off the best fireworks in the state right here."

"Yeah, but what happens when Clarence *finds out* we're lying to him?" Sees your boy talking on the phone for instance," Powell asked.

"Let's pray he doesn't. This is a unique situation, Powell. I realize this goes against the rules, but Steve had to kill one of them before I even talked to him. He killed the other one protecting the woman. I was surprised Steve knew that was going down. Clarence thinks he's just a good old boy holding his ground. That's about the truth too. He's no cop wannabe. He wants *us* to fight this battle. We need to keep him motivated, though. He's our best hope to end this successfully."

"I would have done things differently. You know that right?"

"Yeah, I would say the same thing if our roles were reversed. I hope this doesn't turn into one of those case studies you guys use at Quantico when teaching what *not* to do," Parker said.

"If I get to star in another one of those, I'll be lucky to get the security job that just opened here," Powell said, pointing out the window.

"I'm wide open to suggestions. I don't like putting Steve's life on the line any more than you like staking your career on him. I'm the one who'll have to sit down with his wife if he goes down."

"What have you told him about Clarence? Does he know about the bank robbery?"

"He probably saw it on the news back then, but no, I didn't tell him it was the same guy. I'm afraid he wouldn't do what I need him to do if he found out. He didn't make the connection when I said the name. He didn't mention recognizing him either. Clarence had long hair back then. One of the Nashville reporters has made the connection, but she promised to sit on it in exchange for an exclusive interview later. Now that Clarence is being Clarence, I'm sure that deal is out the window. She's probably airing the story now, before another reporter figures it out."

"I nearly got transferred to Virginia following our last encounter with Clarence. I'm there most days training personnel on the lessons we learned. Armchair quarterbacks wore me out for letting him leave the bank with hostages." Powell said.

"You know my opinion on that. We had the base of his skull in our crosshairs, and you waved me off. I know the accuracy of hindsight, but you—"

Powell interrupted, "You really think your boy can take him out?"

"He's already eliminated the worst of Clarence's sidekicks. Most are hanging out, waiting for a bus to come and take them back to prison. There's one knucklehead we've identified as Michael Watson, who may be a significant threat. He's been coming in and out of the loading dock area. Mikey, the nickname listed on his rap sheet, did time with Clarence . . . was still incarcerated when Clarence pulled the bank job. We don't know how loyal he is."

"I can't imagine anyone being loyal to Clarence. He abandoned his entire crew on his last heist for Pete's sake," Powell said.

"Dumb criminals . . . go figure."

"So your boy has skills?"

"He knows how to load and shoot a gun, but that's been good enough so far. He's bound to be skittish now. I have an idea that should help if I have to lean on him. I'm hoping it doesn't come to that," Parker said.

"You sure he's got the stomach for it? That's the hardest part even for trained professionals."

"He'd walk through fire to get home to his wife. He also showed some fortitude helping the woman in there. Definitely shaky going after Clarence, but he managed to cripple him. I wish he could've taken out Marvin quietly, like one of his previous kills. Blame Steve for that if you want—not that he had any options."

"So how do you intend to compel him, if it comes to that?

"Let's just say I'm one phone call away from having him do whatever I tell him."

"Did you notice he left the vest behind? Too messy I suppose. I would've taken it. Unless I wouldn't need the protection going forward."

"I almost told him to grab it, but I didn't think I'd like his response. I guess I better make that call," Parker said, pulling out his phone.

Chapter 43

2:00 p.m. Saturday

My vibrating phone woke me, but it stopped before I could answer. My mouth, dry as sandpaper, told me I'd been snoring. Not too loudly though, because Ella was still asleep, sitting upright with her chin resting on her chest. I identified the caller and then swished some water around in my mouth.

Today is the day, Steve," Parker said with enthusiasm when I called him back.

"Don't tell me; let me guess. It's the last day of the rest of my life."

"I figured you for one of those glass-half-full kinda guys."

"Give me a reason to be optimistic," I replied.

"Your wife is here."

"What the . . . what do you mean my wife is here?" I yelled, waking Ella.

"Out here in the parking lot, a hundred yards away from you. We're ending this today. I knew you'd be anxious to see her as soon as you came out."

"Where is she exactly?" I demanded.

"She's sitting in the backseat of a patrol car with the air-conditioner running. I tried to help her in, but she wouldn't allow it."

"Listen Parker, Suzy is very fragile. You shouldn't have pressured her to come down here, with all that's going on."

"Who pressured? I offered a ride, and she took it. Suzy told me about her medical condition on the phone. Don't worry, I'll take good care of her."

"That's not your job, Parker. It's mine."

"Take care of business in *there*, then you can come out *here* and take over."

"I *was* keeping her safe in our house. That's how I was *doing* my job."

"Well, Suzy's *here* and she's not leaving. I'm looking at her through the window of my bus right now. She's talking on her phone. She said she had some work to do. I'll be taking good care of her. That leaves you free to take Clarence down. And that's what you'll do."

"Alright Parker, I'll play along, but let me tell you, if something happens to my wife you better cross your fingers I don't make it out."

"That's fine, Steve. I know you're angry, but channel that energy into helping me reunite the two of you. Got it?"

"You could have checked with me before you brought her to your war zone. You have no reason to put her in danger."

"*You're* in the war zone, Steve. We're out here sipping coffee waiting for you to quit pulling shots, so we can *all* go home. Let me set you straight on something: I'm in charge here. If I thought bringing my ninety-year-old grandmother down here would facilitate getting you and the other hostages out alive, I would send a car for her too. Understood?"

I let it go. My wife was here, and there was nothing I could do about it.

Chapter 44

4:00 p.m. Saturday

Suzy was sitting in a police car behind the bus. She knew there would be a lot of waiting around, so she brought her laptop and Wi-Fi hotspot to the scene. She was banging out an email when Parker appeared at the window.

"Sorry the coffee's burnt," he said. "We're shorthanded, and everybody's drinking cold stuff since the temperature's up." He slid into the backseat of the patrol car with a Styrofoam cup in each hand.

"What part of the store is Steve hiding in, Lieutenant?" Suzy asked after he handed her one of the cups and a napkin he'd tucked into his vest.

"Please, Suzy, call me Tom. They're in no immediate danger. Sorry, I can't give you specifics."

"Who's they? I thought Steve was alone," Suzy said, curious why Steve didn't mention he had company.

"Ella, the hostage Steve rescued. She's hiding out with him. I assumed you knew."

"He hasn't mentioned her."

Parker held silent.

"Does she work at the factory with Steve?"

"I think so. I know her husband does," Parker said. "He stayed in the vehicle while she went in to shop. He's been driving us crazy since we got here."

Oh geez, Suzy thought. *Steve's cornered in the store with that nut job she'd heard so much about.*

"Steve knows a woman named Ella," she told Parker.

"From work?"

"Yeah, and before I met him."

"It's a common name. My sister's name is Ella. It's probably not the same person," he said.

I'm pretty sure it is the same person, Suzy thought before saying, "She still has feelings for him. Steve was upset for months when she moved here."

"You aren't worried about *that* are you? If it is her?"

"I trust Steve totally, but I'm not too sure about Ella. She bothers him at work. Her husband even threatened him once. He didn't want me to think he was doing something behind my back so he told me the whole story."

After a pause, Parker said, "I think Steve would have told me if he knew her. I'll bet it's someone else."

"Gary . . . Gary Thompson . . . is that the husband's name?" Suzy asked.

Parker's whole body jerked, and coffee sloshed onto his lap. Suzy gave him the napkin. He never answered her question. He didn't have to.

"Has Steve been able to get his medication?" Suzy asked, figuring her husband told him about *that* at least.

"Medication for what?"

Suzy closed her eyes and shook her head. It was just like Steve to leave out the important detail that he could die within a few days without his medicine.

Chapter 45

6:00 p.m. Saturday

Jimmy was watching Joe fight his restraints in the midst of a nightmare. He noticed his tattoo and wondered if his new friend was old enough to have fought in Vietnam. His thrashing and screams reminded him of his own sweat-soaked nights after he returned from the Gulf. The scrawny chain smoker guarding them was getting anxious, looking towards the bank and back at Joe.

"Wake up, Joe," Jimmy whispered, nudging his feet with his own.

"What—what's going on?" Joe asked, gasping for breath.

"You were having a bad dream, and it's making our boy nervous. He's probably worried his boss will come out and smack him again," Jimmy said, pointing to the sentry glaring at them. "By the way, I know who the sniper is. I've been trying to figure out who came into the store just before all of this went down."

Jimmy stopped talking when one of the ladies waved their captor over. He began granting requests for bathroom visits again, soon after the television went quiet. It was assumed that Bear was back in hibernation. Jimmy watched his employee as her wrists and ankles were untied, and she was led to the restroom. So far, none of the women had reported inappropriate behavior.

"He's kind of a big guy, short blond hair. Looks like law enforcement, but he always comes in with your bunch," Jimmy continued.

"Sounds like a lot of guys. Thousands of people work at the plant."

"Are you a vet?" Jimmy whispered ten minutes later.

"Are you a Marine?" Jimmy restated, sensing Joe's confusion.

"Yeah, how'd you know? Was I saying things in my sleep?"

"Your tattoo," Jimmy said indicating the blurred *USMC* on Joe's arm. He then raised his bound wrists to pull his sleeve back, showing Joe the tattoo on his own forearm: the Marine Corps insignia—anchor above the globe—with the same letters stenciled below.

"What do you think would happen if a couple of squared-away marines such as ourselves tried to belly-crawl out of here when nobody was looking?" Jimmy whispered, gesturing toward the point of sale terminal and the wide-open spaces beyond. "We could find that sniper and truly go to war with these guys."

Joe pondered the idea, then said, "Unless our shooter was out there to cut us loose, I think they would notice us missing before we got far. Then they would drag us over to the door and blow our heads off."

"What if I had a knife?" Jimmy said with a grin.

"If nobody spotted us cutting our ropes, we might have a chance. I thought about doing something the last time I got escorted to the bathroom. That goofball stood there, gun pointed at my head. Maybe I could have taken *him* down, but then what? Go after that gorilla toting a grease gun?"

"Yeah, I thought the same thing when I went. If we get an opportunity, though, we need to act."

"I may be old, but I've still got some fight in me."

"Once a Marine, always a Marine, my friend."

Chapter 46

8:15 p.m. Saturday

Ella gazed off into space as I wiped blood from my neck with the clean part of a towel she discarded. She snapped out of it and studied my wounds. "Why hasn't that stopped bleeding?" she asked. "The pellets barely broke the surface. One of them on your neck is playing peekaboo." She made a motion to remove the pellet, but I jerked my head away.

"It'll stop . . . eventually," I said, wondering if it would.

I doubted she noticed the blood soaking my shirt from the other pellet wounds. A few minutes later she began squirming like a ten-year-old.

"Number one or number two?" I asked.

"Number one . . . too much to drink I guess."

"I think I'll step out for a minute." I abruptly rose to my feet.

"I just have to pee. You never had a problem with *that*."

"I still don't—when it's *my* wife, not someone else's," I said, parting the curtain.

"Get some hand sanitizer if you run across any."

"I'm only going right out . . . never mind," I said as I climbed out.

Avoiding embarrassment wasn't the main reason I was leaving. I wouldn't be any use to Parker if I couldn't stop the bleeding soon. I surveyed the camping aisle, trying not to look at Flattop and the mess I created at the next intersection. I found the first aid kit I was looking for. There were actually two choices available. One was basically a pocket-sized adhesive bandage holder with a few ointments. The larger version held virtually everything an army field medic might carry—except for the morphine. I took the larger kit.

Stalling to allow Ella ample time, I walked past Flattop and spotted a clearance rack displaying half a dozen T-shirts. They all had the same saying across the front—*I'd Rather Be Fishing*—with a large bass pictured below. The message conveyed my thoughts precisely. I was thankful the shirts came in different colors. Ella and Gary always wore matching jackets in the winter, which I thought looked silly. When I returned, she was charging my phone. I didn't realize I'd left it behind.

"So, what did you get me?" Ella asked.

"Sorry, they don't sell a hand cleaner for sportsmen. Not much demand, I guess." I passed her the medical kit.

I stuffed the shirts into the pack while she inspected the contents list on the front. I realized Ella still had some work to do on her hair before she could pull on a clean shirt. Also, she would have to expose herself when she removed my jacket.

"Let me see the damage," Ella said.

I took off my shirt, and Ella studied the wound. The old one, which I had forgotten was there.

"When did this happen?" Ella asked.

"You don't remember shooting me."

"You know what I'm talking about," she said, running her finger down the center of my chest as tears welled in her eyes.

"Right after I got married," I said, reminding her how things were now.

"There was a rumor back home that you'd had a heart attack. Then a few weeks later someone told me you went back to work. I wasn't sure what to believe."

She didn't ask a question, so I didn't feel obliged to respond.

"How many . . . bypasses?"

"None. They just fixed a problem I was born with."

"Why didn't you tell me back then?"

"I didn't know I had it until my wife insisted I have a thorough physical."

Ella turned her attention to the medical kit. "Have you got a knife?"

"I've got my britches on, don't I?" I said, so happy to change the subject I couldn't resist.

"Does your father know you're stealing his lines?" Ella asked, smiling.

"He left me all his material in the will."

"Oh Steve, I'm so sorry. I've thought about him a lot over the years. I remember the first time I saw you after we moved here. You looked exactly like I remembered him."

I turned my head in case a tear rolled out, then removed the knife from my pocket. She sliced the wrapper off the first aid kit, then focused on the pellet holes in my shoulder.

"I guess a lot has happened since you and I split up," Ella said.

Yeah, life got better real quick for one of us, I thought. Not that I blamed her for the life I made for myself after we parted ways.

She stuck the tip of the drop-point blade into each of the dozen or so holes spread across my left upper body, prying until the pellet surfaced. Blood trickled out faster than before. Ella wet a clean towel and wiped the wound, which immediately started bleeding again.

She coaxed one pellet out of my neck with her finger and said, "I'm not touching those other two."

"I was about to suggest that," I said, wincing out a smile.

"Keep pressure on that," Ella said, handing me a fresh towel. "You're bleeding like a stuck pig."

Ella unzipped the canvas valise and opened it like a book. Both sides were crammed with supplies for everything from burns to insect bites. She searched the contents and pulled out a moist towelette in a foil wrapper and washed her hands, giving me a dirty look. She then turned to the "bleeding" tab. The pocket held bandages, alcohol wipes, and larger packets labeled "blood-clotting agent." I grabbed the small manual and flipped through the pages.

"Says here to clean the area, then spread the clotting agent over the wound."

"I've never seen you read the directions."

"First time I needed to," I said reaching for the kit.

"I'll do it," Ella said, wrenching it away.

She removed an alcohol wipe and tore it open with her teeth.

"Thanks for your help. Sorry about the cracks I made about our little accident," I said, feeling guilty.

"You haven't changed a bit, Taylor. Most people would actually be mad. You always used to tease me like that, to make me laugh," she said, smiling as she wiped away tears.

I wanted to hug her and tell her I was sorry for all the pain I had caused—when I wasn't making her laugh.

"This stuff might do the trick, I said, tossing the manual. "At least those large bandages will hold the blood in."

Ella ripped open the clotting agent and sprinkled the powder on my injuries.

"They used this stuff in an old war movie I saw. The soldier lays down on a grenade to save his patrol; the medic runs up and sprinkles magic dust where his intestines are hanging out," I said.

"And he survived?"

"It was only a movie," I said, making her giggle.

Ella positioned a separate bandage on my shoulder and chest, holding them in place until they stuck to the seeping wounds. She then took out a roll of white tape and a pair of round-nosed scissors of the sort I had in kindergarten. She had me pull off a long strip of tape, then she cut shorter sections and laid them across her leg.

"You're good at that, Ella."

"I attended nursing school part-time for a couple of semesters after Gary and I got married. He wanted me to work in a hospital."

"Really? I had no idea."

"There's a lot you don't know about me, Taylor."

"Why didn't you finish?" I asked.

"Gary just wanted me to quit the factory because he was afraid you and I would get back together."

After a short silence, I said, "It's kind of amazing how much our lives got screwed up all because of the few months you and I were a couple."

"I see things differently," Ella said, zipping shut the valise.

"How do you see it?"

"It doesn't matter. Let's change the subject."

"Come on Ella, tell me."

"Well, if you must know . . . I think you screwed up my life when you became a drunk. If you'd quit drinking when I gave you that ultimatum, we'd *both* be happily married—to each other."

"Yeah, I should've gotten some help; no argument there. I finally quit when I hit rock bottom. I always assumed I wouldn't have gotten any worse if we'd stayed together."

"Our breakup may have accelerated things, but you were in a downward spiral. And I wasn't going along for the ride."

"I'm sorry. I didn't mean to hurt you." I never dreamed I would say those words. All this time, I'd felt I was the one who'd been wronged.

"I don't want your apologies, Steve. It's just weird. First, I had this urge to move here. I'm not even entirely sure what my motivation was. I already had Gary trained like a show dog. Something I would've never accomplished with you. Then I have this overwhelming desire to get you to speak to me . . . and for you to be friends with Gary again. You have no idea how much grief *that* caused me—from my husband *and* people at work. Everybody thinks I'm some kind of home wrecker trying to bust up your marriage. It truly is embarrassing."

I was speechless.

"When I saw your truck turning into the store, I had this eerie feeling, like I had to set things right with you because I wouldn't get another chance. Go ahead, make the *Twilight Zone* music—go on do it."

"Doo-do Doo-do Doo-do Doo-do," I said, not giving it the full effect.

"And now we're both going to die in here," she said, looking away.

Neither of us said anything. I didn't know what to say. I was no longer sure we'd get out of this alive.

Chapter 47

Powell studied the monitor, watching for any threats to the hostages at the front of the store. Every once in a while he rotated the camera to view the entire store, hoping to give Steve and Ella a heads-up if someone were approaching their hideout. Parker was trying in vain to catch a few winks in a straight-back chair.

"Parker, check it out. Looks like Clarence is sending someone out on foot patrol again."

"Are Steve and Ella out of sight?" Parker said, jumping up and pulling out his phone.

"Yeah, but who knows for how long. Steve's in and out of there whenever he needs something. He should check with us before he steps out."

"I only tell him what to do when I need something. He's bound to stop taking orders if I hound him. If we get the right opportunity, I'll have Steve take him out."

"He could have got nearly all of them earlier. Clarence was sleeping and I know his two assistants weren't playing poker in the men's room."

"Steve's not going for anymore big showdowns. We'll be lucky if I can get him to pick them off one by one. He got shook up pretty bad going up against Marvin." Parker said, watching the tall, thin ex-con take off his lab coat and exchange his T-shirt for a fresh one in the men's department.

"Are you going to call Steve and warn him?" Powell asked.

"Let's wait and see where he goes. There's always someone walking around out there. No one's found them yet."

A few minutes later, Powell said, "I think he's avoiding sporting goods." The lanky exterminator was ducked down behind a cookware display, watching the department across the aisle.

"They know Steve's hanging around there somewhere. That's where Marvin got killed. And there's another dead body a short distance away, in Electronics. They don't spend much time there either."

"This one must be braver than the others. He's going over there," Powell said a minute later.

"Clarence is putting the squeeze on them to locate Steve. He smacked the last one who came back without his head on a platter," Parker said, punching numbers on his phone.

"He went into the checkout station," Powell said as they waited for Steve to answer.

"Steve, don't say anything, just listen. You've got a guy in the sporting goods checkout. He may be looking to get ammo or something; I don't know yet. Stay with me for a minute until we know what he's up to. Clarence sent him out to find you. If he decides to camp out there, I want you to go over and take him out."

They watched as the gunman surveyed the merchandise in the display case and then dropped out of view.

"The camera angle doesn't tell us if he's crouched down in front of the case or settling in for the night," Parker said, putting his hand over the phone.

"He's tall. I think we'd see his head if he wasn't laying on the floor."

"Probably," Parker said, uncovering the phone. "Steve, I need you to go over there and take care of business. Right now."

"Wait, he's getting up. He's . . . walking out the door," Powell said.

"He's going to find a safer place to take a snooze," Parker said, watching him walk across the aisle back into housewares.

Parker returned the phone to his ear and said, "Never mind, Steve. He moved away from your position. You're eventually going to have to take care of these guys before they catch you walking around. You hear me?"

Parker listened to his short response before hanging up.

"So, he's on board?" Powell said.

"Let's hope so," he said.

Chapter 48

"You'll think about what?" Ella asked when I got off the phone with Parker.

"Anything he tells me to do from now on."

I explained what had happened. We sat without speaking a word, but I could hear the wheels in her head turning. I was hoping the recent threat would keep her quiet.

After a long silence, Ella whispered, "Do you know why I visit you at work?"

This was a subject I *was* willing to discuss. I'd wondered about that for a long time.

"Because you're obsessed with me?" I said, halfway kidding.

"Don't flatter yourself. I just wanted you to like me again—not romantically, but like you did when we first met. You were the only guy who looked at my face when he talked to me."

"Does Gary know that?"

"He thinks I'm still in love with you."

"You kind of like Gary being jealous—that's what I think."

Ella stopped talking, but I couldn't leave it alone.

"So you thought blindsiding me in front of my teammates would wipe away all the hard feelings between us?"

"Yeah, that was wrong. I'm sorry, but that was the only way I could try to have a conversation without Gary wanting to kill you. And I knew you wouldn't say more than a few words before you shut me down—because you hated me so much."

"At no time did I hate you, Ella. I took you for granted, and you made a life with someone who didn't."

"That's sweet, Steve. I was hoping you felt that way."

I wanted to mention that it would've been nice if she'd found someone besides my best friend, but I was willing to take some of the blame for that. I shut out everybody but Jack Daniels and Jim Beam when we broke up.

"You should call him," I said.

She recoiled at the notion. "He won't speak to me. He probably hopes I'll get killed in here. I said something awful to him the last time we spoke."

"Go on, Ella, talk to him. Tell him you still love him," I said, powering up the phone.

"You call him. I don't have anything to say."

"What's his cell number?"

She rattled off the digits as I punched them in, daring me to call the man who once threatened to kill me if I ever spoke to his wife again. But I felt sorry for Gary, out there afraid his marriage was over. I didn't have any hard feelings with him. The old Gary, not crazy Gary. I missed *that* knucklehead. I hesitated a moment, then sent the call.

"Give me that," Ella said, snatching the phone.

"Hi, Gary, I'm okay," she choked out seconds later. She listened for a moment as tears ran down her face.

"I'm fine, honey. Steve and I are hiding out."

I put my finger to my lips, trying to shush her, though it was already too late. I would have told her not to mention me if I thought there was any chance she would. Then I realized what a terrible idea it was to call him. I knew better than to rely on him to keep quiet about the phone. He would no doubt have one of his tantrums and might even blab to the media that he had spoken to someone inside the store.

They talked for several minutes before she closed the phone. The mood between them was more than a little strained, judging from her side of the conversation. On her own initiative, she plugged the phone in and turned the handle.

I recalled the time Gary threatened me. It was during our lunch break, and I was exploring the candy machine for something healthy to eat. I had already nibbled on a diet bar in the break room, but that didn't satisfy my hunger. Ella appeared and began talking before I could get away. Gary exited the restroom seconds later and went into a tirade witnessed by a dozen of my co-workers.

"He still loves me," Ella said.

"Great," I replied, imagining what he said about me.

Chapter 49

Bear sat on the teller's stool behind what he hoped was bulletproof glass. He was watching news reports of the standoff on the television at the end of the counter. He was hoping to hear gunshots from the back of the store, but he doubted Tommy could find, let alone kill, the sniper who had shot him and killed his brother. He hadn't brought the kind of men capable of doing that. He was expecting to get in and out without any trouble. Capable men cost money and he had wanted as much as he could get to make a fresh start.

He saw Tommy's head bobbing through the store a full minute before he reached the checkout lane. It was a wonder he was still alive. Tommy must have hidden somewhere instead of shaking the bushes in sporting goods like he'd been ordered. Bear got angrier with every step Tommy took toward the bank.

"No luck?" Bear said, putting on a big friendly smile as Tommy stopped ten feet away, so nervous he was trembling.

"I searched everywhere, Bear. He must have found a way to get out of the store. Probably took that foxy chick with him. I didn't see her either."

"Yeah, Marvin probably missed one of the doors. He said there was no way for anyone to get in or out. Maybe he lied to me," Clarence said, no longer smiling.

"Maybe they found some other way. Maybe the police cut a hole in the wall s-s-s-somewhere," Tommy said, stuttering.

"Yeah, that's probably what happened. Why don't you come sit down here and help me watch for them," Bear said, patting the stool next to him. "If someone could get out, then surely a SWAT team is about to run up on us."

"I should go help Johnny with the hostages. The cops won't mess with us if we've got shotguns pointed at them," Tommy said, turning to go.

"Sit down," Bear yelled. "Put the shotgun down and have a seat."

Tommy, hesitating, set his shotgun against the wall and sat on the stool next to Bear. Tommy kept his eyes pointed at the floor, like Bear wouldn't see his tears. With the K-Bar knife Bear was holding down and out of sight, he reached around and cut Tommy ear to ear. He then dragged him out to where the bodies of two of his other incompetent men lay.

He looked at Johnny, who was smoking a cigarette beside the water fountain, and said, "Get with the program or you're next."

Chapter 50

12:30 a.m. Sunday July 5

I didn't think I'd fallen asleep, but a moment earlier I was at home watching television with my wife. I tried to remember what show was on, but the dream vanished. I opened my eyes to find Ella wiping her hair with a damp towel.

"You missed a call. I started to answer, but I thought it might be your wife. I didn't know if you told her about me."

"Believe me, she's heard all about you," I said, taking the phone.

"Does she know we're together . . . again?"

"Hold that thought," I said, as I checked the phone and saw the call was from Parker.

"Steve, I've got good news and bad news. Which would you like to hear first?" Parker said when he answered.

I doubted either were good news, but I played along. "The good news is, you've finally come to your senses and sent my wife home, right?"

"No, Clarence killed one of his own men earlier—the guy who was looking for you. That's one less you'll have to worry about. The bad news is, I want you to take care of another one right now. I don't want him making Suzy a widow the next time you venture out for bargains."

"So you like my odds better if I go find *him*?"

"This one should be easy. I wouldn't ask if I didn't think you could handle it."

I hesitated a moment, picturing my wife in a black funeral dress, then said, "Tell me what to do."

"We've had eyes on the criminal pulling guard duty at the lawn and garden entrance. Clarence was rotating them, but he's running out of reinforcements. A few minutes ago, he made himself a bed behind the sales counter back there. Do you know where that is?"

"Yeah, but why bother if he's not hurting anyone?"

"Steve, if I were in there, I'd take out anybody who could possibly stop me from getting out alive. They came in with guns drawn and killed innocent people. They're all fair game, even old dried-up convicts like this one. Just walk over there and put a couple of those hollow points in him. He's probably asleep by now. Make sure he wakes up dead. You hear me?"

"Yeah, loud and clear," I said.

I left Ella holding the rifle, following a brief lesson on how to use it.

Free of the weight of the knapsack and a long gun, I felt light-footed as I cut across the automotive department. Parker made my task sound simple, and I was eager to do it quickly and get back.

With the Glock hanging in the low-ready position, I advanced into the department I'd recently bought a new lawnmower. Reality began to set in. I had to kill someone up close and then get away before the rest of his gang saw me. I pictured them running through the checkout lanes after they heard me shoot. They'd likely spot me coming out and know which direction I was headed. I could see the Glock moving in rhythm with my trembling hands.

I turned right and proceeded down the aisle with flowerpots and yard ornaments displayed on opposing sides. I peeked around the corner to my left. The station was straight ahead, a short distance away. My knees were wobbling like they might fail me.

Fatigue makes cowards of us all, I thought, remembering the famous quote from Vince Lombardi or Knute Rockne. I was too exhausted to remember which.

Chapter 51

"Where is he?" Parker radioed Powell from outside the lawn and garden entrance. Powell was monitoring the camera from the bus.

"He just turned into lawn and garden."

Parker stood outside the chain-link gate that secured the outdoor section of the department. Two members of the Metro Nashville Bomb Squad, sweating in their bulky suits, stood beside him. The plan was to continue reducing the number of armed gunmen. Powell tried to talk him out of it, fearing retribution, but he didn't have any better ideas. So, this was it.

He didn't tell Suzy about his plan, nor about Steve taking friendly fire. The two had been eating sandwiches in the backseat of a patrol car when he got word that the old man they called "Garden Party" was getting drowsy. They hadn't given all the exterminators code names, but this guy had made an impression. Parker believed Steve could get the jump on one sleeping gunman without suffering a scratch. He prayed it would work out that way.

The lookout in the lawn and garden department grew accustomed to seeing movement outside the gate. The police respected this border line, even though it was a hundred feet away from the Plexiglas double doors the explosives were taped to. Earlier, he'd acknowledged the police presence by nodding at the officers, as if they were old friends passing on the street. Once, he even gave a crisp salute that no one acknowledged.

Parker relayed this information to Powell, who suggested he try to communicate with him. Parker then made a large sign, asking the sleepy convict to cooperate. He shrugged and pointed at the explosive device. After that, he stopped looking in their direction.

"Have you got him yet?" Powell inquired a few minutes later.

"No, he made the turn, but must have stopped at the clubhouse for a burger," Parker replied.

"You know golf is a foreign language to me, right."

"He'll be here. Where else could he go?"

Parker waited in silence for Steve to appear. He stood at the far side of the gate, anxious to get an early glimpse of his arrival. Then he pulled up Steve's number, ready to warn him if danger was approaching.

Chapter 52

I willed my feet to move. Parker was waiting for me to finish the job, and I was taking way too long. As I approached the sales counter, I could feel heat coming through the door, even though it was the middle of the night. I held the gun pointed at the cash register but gazed to my right for a moment when I came to the door. Not a smart move on my part, but I couldn't stop myself. The well-lit parking lot was filled with police and emergency vehicles. The scene reminded me of the ending to one of the Die Hard movies, but I couldn't remember which. Perhaps all of them.

Too bad Bruce Willis isn't in here instead of me.

Outside the chain-link gate, I saw Parker and a couple of odd-shaped individuals. Their outline resembled the Michelin Man, but I knew they were members of the bomb squad Parker said was coming. The device taped to the door was a clue as to why they were here. The clearly homemade device had what appeared to be the tilt mechanism from a pinball machine and a battery pack rigged to what must be the C-4 Parker mentioned.

I brought home an old pinball machine after I bought the house. I wanted a pool table, but none of the rooms were large enough, not even the living room. This was months before I met Suzy, who politely insisted a couch would make better use of that space. I'd disabled the high-score killer on that machine, but I didn't have the nerve to disarm the bomb. My whole body was shaking like a washing machine with a couple of bricks thrown in the load.

Parker raised his rifle above his head with both arms, pumping it up and down. He was obviously conveying a message. I doubted he wanted to congratulate me on what a great job I was doing. Tired and scared, I wished now I had refused Parker's order and remained with Ella. If the guy napping behind the counter attacked me, I wouldn't hesitate to defend myself. But killing someone as they slept wasn't working for me. If Clarence Jenkins were in there taking a snooze, however, this would already be over—win or lose.

I inched forward, but it wasn't pretty. I never in my whole life, experienced a panic attack, but I assumed this was how one looked. The shelves inside the checkout came into view, but still no gunman. At the rate I was going, it'd be an hour until I moved the three feet necessary to take him out. I finally caught sight of his worn-out shoes and denim pant legs—and finally the rest of his body.

I aimed my gun and put my shaking finger on the trigger. I was surprised the gun didn't go off. I wished it to happen. My weapon was aimed at something I intended to destroy. This was the test Parker taught in the permit class, for allowing the muzzle of a weapon to point at something. Parker told me to kill him. I didn't feel doing that was wrong; I was just having a hard time getting it done.

It reminded me of another occasion when I was unable to pull the trigger. I was deer hunting with my father. The large buck warily trotted down the trail in front of me. My stand was strapped to a tree twenty yards into the woods. I put the animal in my sights as it entered the shooting lane I'd cleared. I tried to pull the trigger, but I was paralyzed then as well.

I eventually got cured of buck fever, putting several deer and other game in the freezer over the years. Most, if not all of those shots, were directed at animals that had for a fleeting moment, become aware of my presence. Putting a bullet in a human being, asleep and curled up in the fetal position, proved more difficult.

Chapter 53

"Powell, we've got him. He's about to pull the trigger. You got eyes on Clarence?"

"The Bear is still in his den."

"C'mon Steve, the longer you take, the bigger the risk," Parker muttered.

He came unglued when Steve turned his head, staring out the door again. Parker watched him lower his weapon and, even from that distance, he could see that his whole body was shaking.

"Why is he opening the gate? Just lean in and shoot him," Parker whispered.

When he stepped in and stood there without firing his weapon, Parker knew that Steve had stopped taking orders.

Chapter 54

I looked down at the exterminator. He was breathing heavily, but not quite snoring. I turned toward Parker, who was jumping around like a crazy man. I considered just closing my eyes and pulling the trigger. I had another bad idea as I studied the well-aged man with his hands tucked under his chin like he was praying.

I straddled the chaise lounge pad he used for a bed. He had his lab coat balled up, using it as a pillow. I took one hand off the Glock and commandeered the shotgun lying beside him. Hardly the way a skilled assassin would have carried this out, but it was the best *I* could do.

I laid the scattergun on the counter without making even a click when it touched the surface. I moved both of my feet to the same side of his body, having seen enough old movies to realize I could be tripped up and lose my advantage. I figured he would startle when I woke him. If he came up fighting, his next breath would be the last.

I nudged his foot with mine, and his breathing pattern changed for several cycles before reverting to a near snore. I gripped my weapon and gave a solid shot to the bottoms of both his feet, which were still tucked close to his body. He awoke panicked as I stood over him with the Glock and my game face. I'm not sure which did the trick, but he went passive almost immediately.

"If you make any kind of sudden movement, I'll blow you away," I said hoarsely.

"Whatever you say, man," he replied.

"Do you have any other weapons?"

The scrawny, pale convict scanned where his shotgun had been, then said, "No, man, they just gave me the one."

I wasn't willing to bet my life he was telling the truth, but I saw no indication he was lying.

"Get on your belly, and put your hands behind your back."

He did what I said, then turned his head and asked, "Are you the po-lice?"

"Worse than that, I'm an autoworker getting cheated out of a paid holiday."

I spotted a ball of twine on a shelf below the register.

"Put your wrists together," I growled.

The exterminator complied. I holstered the Glock and knelt down. I bound his wrists so he couldn't wiggle loose.

"You're hurting me, man. Don't wrap it so tight. I'm with you now. I don't *want* to get away."

I thought he had a lot of nerve complaining. They took the life of two, maybe three people and meant to harm Ella.

"You're lucky the police are out there. I'd rather put a bullet in your head than waste this string," I yelled, wishing it were so.

"Keep your voice down. I don't want Bear coming back here worse than you."

He was thin but wiry, like those old guys in the plant, who were living on the coffee and cigarette diet. They never suffered from diabetes, but no one was betting they'd live to be a hundred either. I tried to guess his age. Somewhere between fifty and seventy was the best I could do.

"You must be the guy who was shooting at us. What are you, like an ex-Green Beret or something?" he asked.

"Yeah, I'm John Wayne," I said, remembering the *Green Beret* movie.

I wished I were some kind of trained warrior because then I wouldn't be having this conversation. I was halfway through the ball of twine before I had his ankles secured. I then wrapped it between his extremities, drawing his arms and legs up behind him. Examining the hog-tied exterminator, I was satisfied with the results. I needed something to keep him from yelling for his partners in crime after I walked away. My cell phone vibrated before I came across anything useful.

"This is why I hate dealing with amateurs. They don't have the discipline to follow orders. They do things their own dumb way," Parker yelled.

I powered down my phone. If he didn't like how I was performing, he could come in here and do it himself. I was delirious. Those last few minutes of stark terror, though unwarranted, reduced me to a sniveling coward. I looked around for anything I could stuff into his mouth. Not a difficult task, but in my current state, I couldn't think of a way to gag him. Evidently, I missed that episode of MacGyver.

I wanted to give up. It was getting too hard all of a sudden. Then I did something I hadn't done since I quit drinking. I broke down—

completely. I was certainly more emotional since my surgery, but not like this. It began with a whimper. But once the dike gave way, I released everything. I kept my back to Parker and let the mongrel peering up at me enjoy the show.

"It's okay man. I ain't gonna call out to nobody. Bear would shoot me dead if he found out I fell asleep back here."

"Shut up," I gasped, trying to get air into my lungs.

I was embarrassed by my lack of control and wished I'd followed Parker's orders. At least there would be one less witness to my meltdown. I convulsed, barely able to breathe. I knew Parker was trying to get my attention when I heard loud clanging outside. An M-16 butt-plate slamming against the gate was my guess.

"Pick up," Parker yelled just loud enough to hear.

I pulled my phone out and tried to answer, eventually realizing it was powered down. I had no recollection of doing that. My brain was operating on about two cylinders, barely enough to turn it on. My phone buzzed two seconds later. The way my hands were shaking, I couldn't have made the call, even if Suzy's life depended on it.

"Deep breaths, Steve. What do you say we quit killing people awhile and let you get some rest?"

The only response I could give was a vigorous head bob, my back still facing the outside world.

"Great, get him out of there so I can give you pointers, and see if he's wearing a belt."

I gripped his ankles and dragged him off the mat. He looked worried as I slid him out through the gate. His trucker shirt slid up, exposing a thick leather belt. My mind picked up horsepower as I realized what Parker was thinking.

"I'm taking your belt," I said, kneeling down on the concrete and stripping it off.

"Cool beans, man. I should've thought of that."

I put the phone back to my ear, and Parker said, "Now, we need some cloth. You can use that new shirt you're wearing—hey, I don't even like to fish, and I'd rather be fishing right now—or cut a piece off the other fella's. Your choice. Are you carrying a knife?"

"Have I got my britches on?" I replied with a knee-jerk response.

"Yes, you do. Short ones," Parker said, laughing.

The criminal's eyes grew wide as I opened my knife. I leaned over to cut his shirt, but I came up with a better idea. I put the knife back in my pocket and took off his well-worn brogans, then his socks, which had a slight crust on the bottoms.

"I'm starting to have fun, Steve. How about you?" Parker asked.

"Yeah," I replied, not wanting to say anything negative, afraid it would put me back into the dark abyss I just returned from.

I trapped the phone against my ear to free my hands, then held one of the socks against his mouth. When he tried to protest, I crammed it in.

"I hope he has a strong stomach. I smell those socks out here. Now wrap the belt around his mouth. You still got your britches on?"

I nodded and pulled out my knife.

"Punch a new hole in the belt. Get it tight, but not too tight. He's your BFF now. We don't want to upset the bonding process, do we?"

I nodded again and cinched the belt over his mouth, then twisted the tip of the blade until it poked through. He never moved a muscle, eyeballing my shaky knife work. To ensure the belt didn't slip off, I wound the string about ten times and tied a square knot.

"I know this is hard, Stevie, but you have to make sure he can't get loose or yell for help. Slim Pickens there saw you talking to me. If he tells his buddies—ballgame over. I'll have to crash in and let God sort everything out. How much battery you got left on that phone?"

"Twenty-five percent," I said, examining it.

"Double-check the knots before you leave him, and keep your phone on," Parker said, ending the call.

I was embarrassed Parker had to remind me why he wanted him dead and not merely restrained. My inability to shoot him was putting innocent people's lives at risk. I hauled him back onto the pad and verified my knots were good. As I was standing up, I saw a MacGyver necessity at the back of the shelf below the cash register. Duct tape would have been a better choice than the twine or the belt.

I knew it was overkill, but I wrapped tape around the belt and then his eyes, leaving a small opening below his nostrils. Looking down at the top of his head, I noticed that dried blood matted his wispy slicked-back hair. His scalp was still oozing a little. I couldn't recall inflicting the wound, but I wasn't certain.

If he's taking blood thinners, he might have a problem, I thought, remembering my own recent experience.

I stood and unholstered the Glock. I was mentally able now, I hoped, to defend myself. I was tired and hungry. I wanted to be home, snuggled in bed with my wife, eating popcorn, and enjoying an old movie. I would settle for arguing with Ella and eating a bag of jerky.

Chapter 55

"What's the problem back there, Parker?" Powell radioed.

"Steve got cold feet. Actually he 'nutted up' on me for a minute. He couldn't pull the trigger. He's leaving the guy back there, bound and gagged."

"I don't like it. Does he know your boy is talking to us?"

"Yeah, he saw him."

"Steve *cannot* leave him there."

"I know. I got caught up in Steve's problems and gave him a break. I figured we could put a bullet through the door if we had to."

"I suggested we take Clarence out that way on the telephone, but you thought it would set off the explosives . . . maybe all of them. Remember that conversation."

"I remember," Parker said.

"If he wants to take prisoners, he has to bring them home."

"He'll probably want to strangle him."

"Tell him not to. Someone in the media may be curious about what you're doing over there. They may be streaming video as we speak. We can't justify taking him out, now that Steve tucked him in and kissed him good night."

"Yeah, Steve will have enough to live with as it is."

"Let's hope so."

Chapter 56

My cell phone buzzed as I was about to enter the main part of the store.

"Good news, Steve. I've decided to let the two of you get better acquainted.

"What do you mean?"

"You've got to take him with you."

"Take him where?"

"Back to your hidey-hole in sporting goods. You stayed his execution, governor. Now you have to feed and house him."

"How about if I go back and shoot him—rewind the tape and do it right this time."

"That ship has sailed, not that I think you could pull the trigger," Parker said, hanging up.

A minute later, I crouched down beside the criminal and said, "You're coming with me. If you try to run when I untie your feet, I *will* hurt you."

I cut through the twine securing his ankles, and after some thought I freed his wrists as well. I grabbed the underweight geezer by the collar and stood him up. Out of self-preservation, I tried to regard him as dangerous. His estimated 150 pounds and twenty-eight-inch waist made it difficult to actually fear him. He had zero fight in him; probably never did. His wound, if I didn't inflict it, indicated that even his comrades weren't afraid to pop him whenever they felt like it.

I pumped the shells out of his weapon. I wasn't leaving it behind. My intent wasn't to see how many guns I could gather, but I assumed I could take my wife home when I had them all.

"I *will* shoot you if you give me any problems. Understand?"

He shook his head, covered with duct tape and twine. I drew my Glock, hoping he would give me an excuse to do what Parker wanted me to do in the first place. I picked up the roll of duct tape on the counter and slipped it on my wrist.

"Carry the shotgun. You heard me unload it, so don't make me think even less of your intelligence by trying to shoot me."

He held out both hands, feeling blindly for the weapon. I expected him to lash out with it, but he placed the barrel on his shoulder and waited for marching orders. I wanted to ease my task by peeling the tape away from his eyes, but I didn't want him to know where we were hiding. All my knowledge about dealing with prisoners came from watching *Hogan's Heroes*. I figured I was about to witness a real-life comedy show when he moved in with Ella.

"Let's go," I said, turning him in the right direction.

He lifted one of his feet up, indicating he wanted to put his shoes on.

"They'll issue a new pair when you get to prison," I told him.

He looked like a tenderfoot, unable to run ten feet before stubbing a toe and giving up. I wasn't much better. Regard for my own abilities was hovering near rock bottom. The barefoot exterminator, with skin showing well above his ankles, blindly led the way as I directed him from behind.

As we strode along the back wall in automotive, I saw clearly the complications bringing him back to our hideout would create. The biggest one being, there wasn't enough room for three people, even if Ella was agreeable to sharing our space with one of the criminals who tried to assault her. My phone buzzed a few moments later.

"Get Ella and go to the pharmacy. The front door is gone, but you should be able to defend your new hideout's cinder block walls with the M-16."

"That's kind of close to the action isn't it?"

"You need your medicine, right?"

"How'd you know?"

"A little birdie told me. She was concerned," Parker said, as my phone chirped the low battery warning.

"I was thinking about going over there and looking for it . . . in a week or so. If you didn't get us out of here by then," I said, laughing.

"I'm glad you're feeling better. Get that phone charged and call me. I'll make some noise if there's a problem," Parker said before ending the call.

We stopped in front of the twelve-pack coolers next to Ella. I whispered for my prisoner to stay put. I didn't think it would be a good idea if she saw him holding a firearm right off, even though he had so much duct tape covering his head, he resembled King Tut more than the animal who tried to hurt her.

I stood at the edge of the hanging garments and gave a Gomer Pyle "hooty-hoot" that she had despised too much not to remember. She made an opening, and I came forward.

"We have to leave. Parker told us to hide out in the pharmacy."

"The pharmacy? No, thanks. I'm not going anywhere."

"It's got a bathroom . . . and a shower," I said, adding the last part in case a flushable toilet wouldn't lure her out of there. I had no idea what accommodations awaited us. I was hoping for a mini-kitchen stocked with microwave dinners.

Ella stepped out carrying Flattop's rifle.

Seeing the prisoner, she swung the weapon in his direction. "What is he doing here, and why does he have a gun? You were supposed to kill him."

The prisoner fidgeted but remained in place.

"Parker made me bring him back. It isn't loaded."

"Great, just what we needed," Ella said, pointing her gun at his midsection.

"Keep an eye on him. I'll get our stuff."

"Make it quick, because I'm going to shoot him if he so much as breathes wrong."

I put the duct tape and everything else that would fit into the knapsack. We crossed the store, looking somewhat ridiculous in my estimation. Ella jabbed our prisoner with the barrel whenever he veered off course. I followed carrying a shotgun, leaving the rest of the long guns in storage.

Chapter 57

2:30 a.m. Sunday

As we approached the pharmacy, a space constructed of concrete block extending out of the store's front wall, I took the lead and the rifle. Ella balked at the swap but relented when I told her she would have to go in first. Parker was correct; the entryway next to the walk-up window had no door. It was lying amid the debris inside. The twisted hinges were still connected to the jamb. The nearby wrecking bar, with the price tag still attached, clued me into how it was removed. I shouldered the rifle and stepped inside. Parker seemed sure the area was clear, but I feared someone might have returned to get their fix.

The space inside was divided into two parts. The larger room I stood in had multiple rows of metal shelving units where large containers of medicine were stored. Most of them, and the contents, were scattered on the floor. There was another room to the left; its door lay against the wall inside. The pharmacist filled prescriptions in there and customers received their order through the sliding glass window. I could see medicine bottles strewn about in there as well. I motioned for Ella to move up.

She proceeded, jabbing her prisoner with the shotgun every step of the way.

"I don't like it," Ella said, scanning the room.

"Why not?"

"If there was a door and I could lock it—"

"Parker says this is the safest location," I said, cutting her off. "Here, take the rifle and watch out the window. Yell if you spot anyone."

We swapped weapons again.

"What are you gonna do?" Ella asked.

"Charge my phone. It's completely dead," I replied, steering our prisoner to the rear of the storage room.

There was an open area behind the last row of shelves. It was a good place to set up camp. No one could see us from the entrance because the storage racks were backed with the same heavy-gauge metal as the shelves. The downside was that it would be difficult to see if anyone came in, so one of us would have to stand guard.

After removing my pack, I took the prisoner's shotgun and put it in the far corner. I taped his wrists together in front of his body, then pressed him against the wall and told him to sit. Ella came in, abandoning her post, clearly upset. She was muttering to herself, but I figured she was just getting her motor running. Upon Ella's return, the prisoner began humming through his gag—upset about something as well. I figured he must have feared Ella was going to jab him with the rifle again.

"You said there was a bathroom and shower in here. There's only a small sink," Ella said too loudly, considering our proximity to the killers.

"I've never been in here, Ella. I figured there would at least be a bathroom."

"There's no shampoo, only a bottle of store-brand dish soap. I have to wash this funk out of my hair, Steve. I just have to."

"Charge the phone. I'll go out and get a few things."

"I'll make you a list."

"No thanks," I said, taking the radio out of the knapsack.

"You need to get our boat cushions," Ella said, pointing to our prisoner parked on the cement floor.

"How about a sofa and recliner while I'm at it?"

"Just hurry, and don't get the cheap shampoo."

We were both exhausted. That always meant trouble when we were a couple. I plugged in the phone and gestured to Ella. She started to say something but sat down a few feet from our prisoner and got to work. I went out and found a bottle of salon-quality shampoo and another formulated to treat lice, since none of the ordinary shampoos claimed to be effective at clearing out blood and brains. I thought about trying to sleep on the floor. Ella was right; I had to do something about that and soon. There was no way I could carry enough boat cushions for the three of us. Then I remembered the chaise lounge cushion the convict had been lying on.

I wanted to tell Ella to watch for intruders, but I knew it would turn into a lengthy discussion, and I needed to get a charge on my phone. I dropped the shampoo at the pharmacy door and sprinted down the front wall to the lawn and garden department. I was deserting Ella for a couple of minutes, but Parker would know if there was a problem and alert us.

I pulled the last two lounge pads off the shelf and laid them on the counter. I walked into the station and collected the other one, hoping I would remember which one not to use. The convict's lab coat rolled off, uncovering his stash—a carton of cigarettes and a loose pack with matches stuffed inside the cellophane. I grabbed the pack and stuck it in my pocket, recognizing the value of a cigarette to a nicotine-starved prisoner.

Walking in with the pads under my arm, I collected the shampoo and went back to deliver the goods. The first thing I noticed was the phone and radio lay unattended. Walking past the last shelving unit, I discovered Ella kneeling next to our detainee, unwinding the tape covering his eyes. The rifle was lying beside them. I dropped the shampoo and drew my pistol.

"Cut him loose," Ella ordered. "I know this guy."

"Are you crazy? What's his name?"

"Snake," Ella said after thinking for a moment.

I didn't know if she was correct. After a moment, the prisoner nodded his head in agreement.

I couldn't think of the right question to ask to get to the bottom of this mystery.

"I didn't recognize him earlier. He wasn't wearing his lab coat. I thought he was one of the other guys. He tried to protect me when I was in trouble. Untie the gag at least so I can talk with him."

I didn't move.

"He got a beating when he tried to defend me," Ella said, starting to cry.

I holstered my weapon, still holding the cushions under my arm.

"Stack them here," Ella said, standing and helping Snake to his feet.

"I brought one for each of us," I replied, not trying to sell it.

I situated all three pads on the floor against the wall. I put the rifle, radio, and pack on the end, and sat beside them so I'd have a partial view of the doorway, though I doubted I would be able to get up fast enough to stop anyone from entering.

"That'll be more comfortable. We'll spread them out later. Right now, I need the first aid kit. Get it for me," Ella said.

Ella helped Snake sit down and kneeled next to him again, studying his injury as I got up and fumbled through my pack.

"Give me your knife," Ella ordered after I handed her the kit.

I reached in my pocket and gave it to her without comment. The way I was taking orders made me wonder if I'd fully recovered from my meltdown. Our prisoner eyed the cigarettes I removed with the knife. I tossed the pack on the cushion.

"Check with her," I said, pointing at Ella.

Snake's eyes lit up, then faded when Ella shot him a look. That was another issue Ella had with me back in the day. Luckily, she got me to quit before we parted ways. Something I'd forgotten until that moment. I smoked several cigarettes during my whiskey years, but never resumed the habit. I knew I should take the rifle and go attempt to stop intruders *before* they came inside, but I was too tired. Instead, I sat down, laid the Glock in my lap, and charged the phone. Ella cut the rest of the tape and twine, then unbuckled the belt.

"Hello, Sunshine," Snake said after Ella plucked the sock out of his mouth and flung it.

"I was worried about you, Snake. I thought you were dead."

"I was worried about you, too. When I came around, you and Clyde were gone. He didn't hurt you, did he?"

"No, but I did a number on Clyde," I said, unable to stay out of the conversation.

"I'm fine now, but we've been through a lot," Ella told him.

"I'm glad you're okay," Snake said, making puppy-dog eyes at her.

I cranked the phone at a rapid rate, harnessing my frustration with our new roommate.

"Let me see that bump on your head," Ella said, moving in close.

"You still smell . . . nice," Snake said, reacting like he got a whiff of her hair.

"You're so sweet. I'll wash up as soon as I get you patched up."

I stopped cranking and put my hand on the Glock when Ella cut his hands free. I wasn't keen on treating him like a friend instead of a foe, but I didn't have the energy for *that* discussion. He tried to stop her attacker, but he was still the enemy in my book. Snake behaved like a model prisoner while Ella sprinkled the magic dust on his head. I continued charging the phone as I leaned my head against the wall and tried to keep my eyes open.

I woke to Ella and Snake giggling like schoolgirls. I turned on my phone and the battery meter indicated 15 percent. The bad news: I had no cell reception. I noted the time, then turned the phone off. The top of the hour was minutes away. I turned on the radio, appreciating the diversion. Snake, with a large bandage taped to his head now, studied me as I raised the antenna and adjusted the knobs.

"*WKOM* breaking news. I'm Skip Jackson," the reporter crackled. I placed the radio in front of us, and we looked at it like a pre-television family anticipating a new episode of *Amos and Andy*. "There is speculation in the media that the local SaveMart siege is being led by none other than Clarence Jenkins. If you'll remember two years ago, Jenkins was the mastermind behind the bank robbery that left four people dead. He is currently ranked seventh on the FBI's 'most wanted' list. Federal and local police were criticized for allowing him to leave the scene with four of the hostages, none of whom survived. We'll have more on this breaking story as it develops."

I watched as Ella tried to hold back tears. The event, reported on nationally, came back to me. Clarence attempted to rob a bank in Nashville, but the police got there before he could make his getaway. He threatened to kill everyone in the bank unless the police allowed him to leave in an ambulance that was parked outside. He drove away with four of the hostages. The police recovered them a week later. They were discovered inside the ambulance, bound and gagged, behind a vacant building fifty miles away. They died from heat and dehydration. My eyes shot daggers at Snake as I rose to my feet.

"I should have left you back there . . . dead. Your boss is a murdering piece of garbage and so are you."

"I didn't know about all that. I came here with Johnny. We shared a cell at Brushy Mountain. I'd never seen that Bear fella before he picked us up in his van."

"They're going to kill us all," Ella said, sliding away from Snake and looking at him like he'd just drowned a kitten.

"I won't let anyone hurt you," Snake said. "Please don't be mad at me."

I grabbed the rifle and stood where I could see the entrance.

Minutes later, Ella broke the silence. "I should go see if I can get this mess out of my hair. Steve, we could use some food, and I drank the last water."

I wanted to tell her to get it herself, but I needed to get away and clear my head. I also planned to call Parker and wear him out for keeping me in the dark about our captor. My phone barely had enough juice for one call. I decided to check on Suzy instead. If Parker wanted to keep information from me, I'd make it real easy for him.

I was determined to run into the arms of my darling wife. And this new information didn't make me think less of our chances. We'd made it this far. The only thing that *had* changed, and it seemed substantial, was Snake's presence. His being here was like something out of an old Alfred Hitchcock movie, where the unimposing guest might turn out to be a homicidal maniac waiting for a chance to strike.

Chapter 58

Most of the hostages had settled down since Bear murdered one of his own men and threw the body down in front of them. Jimmy liked that there was one less killer to worry about, but didn't like the quiet rage he'd witnessed from Bear, the same quiet rage he demonstrated when he'd killed Gertie. Jimmy wondered how long it would take before Bear lost hope in negotiating his release and resorted to killing all the hostages.

Joe hadn't made any attempt to communicate with him since the killing, but with Bear now sitting in the bank watching television, he slid over and whispered, "You think he's psycho or just evil?"

"A whole lot of both I figure."

"Do you think the police can see what he's been doing? Maybe they'll step up negotiations."

Jimmy shook his head and said, "They can't access the security cameras. Maybe they have another way, but I wouldn't expect them to give in to his demands regardless. He's definitely leaving here in a body bag. I just hope we don't share his fate."

They stopped talking when Johnny, their overseer, came out of the women's restroom. He had dragged his buddies' three dead bodies in there when Bear went back in the bank. He was aiming his shotgun at the hostages again, looking as scared as ever standing just outside the block wall in front of the restrooms. He scanned the area beyond the checkouts, looking ready to bolt inside at the first sign fire was about to rain down on them again.

Jimmy leaned over and whispered, "Did you hear that?"

Joe shook his head. "Hear what?"

"Sounded like people talking. Has to be the sniper and the woman who got dragged off. Johnny looked up like he heard it too, but then pretended like he didn't. He's afraid his boss will send him over there. I guess he's more scared of our sniper than he is of Bear."

"My hearing isn't what it used to be. Where was the sound coming from?" Joe asked.

"Sounded close, maybe the pharmacy. He's definitely not back in sporting goods like everyone thinks. That's for sure."

"He must be planning another attack."

"Let's hope his aim is better this time," Jimmy said, nodding to the bullet hole in the wall.

Chapter 59

I put on the knapsack, then made a big show of gathering the weapons laying around. Ella ignored me as I walked by. From the other room I heard them talking. Their hushed voices were too low to make out what they were saying, but my ears were burning. I laid the rifle and two shotguns on the counter behind the window. Ella came in a short time later carrying both shampoo bottles.

"So you think I have bugs crawling in my hair?" Ella asked, holding up one of them.

"Most expensive, probably the strongest too," I replied.

"Thanks, Steve, for everything. I forgot how sweet you can be," Ella said, before she headed toward the sink.

I wondered how much Snake had told her.

"Hold on a second, Ella," I called out. "I've got something for you."

I searched the pack and took out the bra and T-shirt. I inspected the cups for pellet holes. I had enough reservations already, without making her think I brought her something kinky.

"You asked for these, remember?" I said, handing them to her.

"You went to Victoria's Secret and didn't take me with?"

"Sorry, if you don't like the shirt."

"It's just like yours."

"Not exactly like—" I tried to explain before she interrupted.

"Thank you, Steve. So very thoughtful," she said, clutching the garments.

"I'll be just outside the door if you need anything."

"Taylor, you amaze me sometimes," Ella barely whispered, as she walked off.

I was about to leave, but the sight of pill bottles on the floor stopped me. Not taking my medication was just another way, on the very long list of ways, I could die this holiday weekend.

The recent blood test didn't help matters. My blood was already well below the recommended range when I came in the store. I recalled my cardiologist instructing me on the importance of staying within the upper and lower limits before he released me from the hospital.

He scared Suzy, and me a little, with his worst-case scenarios. If my blood was too thick, as it was now, even a tiny blood clot would cause my artificial aortic valve to malfunction. Too thin and I would bleed out.

I wasn't sure how long I could go without taking the blood thinners. I'd recently had a kidney stone blasted with Lithotripsy. The urologist instructed me not to take the medication for two days beforehand. The procedure would bruise my kidney, and he wanted my blood a little thick. He was drawing a fine line between my kidney bleeding too much and having a blood clot from the procedure enter my prosthetic heart valve.

I scanned each container for the words *Coumadin* and *Warfarin*. Warfarin was the generic version my insurance company kept pestering me to switch to. I didn't come across either of them. Starting to feel desperate, I searched the loose pills for the orange, brown, and purple tablets I took, depending on my test results. No luck there either. I stormed out, fuming at my inability to find what I knew was a common medication.

I checked that my phone was off, then turned left without glancing up at the camera. I was mad at Parker for various reasons, and I wanted him to know it. He would sound off on the bullhorn if someone were approaching. That was his job. He had to help, no matter how I behaved. I would bring some food back, eat, and then talk to my wife. If Parker wanted to have a conversation, he'd better be sitting next to her.

Selecting what was on the menu, I used proximity as my only criteria. Delicious would have to wait until Suzy and I were back home. I was familiar with the nearby options. I had spent many hours studying the supplements and diet products located just outside the pharmacy. My stomach didn't exactly do a dance when my brain announced where I was shopping for dinner. But the rest of my body was glad I wouldn't have a high risk of getting shot again.

I picked up a carton of strawberry-flavored diet shakes, then changed my mind and selected the Chocolate carton next to it. I considered the diet bar options and acquired two boxes—different flavors, both containing chocolate. I typically went for the cheaper version, but today I was eating name brand. I was upbeat enough to appreciate that I might actually lose a pound or two by "holidaying" at the SaveMart.

I made a mental note to write down this funny anecdote when my arms weren't full. It had already occurred to me that this experience could be a great source for comedy material. Getting media interviews might even lead to additional stage time. I thought I could joke about the situation in a few days—if I were still alive. Ella's prediction of our demise kept coming to mind. On my way back, I pocketed a bottle of aspirin, hoping a couple of tablets under my tongue would keep the grim reaper at bay.

Returning, I heard water blasting full force. I could see Ella bent over the sink washing her hair. I set the food down and took out my phone. I speed-dialed my wife's number as I stepped out. I could hear the call going through about the time somebody would see me put the phone to my ear. I didn't normally like playing games, especially with someone who was trying to keep me alive. At the moment though, tired and hungry, I didn't care what Parker thought of me.

"Where are you, sweetheart?" Suzy answered in her sleepy voice.

"Same place," I said, too tired for an update. "Where are *you*, darling?"

"Same place." I imagined her curled up in the backseat of a police car.

"Has Parker talked to you lately?" I asked, sensing she wasn't aware of my crash-and-burn incident with Snake.

"No, I've been sleeping for . . . half an hour," Suzy said. I pictured her focusing on the too-complicated digital watch I gave her for a birthday present. "The last thing he told me was that you were very brave."

"When was that?" I asked.

"I don't know . . . maybe an hour ago." Parker had spoken to Suzy well after my meltdown and didn't tell her about it. I appreciated that. I didn't care what anyone else thought of me, but I didn't want my wife to know I was a coward.

"Babe, I told Lieutenant Parker about you and Ella. Don't be mad. He said you rescued her."

"I can't get mad at you, not even if I tried."

"Where is she right now?"

"She's . . . in another room. We've got a bigger hideout now."

"Please come back to me. I love you *so* much."

"I will baby doll. I promised, remember?"

"I'm holding you to it," she said, laughing as my phone chirped.

"I gotta go, my phone's dying. Love you, darling. I'll call you later."

"Love you too, sweetheart."

After I charged the phone, I would have a long conversation with Parker. It was time to man up and do whatever it took to get my wife home.

I walked into the pharmacy and gathered the food. The shotguns were still on the counter by the window, but the rifle was gone. I went back and found Ella parked in the middle of our makeshift couch, holding it in her lap. Snake was sitting on her far side, getting as close as he dared. Ella's hair was damp, and she was wearing her new shirt. I tossed dinner down beside her. Snake stared at the food, licking his lips.

"No water," Ella commented.

"No jerky either. You found the sink, right?"

"Not real fond of tap water," Ella said, eyeing the shake carton.

"You get all those bugs out of your hair?" I asked, as I sat beside her.

Nothing but silence out of either of them, although I could tell Snake wanted to laugh.

I shook one of the diet shake bottles, opened it, and gave it to Ella. I got one for myself and commenced guzzling.

"Snake says he doesn't think Bear could walk over here if he had to. He could hardly stand the last time he saw him. Isn't that true, Snake?" Ella said, grabbing a bottle for him after she determined that I wasn't going to.

Snake nodded but remained mute.

"He says most of the others wanted to surrender when the police arrived."

"Did he say how many hostages he thought his leader might kill this time? He only needs to kill you and me to beat his record."

"You're still a chocaholic aren't you," Ella said, changing the subject.

I removed two fudge bars from the box and handed the rest to her. She rejected my offer and picked up the box containing the chocolate and peanut recipe. She gave one to Snake, who looked as if he would have preferred the kind I was devouring.

"How many of those candy bars are you planning to eat?" Ella asked as I tore open another one.

"They're meal replacement bars, and I'm curious to find out how many it takes to fill me up."

"I remember during our happier times, you'd get a late-night craving for ice cream and run out for some. You always came back with chocolate. I'll bet you don't remember what flavor I like, do you?"

"Judging by the way you're wolfing down your dinner, I'd guess chocolate."

"Gary loves chocolate too, but he always buys strawberry," she said, turning away.

I shrugged. "Charge the phone and tell him you picked the right guy."

After a few minutes of awkward silence, I rose to my feet and said, "Somebody needs to be out there keeping watch. Will you charge the phone for me . . . *please?*"

I wanted to say "pretty please" but that seemed a bit much.

"I'll charge your stupid phone," Ella said, "but I'm not talking to Gary."

I handed over the radio and phone. She rubbed her wrists, then shook her hands out.

"I'll do that for you, Ella," Snake said. "Chocolate makes me antsy."

Ella deferred to me, pleading with her eyes.

"Fine," I told Snake. "But don't call any of your friends."

Ella shook her head, letting me know she considered the remark harsh. It probably was. The phone didn't even work where he was sitting.

"Can I listen to the radio?" Snake asked as I turned to go.

Ella gave her approval before I could nix his request.

I walked out carrying my pack. I liked that Ella now had someone else to chat with, but I knew I was right in not giving our prisoner too many privileges.

Chapter 60

Parker studied the monitor as Powell was talking to someone on the phone. He was trying to spot anyone who got close to Steve and Ella, so he could give them a heads-up. Powell ended the call and stood beside him.

"That was an agent from my field office. He's been investigating who gave Clarence inside information before the robbery."

"Any leads yet?" Parker asked.

"Yeah, it seems Marvin talked a young lady into helping him case the bank—like last time."

"Did she work at the bank like last time?"

"No, it looks like Marvin was dating one of the nail technicians next door. She told him about the weekly cash deliveries, and Marvin had her get chummy with the bank manager. They're both in custody. The bank manager came forward when he figured out he'd been duped. He didn't want his wife to find out."

"Have they searched the girlfriend's place yet?" Parker asked, still scanning the store for threats.

"They got the warrant a couple of hours ago. Found fake passports and four airline tickets to Mexico—departing from Memphis yesterday. They missed their flight."

"I'd guess mother Jenkins's picture was on one of the passports."

"Yeah, she was brought in for questioning early on but denied knowing anything. They cut her loose after she passed a polygraph."

"Clarence wouldn't have told her about the heist until they were halfway to Memphis—especially with Bubba involved. Has she called anyone yet?"

"Not from her landline," Powell said. "She doesn't have a cell phone that we know of."

"Not likely she would help us talk him out of there. She wouldn't last time. I'm guessing no one told her what happened to Bubba."

"No, and she asked about him first thing. She was watching news coverage when they knocked on her door."

"So let's get Steve to kill Clarence—save her the trouble when she finds out," Parker said, smiling.

"But you said Steve's a loose cannon. He won't follow orders."

"He'll do what I tell him from now on."

"Are you sure about that? Cause that's not the Steve Taylor I'm seeing."

"I didn't say he'd like me afterward."

"He's not exactly the president of your fan club now, but let's change the subject," Powell said." Clarence took losing his brother a lot better than I'd expected, but we'll push him over the edge if we're not careful. He may become suicidal if he doesn't see a way out of this."

"That would save us a lot of trouble," Parker said, turning to look at him.

"He would start killing hostages to force us to do the job for him. That's the way monsters kill themselves, Parker—in a blaze of glory. You know that."

"Try to make him believe he's getting out. The longer we stall Clarence, the better our chances of Steve taking him out; let's take advantage of that."

"How—your boy's gun-shy. He won't pull the trigger," Powell said, watching for a reaction.

"I'll take some of the blame for that. I pushed him too hard—almost to the breaking point. I've got to pay attention to his physical and mental condition. With some food and a few hours shut-eye I think he'll be fine."

"Your decision. We can keep stalling, but Clarence isn't stupid. He has to know we aren't giving him another ambulance.

"I'll put him in an ambulance, all right, but I promise they won't need the siren."

"Sounds like I'm hedging my bets, but I could use a win here. You're technically in charge of this operation, but I can't be associated with another fiasco. I'm on thin ice already with my superiors."

"I get it, Powell, but my focus is on saving hostages, not our careers."

"Probably doesn't hurt that you're, uh, dating your boss."

"Makes it worse actually. I'm not looking to put a spotlight on her or me. Jennifer's been taking some heat for fraternizing with a lowly L-T. I had to stop dodging a promotion so I could make an honest woman of her. This weekend, we were driving to Gatlinburg with her parents, getting married at a small Chapel in the mountains."

"Congratulations . . . on both counts. She's a great lady."

"Thanks, so what were we discussing?"

"How to keep one of those young pups I work with from taking my job because I screwed up again."

"The best way? We get Steve to finish off Clarence, then you and Jennifer can stand in front of the microphones and do your thing."

"You don't think his crew will attempt to hold down the fort?"

"No, and there aren't many left. Mikey, Clarence's old cellmate guarding the truck dock, looks like a brawler, but he's not picking up the mantle when Clarence falls. I'm planning to have Steve take him out to make sure."

"I hate to ruffle Clarence's feathers again. No telling how he'll react when he hears gunfire and another one of his men goes missing."

Someone tapped on the door, and a uniformed officer stuck his head in. Powell and Parker stopped talking and turned their attention to him.

"Sir, one of the family members is asking to see you. I told him you were busy, but he's persistent."

"Which one?" Parker asked.

"Same one as before, sir," the officer replied.

Parker considered chiding the young officer for not answering a direct question with a direct answer, but he knew with certainty who he was referring to.

"Inform Mr. Thompson I'll come and see him the first chance I get."

"I'll tell him, sir," the officer said, closing the door.

"I don't have to remind you Parker, a lot of people are dissecting our actions. I got word the governor is getting involved. She's sending equipment and personnel from the Tennessee National Guard."

"They're just covering their backsides. My bomb squad has a vehicle on-site that can drive through that door. It's been here since day one. You know as well as I do that if we use it, we'll end up killing more people than we save," Parker said.

"Yeah, it's just political posturing. Everybody wants to be on the right side of this if things go south . . . including me."

"Hey, we've got room to park a tank if they want to send it, but I was hoping to save as many lives as possible."

"I'd rather wait him out too. But if we're planning to get Clarence riled up again, we better be prepared for the consequences," Powell said.

"I'll be careful not to poke the bear too hard. I don't think he'll blow a gasket anytime soon."

"I'm still moderately rested. Why don't you get some sleep?"

"Yeah, okay. I'll go talk to the hot head, then visit Suzy and catch a few winks. That lady is something else." Parker hesitated, then handed Powell his phone. "Here, you'll need this if Steve calls."

Chapter 61

I paced the floor in the dispensing area, trying to stay awake. I stuck my head out and saw Snake going to town on the phone charger. Ella was leaning back against the wall with her eyes closed. I had to clear something up before she conked out. I leaned out and said, "Ella, can you come here, please?" She startled and squinted in my direction. Slow to get up, she walked in carrying the rifle. "Where are *you* sleeping?" I asked.

"You woke me up to ask me that? In there, on one of those nice pads you brought back. Why don't you join us?"

"Somebody needs to be out here in case Parker warns us trouble is approaching. I'm taking my cushion and sleeping by the window," I said, my voice rising louder than I intended.

"Fine, you don't have to get testy."

I turned and left in what Ella likely considered a huff. When I reached Snake, I said, "Get up, I'm taking one of the cushions."

He pulled out my earbuds, which I assumed Ella gave him permission to use, and jumped to his feet.

"Give me the phone. You *will* charge it later. The earphones are officially yours now," I said, yanking the top pad off the pile, launching everything laying on it.

Snake's eyes followed the cigarettes as they soared through the air.

"I'll charge it real good man. I don't want you bein' mad at me. I'm real grateful about what you did back there, letting me live and all."

Ella walked in, sat down, and laid the rifle beside her. When she turned her attention to Snake, I grabbed the rifle and stomped out with the cushion under my arm. Ella gave me a dirty look but said nothing. I threw my bed down next to the window, then positioned the long guns beside it. I felt a twinge of guilt for taking the rifle, but not enough to give it back. It was, after all, the best weapon we had to defend ourselves.

I also felt guilty for the way I'd been treating Ella. I needed to stop holding her accountable for what happened twenty years ago. We were in this together, whether we liked it or not. Snake didn't deserve the treatment I was giving him either. He no more wished to be found than I did. I doubted he even *wanted* the police to end the standoff. He probably had it better here than where he was going. There wouldn't be any pretty blondes to cozy up to in prison.

The one thing missing in our new sanctuary was a bathroom. I would have to do something about that real soon. We now had a sink with running water, and that was a big improvement. A *new* portable toilet would look nice beside it.

Acquiring the toilet wasn't the only thing I needed to do before I could sleep. I had to call Parker. He must be plotting his next move, and I wanted details. Also, I needed to find my medicine. That was a priority.

I searched the many drawers and shelves in the smaller room without success. Then I got down on my hands and knees, searching through the hundreds of bottles scattered on the floor. My knees ached in a matter of minutes. I got up and took the bottle of aspirin out of my pocket.

I started for the sink to get some water but spotted a mini fridge tucked in a corner. I retrieved a nearly full diet soda behind various-sized bottles of liquid medication. I twisted off the cap, pleased to hear a generous escape of carbonation. I removed four tablets and washed them down. I took another long pull on the soda and tossed it on the pad. I was glad to be alone; it gave me the opportunity to think about my wife and what it would take to get her home.

Chapter 62

4:30 a.m. Sunday

Parker was attempting to calm down Gary Thompson. The two men were standing behind a strip of yellow tape with the words "Police Line—Do Not Cross" repeated along its length. Gary and the other family members were kept back a safe distance from the building and segregated from the media.

"Your wife is most likely trying to sleep right now. She's as safe as she could possibly be in this type of situation," Parker said.

"I demand to know where they are and what they're doing."

Everybody reacted to these things differently, Parker was well aware. Some were deeply grateful to the police officers for risking their lives. While a few, like Gary, acted belligerent. Parker took it all in stride.

"The last time I checked, Ella was unharmed and waiting patiently for me to free her," Parker said, not willing to give Gary more information than he required. "And don't tell anyone you've spoken to her."

"Are they sleeping together?" Gary shouted.

Parker watched as a couple of the officers in the vicinity turned around.

"Keep your voice down. Steve's wife is here, and she doesn't need to hear your nonsense," Parker scolded.

"Where is she? I want to talk to her."

"If I see you bothering anyone, especially her, I'll have you removed from the premises—and locked up, if I have to. Do you understand me?"

"Yeah, I get it, but I don't appreciate you letting them get friendly in there, while I have to sit out here and pretend like it's not happening."

"Relax Gary. You're worrying about imaginary problems. Go to your vehicle and chill out. I'll send someone to get you if anything changes."

"My truck is inside the barricades," Gary said pointing to the cordoned-off area by the far entrance.

"Where have you been sleeping?"

"I haven't. I've been waiting right here for my wife to come out of that store."

Parker had noticed the way Gary appeared unsteady on his feet. He'd have to find this guy somewhere to lay down.

"Let me see what I can do. Wait here," Parker said.

He gestured to a police officer securing the line.

"Have you got a car I can sleep in for a couple of hours?"

"Yes sir, that one over there appears to be empty," the officer said, pointing to the cruiser Suzy occupied, parked behind the bus.

"Someone's already using that one," Parker said, hoping he wouldn't have to explain why he couldn't share it.

The officer scanned the area for a moment, and Parker cut him off as he was about to speak. "Get me a car. Park it right there," he pointed to a spot.

"Yes sir, right away," the officer said, hustling off.

"Gary, looks like you and I are sharing accommodations," Parker said, holding up the tape to let him pass underneath. "Unless you have a problem with the two of us sleeping together," he added, watching as Gary caught his drift.

Chapter 63

I stepped out and called Parker. Snake didn't have much time to charge the phone before I took it away from him, but the battery meter already showed 12 percent when I powered it up.

"I'm ready to do whatever's necessary," I said before he could speak.

"Steve, this is FBI Special Agent, Powell. Parker is out of pocket for a few hours. You guys doing okay?"

"We're fine, but I need to get out of here. Tell Parker I'm willing to do whatever he asks. I won't fight him anymore."

"He'll be glad to hear it."

"Is he taking care of my wife like he promised?"

"The lieutenant was going to check on her when he left. We'll keep her safe; I promise you."

"Thanks, I appreciate that. Sorry I got you involved, calling 9-1-1."

"Steve, you did the right thing. We'd prefer to deal with them here and now, rather than fifty bodies later at a different crime scene."

I hadn't thought of it that way, but I would have preferred somewhere else; somewhere that I wasn't, I reasoned as my phone chirped.

"That's the low-battery warning. I'll charge my phone as soon as we're done. I don't have service in there, but make some noise, and I'll call you."

"Steve, let me ask you something," Powell said and then hesitated.

"What is it?"

"Lieutenant Parker has a lot of confidence in you, and his men are still pumped about you saving the woman. I'm wondering if you're up for this. I know it was hard for you earlier."

"I doubt Parker thinks too highly of me at the moment, but I'll do anything to get my wife home. He hasn't got me killed yet. I just pray my luck doesn't run out."

"Me too, Steve. I'll give Parker the message," Powell said, ending the call.

I went to the back of the pharmacy and gave the phone to Snake.

"I'd appreciate if you'd stay awake and charge my phone. Leave it turned on so you'll know when it's fully charged," I said, avoiding eye contact with Ella, who seemed surprised by my new attitude.

"I'll get right on it," Snake said, inserting the cable.

I felt stupid giving him my phone, but he would have to walk past me in order to use it. I returned to my private quarters and sat on the counter. I heard Snake and Ella whispering, and a minute later she came in carrying a cushion. She placed it on the floor next to mine, and without saying a word, stretched out on it facing me.

"Things didn't work out with you two?" I said, smiling.

"I told him I needed to help you guard the door. I think it broke his heart," Ella said, trying to look sad, but she wasn't pulling it off.

"Be honest, Ella; you missed the rifle."

"Yeah, but I hoped we could talk. I just want to get along. I don't want you mad at me ever again."

I was too tired for that conversation. I would concede defeat and move on.

"We're fine, Ella. My fault. I've been hard to get along with."

"I understand. Lack of sleep and hangovers always made you ornery," Ella said, scooching towards me, now partially on my pad.

"That's kind of you to say, but I'll try to be more civil. I haven't been myself lately."

"Snake told me what happened. You went over there to kill him, but you brought him back instead. I'm glad you did that."

"What else did he say?"

"That you were unsteady . . . for a minute or two," Ella said, spinning the story to my advantage. Whether Snake told it that way or not I wasn't sure.

"Help yourself to the soda I found in the fridge," I said, after Ella pushed it out of her way and came closer.

"No thanks, I need to get some sleep. Here, if you don't mind."

I wanted to tell her that I'd prefer she did it elsewhere, but I knew that would end our fragile peace treaty. I considered laying my pad on the opposite side of the room, but the proximity to the window and door made this the best place to be, even if I wasn't expecting to be awake much longer.

Why don't you lay down and get some sleep," she said, retreating on her cushion and balling up like a kitten.

It felt like only yesterday she used to sleep like that on the couch, while I watched rented movies on our VCR.

"I'm going back out for a minute," I said, not liking where this was headed.

I set the knapsack on my pad to keep Ella from rolling over on my side of the bed, which was also something I remembered she was prone to do. I was reasonably sure Ella wasn't flirting with me, but according to most of the chick flicks I endured with my wife, these things can get out of control. I'd bunk with Snake before I'd let that happen.

"Hurry back, Steve. You know I can't sleep alone," Ella said as I walked out.

I replayed Ella's last words in my mind. I decided to let it go. I knew what she meant. She'd never felt comfortable sleeping by herself. I couldn't remember if she was afraid someone would break in and harm her or if it was just a phobia. She didn't have a lot of practice at sleeping alone like I did.

After Ella and I parted company, most of my nights were spent solo. I dated pretty often, but most of the women I met bailed before we developed any kind of relationship—especially when I was still drinking. Thank God I met Suzy. We fell in love corresponding by email and talking on the phone before we ever met.

Ella moved Gary in just a month after I was sent packing. I remember not being too surprised she had replaced me so quickly. The fact that my best friend was the replacement made me hate the whole world for a few years.

Chapter 64

I came back with my arms full. Ella was cuddling my knapsack like a teddy bear. She appeared to be asleep, but then I saw her peek as I approached. I dropped the giant bag of kitty litter on the floor.

"What are you doing?" Ella said, sitting up.

"I'll show you in a second," I said, grabbing the small plastic wastepaper basket under the counter. I located a taller version in the far corner. Both were empty and had a liner.

Perfect, I thought to myself.

I cut one corner off the sack and poured the dusty granules into the larger receptacle, generously covering the bottom. I then did the same with the smaller one and took it into the next room. Snake was still cranking, leaning on his elbow, looking uncomfortable on a single layer of padding.

"If you need to take a leak, use this one. 'Number-two' is in the other room. Let me know, and I'll bring it in here for you."

"Thanks, man, I was about to pop."

"How's the phone coming along?"

Snake checked the display. "Forty percent. I'll top her off before I quit."

"Thanks, I really appreciate it," I said.

Snake looked down and nodded. He wasn't expecting praise. I went back to find Ella, but she was nowhere in sight.

"Stay out," she ordered when I whispered her name.

She had chosen the nook between two filing cabinets. I would have put it next to the sink but hadn't considered the privacy issues. I sized up the long but narrow counter surface to see if it was feasible for sleeping. Ella would likely take offense, but I could defend the move by keeping watch out the window until I fell asleep. I decided to reclaim lost territory instead, pushing her bed a foot away from mine.

I lay on my back, feeling secure with the Glock on my belt and the long guns beside me. I would use the countertop as a backup if Ella wanted to pillow talk about our past. As I waited, I thought about how Suzy, and even Gary for that matter, would feel about our sleeping arrangement.

"Ella, you take something in there to read," I said, showing I still remembered her old habits.

"Great idea you had there, Taylor," she said, peering over the filing cabinet

"I'm glad you like it. Don't forget to put another layer of kitty litter on top. I don't want Snake thinking *I* stunk the place up," I said loud enough to get a laugh out of Snake.

"You better get a whole 'nother bag to suffocate that smell when you come in here," she said, vacating the area quickly, making me believe there might indeed be an odor rolling out.

Ella nudged the cushions together with her toe, then sat down and started playing with her hair, obviously wishing she had a brush. I forgot how much that used to annoy me. She lay down, evaluating various positions, finally coming to rest on her back. She was silent, staring at the ceiling. I knew what was coming next and I was too tired to reminisce.

I got up and checked my watch, then reset the blinking clock. I turned on the radio and leaned against the counter. The news at the half-hour mark was about to begin and the local station was already dialed in. I listened to a commercial for a local furniture store having a Fourth of July blowout sale.

"*WKOM* news at the bottom of the hour. Here are the headlines we are following," the newscaster announced. "SaveMart president Brian Stevenson is rumored to be pressuring state and federal authorities to step in and end the siege at the Columbia SaveMart, now entering its third day. SaveMart spokesperson Ann Colson stated that those accounts are false, adding the company wants the matter resolved with only the well-being of its customers, employees, and emergency personnel taken into consideration."

I listened to the rest of the news, none of which affected us, then turned it off. We weren't big news anymore, with no recent shooting or explosions to report. The matter about Clarence being involved in another hostage situation wasn't touched on. I wondered if Suzy knew the beast involved in the botched heist was also the ringleader here.

I turned off the radio and stretched out on the pad. I had planned on retrieving my phone from Snake, but he was still charging it the last time I checked. He couldn't make a call where he was sitting, and I was almost convinced he wasn't looking for an opportunity to call in a hit squad. Or maybe I was just too exhausted to care.

"Good night, Ella."

"Sweet dreams, Steve."

Chapter 65

11:00 a.m. Sunday

Suzy piled either ham or turkey and slices of cheese on a large hamburger bun, then placed the towering sandwich alongside a generous portion of potato chips. Condiments were displayed to one side of her workstation. Napkins and plastic utensils were aligned on the other side. Along with the food, each person could choose between fresh coffee and soda. She had several coolers off to the side containing sports drinks and bottled water in mounds of ice—the only self-serve items on her handwritten menu.

The table, four orange barrels and a sheet of plywood, served as the temporary mess hall for the emergency workers encouraged to stick around at the end of their shift. An extension cord running to the bus powered the coffeepot. Suzy smiled as she slid a plate to the next person in line, who at first glance resembled her husband.

"What can I get you to drink, sir, coffee, soft drink?" Suzy asked.

"I just woke up so let's make it a coffee. You're Steve Taylor's wife, correct? I had no idea you were uhhh . . . crippled," he said, taking the plate and the coffee she poured out of the large pot.

"I prefer the word *disabled* . . . and yes, I *am* Suzanne Taylor. Have we met?"

"Yeah, disabled. Sorry, that's what I should have said. My wife's in there—with your husband," he said, avoiding eye contact as he reached for the mustard.

"You must be Ella's husband."

"Steve told you about her?"

"Oh yeah, he told me about you as well, Gary," she said, causing him to stop what he was doing.

"I hope it wasn't all bad," he finally said.

"Lieutenant Parker said they're not in immediate danger right now."

"How does *he* know what's happening in there?"

"They'll get out unharmed. I have to believe that. I couldn't function right now if I didn't," Suzy said, resuming her work.

"I'm not sure what's more likely: Ella getting killed, or coming out to tell me that she's leaving me for your husband."

"I'm not the least bit worried about *that*," Suzy said with an exasperated laugh. "And I don't appreciate you bothering me with your crazy talk, either."

"I'm sorry I upset you. I'll leave you alone. Thanks for the sandwich," Gary said, skulking off.

Suzy wiped tears with a napkin. When she looked up, she noticed that Parker was staring through the window of the bus at Gary walking past. He didn't look happy.

267

Chapter 66

"You got a phone call," I heard Snake say loudly, like it wasn't his first attempt to wake me. I was having a terrible dream, which I couldn't remember the second I awoke. Holding Ella in my arms, made me think losing her was the nightmare I had awoken from. Then I remembered Suzy and the *real* happy ending written for my life. I blew into Ella's ear—hard—trying to get her off my arm.

She awoke, startled.

"I hate when you do that. What time is it?" she asked, her eyes still closed.

"It's half past eleven. That's what the phone says," Snake answered.

I didn't realize he was still there. Obviously, Ella didn't hear him earlier. She jerked her head around like she expected to find Gary standing there. I crawled over Ella and tried to stand, too stiff to succeed on my first attempt.

Snake handed me the phone.

"Hello," I said, but there was no response.

"He told me to get you. He's gonna call back," Snake said, turning to leave with what seemed like a bit of an attitude.

"The phone worked in there?"

"I went out for a smoke. The phone was in my pocket. Buzzed as soon as I stepped out of the pharmacy."

I bet it did, I thought, wishing I could've seen Parker's face when Snake answered.

"I never got to have that cigarette by the way." Snake said walking back to his area.

I checked the phone for received calls and saw Parker's number. It was fully charged, making me give Snake a pass for abusing his privileges. I would definitely be securing his feet the next time I left him unattended though.

The message he relayed seemed less than life-or-death urgent, and there was no bullhorn action. My head was still fuzzy, but I didn't think anyone was coming to kill us. Parker may have been alerting me that my prisoner was going AWOL.

I followed Snake to the back room and opened a diet shake. I needed to lubricate my tongue enough to talk on the phone. Snake stared at me as I drank it, like he felt I owed him an apology for catching me with his girlfriend. I flipped open the phone and started walking.

"Take me with you," Snake said, removing the cigarette behind his ear.

"Come on." I waved for him to follow.

I guess I was feeling guilt-ridden about him seeing us like that. Technically I hadn't done anything wrong, but I was ashamed of myself for crossing into that gray area. I doubted taking Snake along could reduce Parker's level of respect for me any further. I held up the phone as we exited the pharmacy, expecting he would see or get word I was now awake.

"Wait for me around the corner and don't even think about going for the carton," I said.

Ella, still lying on the cushion, had seen us pass by. I pretended to be focused on the phone so I wouldn't have to explain. I'd slept for over four hours. I felt better, but not great. It would take a cup of strong coffee to render me well. I was trying to remember if my last coffee machine came with a promotional sample, when my phone buzzed.

"Nice job rehabilitating your prisoner. I might be able to get you a job teaching secretarial skills to inmates. I'll have to tack smoking in a public building on top of his other charges when I get in there."

"I guess you'll have to charge me as an accessory on that one."

"Taylor, you are one interesting fella."

"What's happening out there?" I asked, changing the subject before he could explain what he meant.

"We're rattling your neighbor's cage in an hour or so. Should be quiet until then."

"Is it all right if I go pick up a few things?" I asked, awake enough now to be restless.

"Are you taking your new assistant? For a couple of cigarettes, you could get him to be your personal shopper. . . . Yeah go ahead. Powell talked to Clarence earlier. He calmed him down with promises of letting him go. He probably isn't buying it a hundred percent."

"How's my wife?" I asked.

"She's taken over the concession stand out here. You got yourself a keeper there, Steve."

"You're preaching to the choir. Tell Suzy I love her."

"I tell her that every time I see her. Ella's husband finally got some sleep. He hates your guts. Did you know that?"

"I've heard that rumor," I said.

"Don't wander too far. Clarence sends someone out for groceries every few hours," Parker said ending the call.

When we returned, Ella was laying on both pads—double stacked. Snake went into his room and sat down.

"Gary's doing okay," I told her as I passed by.

"He called your phone? He spoke to you?" Ella said a moment later when she joined us.

"No, Parker gave me the message. I'm going out for supplies. You need anything?"

"What now, a slot-car track?" Ella asked, frowning. "You wanted one for Christmas. You almost cried when I told you no, remember?"

"A laptop computer for starters," I replied.

"I'm going too," she said, crossing her arms. "You only think of your own needs when you get stuff. I'll help you make better purchase decisions."

"Sorry, Snake, if Ella's coming I've got to tie you up."

Snake gave Ella a dirty look, something I didn't think he had in him. He rolled over and assumed the position. We both knew there was no talking her out of it.

Ella followed me, holding the rifle in the crook of her arm like she'd carried a long gun in the field before. I pictured her and Gary wearing identical upland jackets. Ella broke off and turned into the personal hygiene aisle. I backtracked and followed her. She leaned her rifle against an I-beam and began picking up items. She handed them to me as she went down the row, filling my arms with toothbrushes, toothpaste, mouthwash, a can of aerosol deodorant.

I walked off and located an empty shopping cart two aisles over, and placed the merchandise in the kid seat. When I returned, Ella was holding several more items and looked annoyed.

"We didn't need a buggy," Ella said.

"I might need another one before I get through," I said, spinning it around in the opposite direction.

Chapter 67

Ella picked up her rifle and followed as I took off toward the rear of the store. After a quick stop for burglary tools, I hustled toward the electronics department. The cart I was pushing was conspicuous, but at least none of the wheels were squealing. I kept my eyes open for trouble, not willing to trust Parker to warn me we were about to get shot. The last time he did that, he was a few seconds late.

I stopped at the cross aisle, staring at the electronic department's checkout. There was a dead body there if nobody moved it. It made me realize how much danger we were in.

"Ella, how about I take the rifle and go first. This place is bringing back bad memories. Somebody may be waiting for us to come back."

"I know what to do, trust me," she said, stepping past me.

"Fine, but flick off the safety—and stay in front of me."

She gave me a dirty look and ventured across, with me pushing the cart right behind her.

"Turn right and go down the next aisle," I whispered when she began staring at Old Fabio's dead body.

I often browsed the computer selection after work. I would have likely purchased a new laptop this summer, but I'd been staging a personal boycott of the store's high-end items—when it suited me. Suzy also reminded me that my desktop was barely two years old. I wasn't even sure it was possible to buy a computer at that hour. I knew for a fact the store wouldn't sell a firearm in the early hours of the morning.

I got in a little dustup with several employees involving an over-under shotgun, which I had decided I had to have sometime during my shift that day. My neighbor had invited me to shoot skeet with his buddies the next morning. Being my first time, I didn't want them to think I was a rube.

I found a stock person to get them to unlock the gun cabinet, but she told me it was impossible to sell me a gun at that late hour because I could use it to rob the store. I fought the urge to tell her I would come back in the morning—to buy a gun to rob the store. Instead, I asked to speak to the manager. He was summoned and told me SaveMart personnel weren't allowed to sell firearms later than 10 p.m. He sympathized with me but said he would get fired when the general manager came across the paperwork the next morning.

I wasn't happy, but it turned out for the best. The next morning, after three hours sleep, I competed with my father's Browning. They never invited me back. Maybe because I'd outscored them while making wisecracks about their fancy over-unders.

Ed's ring held many keys. I hoped he had the one for the new-in-the-box laptops stored in the locked storage below the display. I had a contingency plan just in case. I acquired a large flat-blade screwdriver and a ball-peen hammer. I was hoping the first would force open the locking mechanism on the glass door, but I was prepared to use the second tool to *authorize* my purchase if necessary.

I tried all the keys in the lock and was disappointed when none of them fit. I went to plan B and stuck the tip of the screwdriver between the sliding glass doors, but the lock held. Kneeling down to inspect the situation more closely, I detected the fatal flaw in my strategy. The glass was thick and reinforced with wire mesh. It would take a lot of effort to get at the computers, including going back for wire cutters and maybe a bigger hammer.

"What do you need it for, Steve? If you had a real phone, you'd know the store doesn't have Wi-Fi. You're not going to be able to play secret agent with it."

I nodded, too embarrassed to tell her I wanted it to watch movies. I hadn't thought of using it to help our situation. "Let's swing by sporting goods on the way back. I want to get one more thing."

"Come on, Steve, you don't need anything else," Ella said, unwilling to proceed.

I swung the cart around her and took off. I assumed she would follow me. The item I wanted in sporting goods wasn't merchandise. It was the vest Flattop was wearing. I was hoping to talk Ella into wearing it. We entered sporting goods from the back aisle. I pushed the cart up near the gun cabinet, where the road was blocked by the pallet and a dead body.

"Wait here, and let me know if you see someone," I said.

"You'll hear me shooting if I do," Ella said, scanning the area beyond the checkout.

As I was about to step over Ed, Ella whispered my name.

"I know how to shoot one of those," she said, pointing at the gun cabinet.

"What's that?" I asked.

"The crossbow. Gary and I both have one." She stepped up to the display to get a closer look.

I wanted one myself, ever since Tennessee legalized them for the archery deer season.

"Are you any good with it?" I asked.

"Yeah, we practice all summer. We shot them at the cabin last weekend. I can usually hit the bulls-eye from thirty yards."

I was a little impressed since I'd never held a crossbow, nor could I hit a target with any type of archery equipment. I was forced to sit out the early hunting season, waiting to join the mobs during the firearm season.

"Gary bagged a ten-pointer with one last year."

Not for the first time in my life, I was jealous of Gary. I missed a nice buck with a high-powered rifle.

"Let's get it," I said, digging in my pocket for the keys.

"This one right here," Ella said, pointing to the significantly more expensive model. "Gary wanted that one, but we ended up with shoddier ones that came with a bunch of accessories we thought we needed."

"What accessories *do* we need?"

"It's already strung, so just a package of bolts."

"Bolts—it's not fully assembled."

"Short arrows . . . over there," Ella said, pointing to the archery supplies next to the shotgun shells.

This was the one section of sporting goods I was unfamiliar with. Ella steered the cart the long way around to get the ammunition as I lifted the crossbow out of the display.

"Practice tips or broad heads?" Ella whispered, holding a box of each.

"Definitely broad heads," I said, deducing which type was used when trying to kill something. My mind raced as I imagined the advantage of a weapon that didn't make a loud bang when you pulled the trigger.

I put the crossbow in the cart and went over to Flattop's body and removed his vest. I scraped off chunks of brain on the edge of a nearby shelf, then slung it in the bottom of the cart.

"It might come in handy," I said, pushing the cart.

"It certainly didn't help him," she replied.

Chapter 68

1:00 p.m. Sunday

Parker was approaching the canteen to check on Suzy. She was reaching to pour a gallon jug of water into the large coffeemaker when she noticed him.

"Hi, Tom. I'll fix you a plate in one second."

"Was Gary hassling you?" Parker asked, taking hold of the container to assist her.

"I'll do it," Suzy said, wrenching it away. "I'm sorry Lieutenant, but I can manage. And, no, Gary wasn't bothering me. He's just upset and scared. He chose to vent his anger on me, and I can deal with that too."

"If he *is* a problem . . . I'll have him removed."

"No, as a matter of fact, I want to have a chat with him after I get caught up here."

"Don't hurt him or I'll have to arrest you." Parker said with a smile.

"Funny, Tom, but I'll set him straight my way."

"He doesn't stand a chance. I see it in your eyes."

"What's Steve up to?" she said, changing the subject.

"Currently, he's taking advantage of SaveMart's Fourth of July discounts. I'd tell him to stay put, but I doubt he'd listen. My guys are betting on what he'll take next. The last I heard, the odds favored a new laptop," Parker said, leaving Ella's name out of it.

"He wants one—mostly just to watch his shows," Suzy said shaking her head. "I hope he has a plan to pay for it."

"Don't worry, these guys have cost the store millions in lost sales. When the SaveMart people figure in loss of refrigeration and getting rid of some of the other bad smells in there, the total will likely run into the tens of millions."

"Wow. They can't be too happy about that."

"They told my boss they're self-insured, like that's something to consider when forming our strategy. These criminals apparently knew the bank held a significant amount of cash. It's still in the vault, according to their security chief. They couldn't get into it. The store held a full day's worth of cash in a lockbox as well. They probably got that money, so don't be concerned about any mischief your husband gets into. I just like giving him a hard time. Steve has a unique sense of humor."

"Yeah, but don't let him know you think he's funny. He'll get the big head."

"I'll try to remember that," Parker said laughing.

"Kinda sounds like he's having fun in there. Steve loves that store. He's always coming home with stuff he doesn't need. The next morning he swears he'll never go back."

"Actually, he recently acquired an item that could be *very* useful," Parker said, walking away so he wouldn't have to explain.

Chapter 69

"Gary, can I talk to you?" Suzy called out, as she rolled up to the police car he was leaning against. He still had VIP status; Parker told her that he was keeping him close to keep an eye on him.

"I was told not to speak to you anymore."

"Well, I need to say something to you, so I guess you can just listen."

"I apologize for what I said earlier. I was way out of line. That wasn't like me."

"Forget it happened, Gary. I understand how difficult this is for you. It's hard to think clearly, sitting out here waiting for good news. I'm scared too."

"Ella told me she wanted a divorce before she went in the store. I was being stupid, acting like a jealous idiot."

"Have you spoken to her?" Suzy asked, not sure if he knew Steve had a phone.

"Once. She still loves me, but—and I don't mean to upset you—our last fight was about Steve. He was about to go into the store, and Ella told me to stay in the truck. I told her I was going whether she liked it or not. She lost it . . . said I'm the reason your husband won't have anything to do with her. Then she told me to pack my bags—leave right then if I wanted to. Now they're both in there together."

"Steve told me getting over Ella was painful, but we have a life now. I trust him completely."

"Steve's not the one I'm worried about," Gary said.

I'm the one you *should be worried about,* Suzy thought, watching Gary walk away.

Chapter 70

Joe watched the ringleader hobble out of the bank and shout for Johnny. Bear was a scary-looking guy, but his bloody leg wound limited his mobility to the point he needed a wheelchair. All he had done in the way of first aid was to wrap it with brown paper towel from the bathroom.

"You don't want me coming in there to get you, Johnny," Clarence boomed, as he turned toward the restrooms.

"His roar sounds more like a lion than a bear," Joe whispered to Jimmy.

"Every time he gets this upset he kills somebody. This time it might be us,"

Joe nodded and said, "I was thinking about the guy you were describing, who you thought might be the Sniper."

Jimmy confirmed Bear was still busy with his own problems before responding, "Yeah, the guy comes in maybe once a week. He always tells my employees what a great job they're doing. Our shooter could teach that guy a few things about motivation."

Joe nodded. "Tell me what he looks like again?"

"Six foot, maybe 210 pounds, athletic build, blond hair kinda thin on top. A lot of your people come in here late at night, but he's the one who makes everyone smile and even laugh sometimes. The girls always talk about him after he leaves," Jimmy said, gesturing to the elderly women in front of him. "He may be a boss out there. . . . No, on second thought, he doesn't dress like one. Usually he wears shorts, even when it's too cold for it."

"Does he wear glasses?"

"Yeah, now that you mention it, he does."

"Sounds like one of my guys."

"Is he ex-military? Our guy would almost have to be."

"No, I don't believe so. He's in good shape though, and he looks GI. I know he hunts—takes vacation days during deer season. He rarely bags anything," Joe said, remembering Steve joking about it.

"Sounds like him. Our sniper is no great shot, that's for sure. I had a conversation with him a few months ago. He needed a new shotgun—in a bad way, but it was too late to sell him one. He cracked me up. He really wanted that gun."

That has to be Steve Taylor. Joe envisioned his team leader shooting overhead, killing a couple of the guys wearing lab coats and wounding their leader. Chatter from the criminals indicated the cute blonde from work was no longer in danger. Someone—had to be Steve—killed the guy who had taken her on a forced march. Maybe Steve had more skills than he let on. Then another thought hit him: if Steve rescued her, they were certain to be holed up together. Jimmy had heard them talking. Everyone knew Steve had issues with the woman. But no one knew exactly why she came around bothering him. It was a topic Steve refused to discuss.

Joe looked over and saw Bear disappear behind the block wall in front of the men's room door.

"Was his name Steve?" Joe whispered.

"He didn't say. Let me ask Clara; she might know. He always pays at her register."

Jimmy whispered the woman's name to get her attention. "What's the name of your boyfriend from the factory?" Jimmy said as loud as he dared.

The sixty-four-year-old woman, married for forty years with five grown kids and three grandchildren, looked bewildered for a moment before she comprehended. She shook her head as though unsure.

"Is it Steve?" Joe asked, leaning toward the woman.

The woman looked up and to the left, searching her brain.

"I think so, but I'm so worn out I can't remember for sure," she whispered back.

"Shut your mouths back there, or I'll tape 'em shut," Bear said, silencing them.

"Johnny, you can't hide in there forever," Bear yelled, banging on the door.

"I'm coming out, Bear. I had to answer the call of nature."

Bear stood next to the water fountain waiting for him. "You're lucky I'm shorthanded, now put a gun on the hostages. Can you handle that?" Bear said as Johnny walked by him, dodging most of the blow his boss delivered with his open hand.

"I'll shoot anyone who gets out of line. You can count on me," Johnny said as Bear headed back toward the bank.

Joe whispered, "Steve Taylor. Is that his name?"

Clara smiled and nodded.

Joe leaned in and whispered to Jimmy, "I'm not sure if that's good news or not. I was kinda hoping for somebody like . . . Chuck Norris."

Chapter 71

5:00 p.m. Sunday

Suzy was about to take action without getting prior approval, when she spotted the Lieutenant walking away from the bus.

"Lieutenant Parker," Suzy yelled, pushing the wheels of her chair as fast as she could to reach him.

"What can I do for you? And please call me Tom," he said, kneeling in front of her.

"Do you mind if I take a few sandwiches over there?" Suzy said, pointing to the group waiting for their family members to be released.

"They could definitely use it. I'll get someone to assist you."

"That's okay, I've got it," Suzy said, peeling off.

She put a large Styrofoam platter stacked high with sandwiches on her lap, then wheeled her chair to the group that was praying together.

Suzy gave the officer a big smile as she approached the yellow tape.

"Lieutenant Parker told me to deliver this. You can have one if you like."

The officer smiled and took one, then lifted the barrier to let her pass underneath.

An older woman who looked like she'd just left a beauty parlor, despite the heat and humidity, spotted her first and walked over.

"Is this for us?" the woman asked.

"Yes, I hope you like ham and cheese with mustard. That's all I have left," Suzy said, raising the platter. "I wanted to make sure you got fed before I ran out."

"That's awful kind of you, sugar. Someone brought us that big jug of ice water earlier," the woman said, pointing at the yellow insulated container and paper cups. "We haven't eaten much. Nobody wants to leave. We're afraid something terrible will happen if we stop praying."

"Sir, may I set the food on your car?" Suzy asked the officer as she laid the platter on the hood of his cruiser.

"For a little while, ma'am. I may need to move the car if I get a call," the young officer said, looking around to see if any of his peers had seen him get taken by the lady in the wheelchair.

The rest of the family members stared from a distance.

"Come on everybody, help yourselves," Suzy called out to them.

They all moved toward her.

"Who wants coffee and who wants a soda?"

Ten people with fear and fatigue showing on their faces timidly made selections. Most chose the hot coffee even though they were standing on pavement in direct sunlight.

"I'll get it right away. I just brewed a fresh pot," Suzy said, turning her chair back toward the canteen as someone behind her shouted, "Wait!" Suzy turned her chair around and saw the older woman she had spoken with earlier.

"Please, let me help you carry something," the woman said.

Suzy would have dismissed her out of hand, but she saw tears in the woman's eyes and understood that, like herself, she needed a task to keep her mind off the possibilities.

"Officer, I'm not sure I'm able to carry the next load by myself. Would it be okay if this woman assisted me? I'm sure Tom, I mean Lieutenant Parker, won't mind."

"Uh—I guess that would be okay," the young man said, confirming that no one was watching before he raised the barrier to allow the woman into the hot zone.

Chapter 72

I was standing guard outside the pharmacy when Parker called. "We need to take care of some loose ends that might cause problems later. Do you think your prisoner will give me some information?"

"I think so. He seems to have crossed over from the dark side."

"That's great—Obie-Wan—put him on."

"Snake, come here for a minute," I said sticking my head inside the pharmacy.

In spite of Parker's snide comment, I felt cocky. The police needed information from Snake, and I was the reason he was still alive. Ella accompanied him, curious about what was happening.

"Here, talk to him," I said, passing Snake the phone. He seemed eager to help.

He listened to Parker for a moment before he responded. "No, you can't trust that one. I heard him and Bear were pals in the joint. None of us like him because he snitches on us. If Bear would count on anybody, it would be Mikey now that his brother has gone missing."

Snake nodded as he listened again. He replied that he didn't know anything about Bear or what his plans might be. Snake listened for another moment and said, "You're welcome. Anything else you need, just ask. I'm on your side now."

Snake went quiet, nodding his head again.

"He's right here," Snake said, handing me the phone.

"Yeah, he's with us now," I said, bragging on him.

"That's awesome, but he told me the convict guarding the loading dock is more dangerous than most of the others. And he and Clarence are tight. I was hoping Mikey was back there waiting for the paddy wagon to come pick him up, but it sounds like he'd come back and help Clarence when you start shooting at him again."

"Don't tell me I've got to bring *him* back here too."

"You're in luck there. If Mikey's a bad dude, I don't want him near you. We don't need Clarence knowing we killed him either. Powell is trying to make him believe we're willing to release him with a hostage. If he hears a gunshot back there, he'll have more doubts than he does already. He'd likely kill some hostages."

"Tell me what to do," I replied, wishing once again that I'd shot Snake when I was told to.

"Are you any good with that crossbow, or were you hoping to learn how if you ever had some free time?" Parker asked.

"Ella knows how to shoot it. We haven't been able to draw the string back, though."

"See what you can do about getting that thing to work and get back to me," Parker said. "Call me soon."

We all marched back inside the pharmacy. "We need to do some target practice with your crossbow," I told Ella.

"What do you mean?"

"Parker has a job for us," I said, trying to sound optimistic about having to risk our lives again, this time using the weapon of choice from the Middle Ages.

Chapter 73

Suzy became quick friends with Kathleen as they served emergency personnel the remaining food and beverages. After a few minutes of telling how they happened to be there, they figured out their spouses worked together. Gary was standing twenty feet away for some time, looking like he wanted to join the conversation.

"Gary, we could use some help over here," Suzy yelled, waving him over.

"You know that guy? I thought we'd run out of food before he got the nerve to step up," Kathleen whispered, as Gary made his way.

"Yeah, he's one of us. Let's give him something to do. He's in a bad way right now."

"Gary, honey, could you do us a favor and drain the water out of the coolers?" said Kathleen. "Then put the stuff on whatever ice is left. The ham is getting waterlogged sitting on the bottom." She gave him a sympathetic smile as Suzy slid a plate to the police officer next in line.

"I think we're about to get wet," Suzy said, pointing at lightning strikes in the distance.

"Probably just heat lightning," Kathleen said, pushing a plate to someone dressed in a protective suit with the words "Nashville Bomb Squad" stenciled across the chest and two bottles of Gatorade under his arm.

It was still sweltering hot, the sun's rays poking through the towering cumulonimbus clouds. Not unusual for a summer evening in the south. Suzy noticed the officers wearing protective equipment were especially grateful for the iced-down liquids.

"Anything else I can do for you? I get how staying busy keeps your mind straight," Gary said when he finished the task.

"Go to the store for us. We're running out of everything," Suzy said.

"Yeah, get some ice cream. That'll cool these boys and gals down," Kathleen said, as a female officer stepped up.

Suzy smiled and said, "We'll need a lot of ice to pull *that* off."

"Let's whip up some iced tea and lemonade too. I see the need for Gatorade, but get me some tea bags, lemons, and sugar, and I'll make them forget all about coffee and sodas. I'm a Southern gal, if you couldn't tell. I came here from Michigan, but I was raised in Atlanta. Met Joe while he was on leave from Parris Island."

"What a coincidence. I lived in Atlanta when I met Steve."

"Let me hear you say, Marietta. Then I'll know if you're really a Georgia Peach," Kathleen said laughing.

"Mar-etta," Suzy said, the way the locals pronounce it.

"You've been coached, sugar. I made you for a Yankee the first time you spoke."

"They taught me that when I transferred to the office in Mar-etta," Suzy said. "I'm originally from Minnesota—the Twin Cities, then

Arizona, Connecticut, and Georgia. I moved to Tennessee when I married Steve."

"How do you like it here?" Kathleen asked.

"I miss Atlanta, but not the traffic. Steve thinks I'm safer living in a small town, but I can take care of myself."

"I bet you can. Joe and I got here by way of Detroit and Oklahoma City. We're hoping this is our last stop. We plan to retire here."

"Better get cold brew tea bags. We don't have any way to heat water unless we dump the coffee. I'll make a list for you, Gary." Suzy dug in the small purse hanging on her brake lever.

"I'd like to help you ladies, but my truck is off-limits, and I really don't want to leave. I need to be here when my wife comes out," Gary said.

"Here, take the Caddy. It's out there," Kathleen said, lobbing him the keys and pointing to the back of the parking lot. "I was parked by the front door when I heard the first explosion. I just sat there for a minute praying Joe would come out. When the cars exploded at the back of the parking lot, I fled to the exit. About a hundred police cars surrounded me. For a minute, they thought I had something to do with it."

"Where should I get all this stuff? Gary said, eyeing the list Suzy was preparing.

"Go down to the PricedRight," Kathleen said, "Get some Styrofoam coolers, pack the ice cream in there, and we'll start serving as soon as you get back."

"I've got an idea," Suzy said. "Buy some root beer. Steve says nothing cools you down like a root beer float." The thought of it made her tear up.

Kathleen waved Gary to go, and then bent down and hugged Suzy. "Aw, sugar, he's going to be just fine. You'll see."

"You don't know my husband," Suzy said in her ear. "He's liable to do just about anything . . . if the police tell him . . . it will end all this and he can take me home," Suzy said, sobbing. "That's why the lieutenant brought me here."

I know, sugar. We just had our first grandbaby. I've been expecting Joe to run right through that door so we can go see him." Tears streamed down Kathleen's face. "What do you say we keep tending to these fine police officers and let them worry about our husbands?"

"That sounds good to me," Suzy said, glad to have Kathleen around to cheer her up.

Chapter 74

"You almost had it, Snake. You're a lot stronger than you look," Ella said, making him blush a little.

I watched from the other room. Snake pulled the string on the crossbow about half as far as I figured it needed to go, then ran out of steam. I was hoping he'd be successful so I wouldn't have to impress Ella with how little I knew about this weapon.

"What do you need?" I asked, sitting beside Ella to offer assistance.

"A cocking harness . . . rope with handles at each end. That's the one accessory we did need, but give it a try," Ella said, yanking the crossbow away from Snake and passing it to me.

I studied the weapon, trying to comprehend which were the moving parts.

"This one has a two-hundred-pound draw weight. I think ours is only one-seventy-five, and Gary can barely cock it manually. Go back and get whatever gadget they sell."

Not willing to be outdone by Gary, I put my feet inside the bow and heaved the string back with both hands. It was awkward, but I had a lot of leverage in this position. On the first attempt, I was able to bend the bow more than Snake had.

"Stand up, you're doing it all wrong. You're supposed to put your foot in the stirrup—see, at the end there," Ella said, pointing at something, but I ignored her.

I tried again—really digging in with my legs. I heard something click, and the string caught.

"You did it," Ella said, giving me a kiss on the cheek.

Snake looked dejected, like I'd kicked sand in his face.

Ella leaned over and gave him a quicker peck, making his face turn bright red.

"Come on, Romeo. How about I take you out for another cancer stick," I said, rising to my feet.

"I thought you'd never ask."

"You used to be able to hold a grudge better than that, Taylor," Ella said, retrieving the pack hidden under the pad. "All the way out too. I don't even want to smell it."

"Go around the corner," I said, pointing the way after we left the pharmacy.

Snake removed a windproof lighter from his pocket.

"Where'd you get that?" I asked, embarrassed I hadn't at least patted him down. Frisking your detainee was a no-brainer—TV Cop fundamentals.

"At a PX in Nam."

"You aren't old enough to have fought in Vietnam."

"101st Airborne," Snake said, showing me the lighter with an insignia and the words "Screaming Eagles" etched underneath.

"So, why were you in prison?"

"Bad checks mostly. I was living on the streets for a few years. Had a lot of troubles when I got stateside. I just got out again last year. I had a decent job, and my parole was up next year. I should've never let Johnny talk me into this mess," Snake said, balling his fists up like he wanted to hurt somebody.

"Tell me about this guy you and the lieutenant discussed. Is he a vicious killer or what?" This was the real reason I had suggested a butt break.

"He ain't nothing. Some of the guys said he was pals with Bear. He's sneaky, though. Maybe you ought to let him be. What if something happens to you? Please don't leave me tied up in there. I'll stay put, I promise."

"Don't worry, I won't let this guy take us out. Like you said, he ain't nothing. I appreciate your cooperation—and your service—but I won't leave you free to walk away."

"Don't let anything happen to Ella," Snake said, looking me in the eye.

"I'll do my best. Smoke your cigarette. I'll step out of your airspace and make a phone call," I said as he sparked the lighter.

"Hello, sweetheart. Everything okay?" I said, hearing loud noise in the background when my wife answered.

"Hold on," Suzy said, followed by static and rustling sounds. "There, that's better. You'll never guess who I met."

"Gary Thompson," I ventured, agonizing over that scenario since she got there.

"Yeah, him too. I also met the nicest lady. We got talking and discovered her husband is Joe, your boss, and she's from Atlanta."

"Joe's wife. I saw her in the parking lot. Is he okay? Has she heard anything?"

Joe's the kind of person who doesn't take any guff. I feared he might have gotten hurt trying to be a hero like Ed, or Snake evidently, according to Ella.

"The lieutenant said he was doing fine. I'm not sure how he could be so certain."

"I'm sure he knows," I said, guessing Parker hadn't told her about the camera. "That's great news. Tell her I said hello."

"I will. I love you, darling. Please stay safe."

She started to cry and I wanted to cheer her up before we ended the call.

"I heard you're feeding the troops out there, baby doll."

"Yeah, you know how I get when I'm worried. I start cooking and cleaning the house," Suzy said, trying to laugh, but her sniffled-back tears gave her away.

"I'll see you soon, I promise."

"Call me later," Suzy said, hardly able to get the words out.

My poor wife, who could see the bright side to just about any situation, was losing hope. And hanging out with Gary. That was enough to make me want to grab Flattop's rifle, put it in full auto, charge into Bear's camp and kill everyone who wasn't tied up. But I knew that was a bad plan. The smart play was to follow Parker's orders—kill the exterminator on the truck dock and then kill Clarence.

"Give me one of those bolts," Ella said when we returned. Snake went to sit beside her and she said, "Don't sit next to me, chimney boy."

I cut the plastic tray open and gave her the short arrow. She armed the weapon and checked its various components to be sure everything was copasetic. Then she removed the bolt and handed it to me.

"You'll have to get up close to hit someone with this, Steve."

"Me? Who said anything about me shooting it?"

I stepped out and called Parker.

"Ella says the crossbow is ready to go"

"Take him out quietly, if possible. Shoot him with a firearm if you have to, but high-tail it back to the pharmacy."

Parker explained the best way to accomplish our mission, then wished us success.

When I returned, I picked up the duct tape and knelt down in front of Snake. "You know the drill."

"Please, Ella," Snake cried, "tell him I gotta be able to protect myself. Just leave my hands free and give me the scatter gun."

Ella didn't respond, but it was obvious she wanted to help him out.

"He thinks we're not coming back," I told her. "I'm not leaving him with a loaded weapon." I proceeded to restrain his wrists and ankles with duct tape, and then placed a piece across his mouth.

I had a lot more respect for him since learning he fought in a war I was too young to die in. But having watched a thousand cop shows, I knew the protocol.

"Steve, are you taking the shopping cart? You might run across something?"

"It's showtime, Ella. Let's get serious."

We needed to behave like professionals. I knew something she didn't; if the exterminator went down as planned, things would never be the same for her. Knowing what we were about to do left no room in my soul for humor. That it was police sanctioned, as well as something we had to do to stay alive, brought little comfort. I put my arms through the straps of my well-stocked backpack and collected the rifle.

"We're still using the crossbow aren't we?" Ella asked, as we walked out.

"That's plan A. This is plan B thru Z," I said, patting the 30-round magazine and taking point.

"When do I put a bolt in this thing?"

"When I'm not walking in front of you."

Parker had told me the exterminators were accessing the truck dock by entering the double doors on the far side of the shoe department. He thought we could use the entryway in automotive, but we'd have to backtrack a little. I pushed the left-side door slowly. I shouldered the rifle as I held the door open with my foot. We were in a staging area where off-loaded merchandise was placed.

"Are you sure that thing is accurate?" I whispered as we stooped down behind a pallet of shrink-wrapped oil filters.

"You ever throw darts? It's kinda like that."

Chapter 75

Powell rang the customer service desk after Steve and Ella were out of sight. Bear answered a minute later.

"When are you gonna let me out of here, before or after I start shooting hostages? You have to admit, I've been patient with you. Give me some wheels and back off. If anyone else dies, that's on you."

"I'm working on it. With your—how should I put this—reputation, that's taking some time. I'll get it done, but you've got to continue to be patient," Powell said.

"What's with all the racket outside?" Bear asked, hearing someone sound off on the bullhorn.

"Crowd control," Powell said. "We're moving everyone back."

He hoped Steve and Ella weren't forced to use a firearm. No bullhorn in the world would cover the noise an M-16 makes, even behind a block wall fifty yards away. He worried how Clarence would react, especially if he were still on the line discussing nothing new or significant.

Chapter 76

7:30 p.m. Sunday

"I asked a cop—a guy Ella and I bowl with—to let me park the car here," Gary said to the ladies as he got out of the shiny Cadillac.

He popped open the cavernous trunk using the remote. Inside, there were three Styrofoam coolers with a giant-sized container of premium ice cream in each. The other perishable items were stuffed in around the ice cream. A dozen bags of ice were stacked beside the coolers, water beginning to pool in the bags. Gary unloaded the trunk and dumped the ice into the larger coolers. Suzy reached for her purse, and Kathleen was fishing bills out of her pocket as he finished.

"Thanks, Gary. How much was all that?" Suzy asked.

"You don't owe me anything," he said, looking away.

"We'll let you pay a third, but no more, now give us the receipt, Gary," Kathleen demanded.

"They wouldn't take my money. Someone recognized me from TV coverage. People were—"

Gary couldn't go on. Suzy held one of his hands with both of hers as he struggled to continue.

"Word got around the store and people surrounded me, arguing over who would pay," Gary said, gaining control of his emotions. "The manager came out and said everything was on the house. He even offered to let me go back for anything else I wanted. Then people squabbled over who would help me take the stuff out to the car. I cried like a baby, while ten people abandoned their grocery carts and walked out with me."

Chapter 77

Ella held the drawn but not yet loaded crossbow against my back, as we approached the two loading dock bays. If she accidentally pulled the trigger, I would probably die—from either the scare or the shotgun blast of the gunman alerted by my scream. When we located our target, I would give Deputy Fife one of her bullets, then step aside and put our target's vital organs in my crosshairs.

I saw Mikey in the orange glow of the overhead lighting. We were in luck. The criminal had helped himself to a boom box and was playing a Vince Gill song loudly enough that I didn't think he would hear our approach. Sitting on a tall stool a couple of feet behind the shipping clerk's desk, he had a shotgun across his lap. Since he was facing almost directly away from us, I thought Ella could put one between his shoulder blades before he knew what had happened.

We were still thirty feet away when I whispered, "You can do this," in her ear.

"You want me to shoot him in the back?"

I nodded my head. I saw no dishonor in killing him the simplest way possible. I didn't care what John Wayne or the Lone Ranger had to say on the subject.

"I'll set up on that support beam. Get close and take your shot, then run straight back and get behind something. Don't look back. I'll take over from there," I whispered, handing her the bolt.

Ella nodded and loaded her weapon.

When I had the rifle steadied on the I-beam—ten feet ahead and to her left—she slinked like a cat toward the target. I laid the crosshairs inside his left shoulder. His head swayed with the music from "Pocket Full of Gold."

Out of the corner of my eye, I watched Ella raise the weapon and become a statue. I knew what she was feeling. I had been there myself. If she couldn't do it, I was almost certain that I could. I didn't think I would give her any lip about it either.

As the song was ending, he began fidgeting in his seat, no longer mesmerized by the melody. I held my breath and began to apply pressure on the trigger as I waited for him to turn and notice Ella. A moment later I heard a snap and then a hiss. I could see through the scope that the bolt hit him inches from my crosshairs.

I ran at him as Ella fled her first assassination attempt. I doubted the miniature arrow would drop him—even with the excellent shot. I planned to jump in and finish him off with whichever end of the rifle was required. But before I got halfway, he tipped over and hit the concrete.

He lay gasping for air, the broadhead sticking out of his chest. I opened my knife and slit his throat. Not like a commando, but like I had done on occasion with a deer I didn't care to watch suffer.

Chapter 78

"How'd it go?" Parker asked, calling as we neared the pharmacy.

I stood outside, observing Ella as she made a direct path to the filing cabinets and bent over, still holding her weapon.

"Ella can shoot a crossbow," I said, giving credit where it was due.

I've long appreciated that women can learn to do any task a man can do. I'd seen it too many times to be totally surprised by Ella's abilities. I'd already commended her on the great shot. I thought about telling her how brave she was, aiming the crossbow without the slightest tremor. Later maybe, if she still came to see me at work.

"That's great. Clarence didn't hear a thing."

"I'll bet you make decent money doing this. I may find a job in law enforcement when I get my thirty," I said, believing for the moment that murderers and robbers were no match for autoworkers with a background in the shooting sports.

"Don't get the big head now, Steve. I may hire your wife, though—to cater these events in the future. Suzy and another lady bought ice cream. They're serving root beer floats as we speak."

"Tell her to save one for me."

"We've got some weather moving in. I wouldn't be surprised if we had a power outage in the area."

"Tornadoes?" I asked, thinking about my wife camped out in the parking lot.

"No, the storm was big in Arkansas, but it's tapering down. Don't worry, I'll keep her safe."

"Thank you," was all I could manage.

"I know a position where you can take out Clarence later—after you calm down. Your new rifle barely has any recoil. You won't miss," Parker said.

I hoped he was right. I wanted another chance to kill Clarence and take my wife home. His reference to ice cream made me hungry, and I thought about our options.

"We're sick of eating diet food. You got a problem with me slipping out to the grocery aisles and grabbing some chow?" I asked, expecting my request to be denied.

Parker remained silent for a long count, then said, "Steve, I wish you wouldn't, but I don't think there would be much risk at the moment. If you want to take your weapon and get something quick, you should be okay."

"Thanks, I'll keep my eyes open," I said, taking his reply as a full endorsement to fill the grocery cart with items that could possibly be our last meal—in the store anyway.

"Get some rest after. I'll get back with the particulars of your next assignment."

"I doubt I'll be able to sleep, but I'll try," I said.

"I know I won't," Parker said, ending the call.

Chapter 79

10:00 p.m. Sunday

I cut Snake's hands loose and gave him the phone, ordering him to charge it until I told him to stop. He mumbled something through the tape, but I ignored him.

"Are you going to uncover his mouth, or do I have to?" Ella asked, returning without the crossbow, looking pale.

"I will. After I go out for some real food."

"I'll do it. I kind of like talking to the putz," Ella said, putting a hand to her mouth when she realized he could hear just fine.

"I like talking to you too, Ella," Snake said after she removed the tape.

She sat down beside him and asked, "What was that guy in prison for?"

"I never heard. Everybody lies about that anyway—except me," Snake said, making eyes at Ella.

"What kind of food are you getting, rice cakes and cottage cheese?" Ella asked, color returning to her cheeks.

"Whatever is closest and unspoiled. Probably lunch meat. Who says preservatives are bad for you?"

"I hope Gary still wants me when this is over," Ella said to no one in particular.

"He will," I said, as I reached for the knapsack. "You two are a match made in heaven."

Snake, looking puzzled, asked, "Who's Gary? The way you two bicker, I thought you were married."

Ella and I looked at each other, laughing out loud.

"I'll marry you if Gary doesn't want you," Snake said.

"That's sweet, but I don't think a conjugal visit is going to work as a honeymoon for me," Ella said, looking him straight in the eye to make sure he got the message.

I felt sorry for him. I knew firsthand how painful Ella's rejection can be.

"What are you doing?" Ella asked, as I emptied the pack and then laid the first aid kit in the bottom to give it some structure.

"Making room to put stuff. Any requests?" I asked, looking at Ella and then Snake.

"I figured you were taking the cart."

"Come on, Ella, give me a little credit."

To be honest, I wanted to take it, but pushing the cart past the exterminators' headquarters was an unnecessary risk. I had lost count, but when I did a tally I thought only one or two of Snake's pals were left—and Bear, of course.

"I'll take anything with hot sauce on it," Snake said. "If I had a lifetime supply, those beanie-weenies in prison wouldn't be half bad."

"I'm hungry for steak," Ella said.

"Are you going to eat it raw? Lower your expectations, maybe to a roast beef sandwich," I said, wondering if lunch meat really had enough preservatives to last through the "on again-off again" refrigeration it had been subject to the past few days.

"Hoss, how's about cutting my feet loose and let me use the big can before you leave," Snake said.

I wanted to comment on his nicknaming me after my favorite *Bonanza* character, but I didn't sense it was intended as an insult. At the age of eighteen, I was flattered when my first supervisor called me Hoss. It was one of the first impersonations I learned to do when I was a kid. I remember my father getting tired of me calling him "Paw" in a husky voice.

I cut the tape around Snake's ankles. He laid the phone and radio on the floor at the far end of the cushion and stood up, waiting for me to escort him.

"Go, already," I said, sitting beside Ella.

Ella was quiet. I figured she was nervous about being left behind while I went out for the food.

"I'll leave the rifle with *you*," I said, breaking the silence.

"But you might need it."

"Nah, I'll go pick up a few things and come right back. You should guard the door with it while I'm gone."

I didn't intend to get too close to the enemy's base of operations, but I still had an uneasy feeling about this expedition. Packing plenty of bullets helped me feel a little better. I'd seen a dozen movies where the revolver of the guy in the white hat clicked on empty cylinders.

Ella got up and grabbed Flattop's vest. I'd forgotten about it. One of us should have donned it when we took out Mikey.

"Here, put this on."

"I won't need that, Ella. You wear it."

"No, put it on. I scrubbed it clean."

I obeyed—arguing would only delay my departure. I stood and Ella held the vest up. I stuck my arms through the holes and secured the wide Velcro strap.

The vest rendered the knapsack tight, but I didn't bother making adjustments. I wanted to get out of there before I lost my nerve.

Snake came back and sat down.

"Sorry, Snake, I have to do it," I said, picking up the duct tape.

I hesitated a second because there were only a couple of layers remaining on the roll.

"He'll be okay," Ella said. "He could have run out if he wanted to. I think I could take him if he tried any funny business."

"I won't hurt you, Ella. And I'll fight anyone who tries to," Snake said, looking offended.

I headed for the door, and Ella grabbed the rifle and followed me out. We stood together awkwardly at the pharmacy exit. She placed the rifle against the doorway, and we hugged each other for a long moment.

After we broke our embrace, Ella said, "Taylor, be careful. I'm starting to remember why I liked you. I want you and Gary to be friends again. I'll broker that deal if it kills me."

"We'll have to get some sleep later. Parker says we're getting out of here soon, probably in the morning. We might not get another chance before our shift tomorrow," I said, unable to keep a straight face.

"Yeah, I know, blackout day," Ella said, shaking her head.

I wanted to leave her smiling—something I rarely managed to do when we were together.

Chapter 80

I passed by the checkout lanes, giving them a wide berth. Spending time with Ella had enabled us to heal old wounds, and maybe someday I could have a conversation with Gary without getting flogged. I doubted we would ever be buds again, but then again, what were the odds Ella and I would spend a holiday weekend settling our differences? *Anything* was possible.

As I approached the wide lane dividing the grocery section from the other departments, I couldn't get Suzy out of my mind. I reached into my pocket for the phone and freaked when it wasn't there. I felt my other pockets, expecting the relief that comes with discovering I'd put it in a different one this time. I hadn't. The phone wasn't on me.

I thought for a moment, and it hit me. I left the phone back in the pharmacy. Snake was charging it before he left to take care of his business. I saw it on the floor, still attached to the radio. I intended to grab it but got distracted. I checked to see if I had forgotten anything else. The Glock was indeed on my belt, and the spare magazine was in my front pocket.

I considered going back for the phone, but crossing both ways again seemed more dangerous than hustling over for food. The deciding factor was the likelihood Parker, or even Ella, would tell me to stay there and have another diet bar for dinner. I would not be returning without the grub. I was tired and hungry. I had my heart set on a good meal and some quality, full-belly sleep for a few hours afterward. I'd have to wait until I got back to have a conversation with Suzy.

I regained my composure, then quick-stepped across the main corridor and proceeded down the closest aisle. I grabbed some thick cardboard plates and heavy-duty plastic utensils, then scampered up and down a couple of other aisles taking anything that looked tasty. The can of beans didn't have an easy-open lid, but I knew from my bachelor days that I could open it with my pocket knife.

I was about to go across the meat aisle and pick up a couple of large packages of sliced roast beef, but thought how good the beans would taste with a steak. I could get an electric grill on my way back. I'd thought of that earlier, when Ella mentioned wanting a steak but kept it to myself. Now I wanted a steak—and to do something nice for Ella. I may never have another chance, despite what she said about us all being friends again.

Chapter 81

Johnny blew smoke rings, thinking over his options. He had the choice of staying with Bear and getting killed or hiding out on his own and going back to prison. Overhearing his leader negotiate with the police, he knew Bear was only taking one of the hostages with him—if they actually allowed him to leave. Johnny was thinking about the best spot to hide, when Bear yelled for him from the bank. He stubbed his cigarette in the drinking fountain and ran in.

"The cops are talking a big game, but I'm not seeing any results. Go get Mikey and Snake. I need all of us up here to remind them I still know how to get what I want."

"Good idea, Bear. . . . Glad to do it."

"And, Johnny, don't say anything about what I've told the cops. I'm getting us *all* out of here."

"I won't say nothing about it. Count on me," he said, thinking his best option now was to tell Mikey he was swapping places and then find a safe place to wait for the dust to settle.

Chapter 82

Parker was standing outside the bus, talking to a couple of his officers, when Powell stuck his head out the door and said, "Lieutenant, can I talk to you?"

"I told him he could go," Parker said, coming up the steps.

Powell closed the door and said, "He shouldn't be roaming around out there. If they see him on the phone, Clarence will know we're coaching him."

"Is he? Talking on the phone?"

"No, I just wish he'd stay put."

"Yeah, I didn't like it either, but I need him to follow orders later on. He only says no to me when he's tired and hungry," Parker said, annoyed that he had to explain himself to Powell.

"He makes me nervous running around like he owns the joint."

Parker sighed. "Tell me about it. That boy's gonna give me an ulcer before this is over." He put a hand on his stomach.

"How does he expect to cook those steaks?" Powell asked. "I saw him put three in his backpack."

"Probably get a grill and some lawn chairs, have a cookout on the pharmacy patio," Parker said, making them both laugh.

"What's this?" Powell said, after swiveling the camera back to view the hostages.

One of the convicts was walking through a checkout lane.

"There appears to be more than one person out for a stroll," Parker said.

"I don't think we want Clarence finding out he's down another man."

"I'm on it." Parker pulled out his phone.

"If your boy had stayed put, this wouldn't be so complicated."

Parker sent the call and prayed Steve had reception.

"*Ella*—I was expecting Steve to answer," Parker said, watching Powell's reaction.

Chapter 83

"Bear... I've got... bad news," Johnny said out of breath.

Bear rose from a stool behind one of the teller stations, as the weakest link in his crew came running into the bank.

"Mikey's dead. I couldn't find Snake. He's probably dead too. I guess it's just you and me now."

"I didn't hear any shots fired," Bear said, not willing to take anything he said at face value.

"Somebody broke a spear off in him and cut his throat. We got some kind of monster out there."

For the first time, the bank's phone rang.

"Tell me where he's at, or I'll start killing people until you do," Clarence bellowed into the receiver.

"I told you, we don't have any communication with him. I wish we did," Powell replied.

"You knew I found out Mike got killed. That's why you called. Don't play me for stupid."

"I *called* to inform you I have the green light to let you go—with only one hostage. We want this over. My boss called me back, said you could take your van."

"I know you're probably lying, but I'm not leaving here in that old van. Get me something nice."

"We'll get you a limousine—anything you want," Powell said.

Clarence hung up.

I'll bet they don't give me an ambulance again, Bear thought, cracking a smile.

Chapter 84

Parker studied the monitor with Powell standing over his shoulder, as Clarence hobbled toward the hostages.

"What's he doing?" Powell asked.

"It's not good. You can bet on that."

"He's talking to the manager," Powell said.

"Yeah, James Martin. He's a part-time deputy. All the county guys here know him. I wanted to get him in the game, but not like this."

They examined the grainy feed on the monitor as Clarence stood, pointing the rifle at Jimmy's chest and shouting at him. The camera's microphone was too far away to comprehend what he was saying. Clarence put the muzzle against Jimmy's temple and said a few more unintelligible words. The other hostages turned their heads, expecting him to pull the trigger.

"He's asking questions, but he doesn't seem to like the answers," Powell said.

"Where's the something-something," Parker said, trying to decipher.

Clarence drew his knife and cut the rope securing Jimmy's ankles. Then he snatched him by the collar, yanking him to his feet. He put his arm around Jimmy's neck and pointed the rifle in the direction he wanted to go.

"What's he doing?" Powell asked.

"Let's hope he needs assistance getting to the restroom, but I don't think—wait. They're going to customer service."

The last thing they could see on the monitor before they passed out of sight was Clarence picking the manager's pocket and removing a ring of keys.

"What else is back there?" Powell asked as Parker unrolled the floor plan.

"Security surveillance room," Parker said, pointing to it. "I was hoping to access the cameras remotely. Someone from corporate told us they didn't have that capability. I'm surprised it's taken Clarence this long to think of it."

"We should cut the power."

"They're on a battery backup like the lights . . . for shoplifters. They did mention having *that* capability."

"I told you we should keep the power off. The batteries would have been dead by now," Powell said.

"No, you didn't," Parker said, raising his voice.

"I should have," Powell muttered under his breath.

"The batteries in *our* camera last a week," Parker grumbled.

"You better get your guys ready to storm the doors. I think we're about to witness the old Clarence Jenkins."

"They were born ready. Let's wait and see what happens for a second before we blow the store up."

"I hope Ella's out of sight. The last I checked, they were standing outside the pharmacy," Powell said.

Parker called Steve's phone.

"Ella, get down and stay down. Bear's viewing feed from the security cameras," Parker said, waiting for an acknowledgment before hanging up.

"Guard units one and two, get in position to make entry. Wait for my command," Parker said over the radio. "No telling what he's going to do when he comes out," he said to Powell.

They stared at the monitor, the camera aimed at the point they lost sight of the pair.

"Here they come," Parker said a minute later.

"He's taking him back to the others. I thought he was a dead man," Powell said.

"Don't lose it, Clarence," Parker said, as the leader tied up the manager and struggled to his feet.

Clarence scanned the ceiling; his rifle pointed at the hostages.

"He thinks we've got him on the security cameras," Powell said.

"Unit one, start rolling to the south entrance," Parker radioed, putting one of the National Guard units in motion toward the door farthest from the hostages.

"Those yellow poles going to be a problem?" Powell asked, pointing out the window.

Parker scowled but didn't respond. Both men remained silent as Clarence gripped the rifle and put the muzzle on the floor. He then turned and walked away, using the weapon as a crutch.

"Stand down—I repeat—stand down. Do *not* hit the door," Parker ordered as Clarence proceeded toward the bank.

"What's this? He went right past his office," Powell said.

"Get that armored vehicle out of there. Bald Eagle is headed for the south door. Clear the area. Don't let him see anybody out there," Parker yelled into his mic.

"Maybe he's getting a shopping cart to lean on. No, he's climbing on the scooter," Powell said.

"That's bad. He must have seen Steve on the security cameras. He's going after him," Parker said. He zoomed in the camera as Clarence shot through the archway—his rifle laying across the basket.

"I want a couple of guys squawking on the bullhorn. Make some real noise so Steve knows we've got a problem," Parker barked over the radio.

Chapter 85

I went to the bread section of the deli and picked up some three-day-old Ciabatta. I was about to head over to housewares and get the grill—and an electric can opener since they were nearby—when I heard shouting from the front of the store. It was probably Bear, but I wasn't sure. I'd heard plenty of loud voices coming from there before, so I wasn't too concerned. I did take the precaution of exiting the area by way of the back wall. No sense taking unnecessary risks.

The back wall in the grocery department was the dairy section. Seeing the personal sized milk containers, I opened the door and took out three bottles of chocolate milk. Feeling guilty, I put one back and replaced it with strawberry.

Putting the milk bottles in my pack, I heard a muffled sound—the bullhorn—coming from the front of the store. There were at least ten rows of grocery products between me and the police outside. Making out the words was impossible.

Parker was warning me about something. He'd most likely called and discovered that I had forgotten my phone. I was going back, but I had to make a stop on the way. I'd wasted my time procuring these fine steaks if I returned without some kind of appliance to cook them on. A toaster oven would do in a pinch. I would keep to the rear of the building and swing back through housewares. I could be grilling steaks in five minutes if I hurried—and didn't have too many options to choose from.

Chapter 86

Parker tracked the scooter as it sped down the aisle. Clarence slowed as he approached the last grocery lanes. He turned left into the next-to-last aisle and parked behind an I-beam.

Parker yelled into his mic, "Get in there and cut down those barrier poles—in front of both entryways. I want to be able to drive my grandmother's Oldsmobile through there if I have to."

"That must be close to where he spotted Steve," Parker said, zooming the camera out to locate him.

"Maybe he's already back in the pharmacy. He's been gone a long time."

Both men gazed at the monitor.

"There he is," Parker said, seeing Steve peek around a tall freezer case.

"He's stepping out," Powell said.

"Don't do it, Steve . . . stay where you are . . . you're not listening to me, Steve. He's turning the corner . . . and headed . . . straight for Clarence," Parker said, slamming his fist on the table.

"Cut the lights. Cut the lights," Parker yelled loud enough for anyone nearby *without* a radio to hear.

Chapter 87

The wide aisle I peered down reminded me how this nightmare began. Thirty yards in front of me, I could see the full spectrum of Gatorade on display and beyond that the entrance. The bullhorn had been steady for several minutes. I inched forward, turning the corner. There was an I-beam at the end of the next aisle. These bulletproof pillars almost certainly saved my life once already. I moved toward it, intending to remain there until I could figure out what the problem was.

My guess was that Clarence was about to kill another hostage or maybe all of them, and Parker wanted me to go stop him. As I approached the I-beam the lights went off. I pressed my back against the girder as the backup lights popped to life. The last thing I saw—in my peripheral vision—was the butt end of a rifle.

Chapter 88

11:00 p.m. Sunday

Suzy and Kathleen shared the Cadillac's spacious back seat. Gary sat shotgun in the front seat. The three amigos were recently drenched in a sudden downpour. They'd climbed in the car, just as lightning strikes sizzled down on the surrounding hills. The rain had ended, and the moon was now peeking through nearby thunderheads.

"Something's up," Suzy said. The police vehicles and personnel were scrambling around the parking lot.

"I'll go see," Gary said, reaching for the door handle.

"Keep your shirt on, Gary," Kathleen said. "The lieutenant said he would update us when he knew something. He doesn't need you bothering him right now."

"I need to know why all the sudden commotion out there."

"I'm with Gary; something's going down," Suzy said, watching two policemen use a portable saw to cut down poles in front of the door where Steve's truck was parked.

An officer wearing a helmet and body armor ran toward the car. Suzy pressed the window switch to ask what was happening, but the glass didn't go down. She yelled into it, but he didn't respond.

"Get that car out of here—now—back of the lot," the officer said, pounding on the hood to get Gary's attention.

Gary slid across the long bench seat to access the controls, as a large armored vehicle rolled past the Cadillac. "This isn't just the police anymore. That's the National Guard," he said, reaching across the front seat as Kathleen held out the keys.

"I'm getting out," Suzy said, opening the door. Using her upper-body strength, she transferred back into her wheelchair quicker than an able-bodied person could have exited the vehicle.

"We'll put your chair in the trunk. It's too dangerous out there," Kathleen screamed after Suzy closed the door.

"I'll find you when I get back," Suzy yelled, as a Humvee drove by, splashing her.

Chapter 89

Powell watched the monitor while Parker stepped away to call Ella. She and Snake were hunkered under the counter beneath the window, the only place inside the pharmacy with cell reception.

"Stay put," he told her. "I may have to turn the lights back on."

"I don't like this. Why isn't Steve back?" Ella said.

"I need you to be tough as nails for me, Ella. Clarence spotted Steve on the surveillance cameras. He got him."

"Oh my God! Is he hurt? What did Clarence do to him?"

"He's taking Steve up front with the hostages," Parker said, hoping to give the impression that Steve was okay and not about to get killed, though he knew very well that Steve might be dead already.

"How can this be? Is Steve fighting back? I thought Bear could hardly stand on his bad leg. That's what Snake told us."

"Steve's unconscious, Ella," Parker said, straining to see the monitor from ten feet away. "He's almost there now."

"God help him," Ella whispered.

Parker came up behind Powell and looked over his shoulder at the monitor. He watched Clarence drive the scooter through a checkout lane, dragging Steve by one of his ankles.

"He didn't shoot him," Powell cheered.

Parker covered the phone too late to keep Ella from hearing the best news possible—Clarence Jenkins didn't square things with Steve for killing his brother.

Chapter 90

Suzy rolled up to the bus just when she saw Parker running out.

"Suzy, I need you to get back with the others."

"What's happening in there? Please tell me."

"We have a situation. That's all I can tell you right now. Cadet, accompany this woman to the back of the parking lot, where the family members were relocated," Parker ordered a young man in uniform.

"Tom, please, is Steve in danger?"

"Suzy, go with him. I can't have civilians this close anymore. I'll come and see you when I know something."

"Okay, I'll go . . . I'm sorry to bother you," Suzy said, wheeling around. She wasn't sorry. She had another idea how to find out what happened.

"I've got to take you, ma'am," the cadet said, gripping the handles on the back of her chair.

The young man didn't know what he'd stepped into. Suzy grabbed both large wheels with her small but powerful hands. He was unable to proceed.

"Stop. *I* will follow *you*," she demanded, looking back at him.

The green reservist nodded. He stepped in front of her and led the way. Suzy stayed on his heels.

"I really appreciate your assistance," she said stopping, as they neared a police car where yellow barrier tape was being rolled out.

Suzy assessed the young man as he turned around. He wore a police uniform but carried a flashlight on his belt where his gun should be. He smiled, relaxing somewhat, now that she was being nice. Just as she intended.

"Glad to be of service ma'am. Have you got family in there?" he said, making it obvious he was new to the scene.

"I'm a friend of Tom's. He lets me watch him work—until it gets dangerous. What happened in there? I'll bet you know every detail."

"They were about to enter the building, then Lieutenant Parker decided not to. I'm not sure why, to be honest."

"Were you going in?" Suzy asked the acne-faced young man who didn't fill out the shoulders of his uniform the way most of the other policemen did.

"No ma'am, I'm not an officer yet. I just graduated high school. I did overhear that someone got knocked out and taken hostage, though."

She followed as they neared another young man with a flashlight sidearm, who manned the new police line at the very back of the parking lot.

After they ducked under, Suzy said, "Thank you so much. I'll be sure and tell the lieutenant how helpful you were."

She offered her hand, and he took it. She squeezed his fingers and clamped onto his wrist with her other hand. Then she tugged him down to her level, startling him.

"Was it a man or woman who got hurt?"

"I-I-I-It was a man," he stuttered.

Chapter 91

My next conscious moment came when my head bounced off the metal strip running across the floor between cash registers. This revived me like a flashlight that needed a smack to light up. Someone bald and very large was towing me like a boat—behind a scooter. I thought I was dreaming. Everything went blank again a moment later.

Through the fog of my headache, I heard a woman freaking out about somebody's head bleeding. I figured she must be referring to me. I tried to tell her I was okay, but the words came out incoherent—as if I were talking in my sleep.

A male voice said, "He's moaning again." I couldn't place the voice, but it sounded familiar.

The bright light above me made it difficult, but I forced my eyes open. I was lying on the floor with my ankles bound and wrists tied behind my back. Somebody, a younger man, was leaning against the end of the next checkout counter.

"The police know you were captured," the man said, nodding to the entrance.

I raised my head, as much as that was possible, and saw lots of flashing lights and the fuzzy outline of people standing at the door. I tried to recognize something familiar, but I couldn't even remember my name let alone what I was doing—or where.

Chapter 92

12:30 a.m. Monday July 6

"I thought that's what you wanted. I can have a car ready in fifteen minutes. Why wait?" Powell said.

"I like my chances better in daylight. If I see anything that looks like you got a sniper out there, I'll slaughter all them old ladies," Clarence replied.

"I turned the power back on like you asked. I'm trying to work with you. We don't want anyone else to get hurt."

Powell's options had nosedived since Steve's capture. Given Clarence's current mental state, Parker instructed him to get Clarence out of the store before he finished off Steve or killed any more hostages. They would deal with him when he stepped out.

"Take your buddy along. I'll give you a thirty-minute head start."

"Sure you will. And don't worry about who I take," Clarence said, giving Johnny, who was watching intently, a smile of encouragement. "Make sure I've got a car out there by six."

The line went dead.

Powell hung up. "I don't like it, Parker. He knows we won't allow him to drive out of here. He's not that kind of stupid."

"He still halfway believes he'll get out of this. We'll have to calm him down, make him think he'll get away . . . again. He'll have to disarm the bomb, and that will give us some options."

"I don't see him trusting us . . . and walking out. He knows we were lying about our involvement with Steve," Powell said.

"How does he know? Steve didn't have his phone. Use *that* to convince Clarence we've been straight with him."

"Yeah, that bought us some credibility, but not much."

"I have one ace up my sleeve, but I hope I'm not forced to play it," Parker said.

"If you're talking about Ella, she's good, but I doubt she can get close enough to put him down with her crossbow."

"I'm not even thinking about using her like that. Clarence is too wary now. He'd kill hostages, figuring we sent her."

"This is beginning to remind me of our last encounter with Clarence."

"Steve's starting to come around," Parker said, rising from his chair.

"Are you kidding? He's tied up and most likely has a concussion. What can *he* do?"

"We'll have to wait and see how things play out. You need to make Clarence believe he'll go free. I'm pretty sure I know who he'll take with him," Parker said as he exited the bus.

Chapter 93

My first valid memory was of my wife. It came to me like a dream, only I was not asleep. Suzy was waiting for me to run out and wrap my arms around her. I had an ache in my heart that was beyond unbearable. I could almost sense she knew what happened to me. I had a mental picture of her agonizing over my blunder.

The thought of her suffering because of my mistakes helped bring me around. I still had a chance to survive this. I was, after all, still alive. The police were outside plotting strategies to end this with as few casualties as possible. My capture changed everything.

I scanned each face as they stared back at me. I definitely recognized Clara and the woman from work who parked across from me. I recognized a few others as well. Then I saw the face of the familiar-sounding man I'd heard earlier. It was my boss, Joe Duncan. I nodded to him, and he nodded back. I turned toward the young man sitting behind me, and he forced a smile. When I tried to speak, my voice rattled like a five-pack-a-day smoker.

He looked around, then whispered, "Sorry sir, I didn't know why he wanted to go in the security room. He threatened to kill me if I didn't take him in there. I've got a wife and three little girls."

I nodded, wanting to tell him it was okay, that it wasn't his fault.

"He saw you on the monitor. I prayed you'd be able to take care of him, like you did the others."

Everything I heard told me I played a significant role here, so I willed myself to focus.

"Are you the manager?" I asked.

"Why, you got a complaint?" he whispered, a big grin on his face.

My standard "Ten thousand union comedians on strike and you're crossing the picket line for free" comeback came to mind, but I didn't have the energy.

"The police know about you," I said.

"I'm not sure what you mean. You're probably still dazed. You've got a doozy of a head wound. A while ago, you tried to get up, mumbling something about a blackout."

"Former military and part-time deputy, right? The police were discussing how to involve you somehow."

"Yeah, I've seen some of my buddies at the door. Me and Joe talked about trying to take these guys out, but we don't like our chances. The big guy hasn't been *right* since his brother got killed."

"I'll take the blame for that one. I had no choice. Name's Steve by the way."

"Mine's Jimmy. We've met before. That old jarhead says he knows you," Jimmy whispered, gesturing toward Joe.

I was hoping I could help Joe and everyone else. Now, thanks to my stupidity, we are all likely to die. I prayed. A miracle was the only thing that *could* save us now.

My wound had stopped bleeding. At least I couldn't feel blood running down my neck anymore. It appeared that not taking my medication had this one positive aspect. I tried not to worry about the injury sending a blood clot to my heart.

I observed red stains on the block wall by the restrooms. I sort of remembered shooting at the criminals earlier. I didn't see any bodies, and I wondered if killing them had been a dream. Then I recalled the security guard and looked where I saw him earlier. He was gone too. I scooted across the floor to Jimmy.

"Where's the security guard . . . and the people I shot?" I whispered.

"Johnny, the little weasel over there, moved his pals' bodies into the ladies room. Stan, my security guard, died yesterday. I talked Johnny into putting his body out of sight too. He got walloped with a rifle stock. I watched it happen."

I did as well, but said nothing. I was too fixated on the knowledge that I had the identical injury, inflicted by the same person.

"Jimmy, I know my gun was taken, but did he empty my pockets?"

"Are you kidding? He took your gun, knife, bullets, spare magazine, car keys . . . I was expecting him to pull out that over-under shotgun I wouldn't sell you," Jimmy said, smiling.

"I had too many shotguns already. I took a rifle I had my eye on instead. You probably heard me shoot it," I bantered back.

"Oh, yeah. I heard it. By the way, I've got a small knife they didn't find. I'm not sure how we could use it, or if we should, but Joe and I were discussing some options."

"Good to know. We can try to cut ourselves loose, if the opportunity arises.

Looking out the door, I saw the green signal light.

"Jimmy, the police have a camera in the ceiling right behind us. Nod your head so they'll know I'm well enough to tell you about it?"

Jimmy glanced around, then gave an exaggerated nod several times. The green light flashed twice. It was dark outside, and the signal was easy to see. I nodded toward the door, and Jimmy watched the signal repeat a moment later.

"We're not in this alone Jimmy. I've been working with the police. They'll figure a way to get us out of here."

"I wish they would hurry. My wife and babies gotta be scared out of their minds."

The light changed from green to red. I turned and saw Bear driving a scooter out of the bank, his rifle across the basket. He was steering with one hand, chugging milk with the other. He and Ella appeared to have similar tastes.

Several of the hostages were licking their lips, seeing him slug down the milk. I could tell by the garbage on the floor, food and drink were served at some point, but I guessed it was many hours earlier. My own throat was as dry as sandpaper, but we had greater problems to deal with.

Because I was sitting up now, I realized too late, I could not pretend to be unconscious. Bear swung the scooter toward me, gripping the rifle as he approached. Before he reached me, the phone on the customer service counter rang. He shot me an angry glare, then turned the scooter and kept driving. He didn't hurry, assuming correctly they would let it ring until he picked up.

Bear argued with someone, Powell most likely. At the door, I beheld a sight for sore eyes. Illuminated by the light inside, Parker stood as close to the door as he could without touching it. He seemed to be staring me right in the eyes as he gave the high sign with both hands, looking like Arthur Fonzarelli.

Parker walked away, just as Bear hung up the phone.

"Listen up," Bear said. "They assured me I'm getting out of here with one of you for insurance. If they keep their promise, maybe the rest of you won't have to die."

Bear rode over and stared me down. "You're not so lucky. You're leaving with me."

He turned the scooter and accelerated back to the bank. Bear's lone accomplice avoided eye contact with his leader, scowling as he passed. A few minutes later, I leaned over to Jimmy.

"I probably shouldn't go on any joy rides with that guy."

"I know that's right. He's talked about killing you since the very beginning."

"And I'd have to ride in the basket," I said, coping with fear the way I normally did.

Jimmy looked like he wanted to smile but didn't feel quite right about it.

"Don't worry about me, Jimmy. I'm certain the police are cooking up a scheme to rescue us. We need to be ready to help out any way we can."

"What do you think they're planning?"

"Worst-case scenario, they'll drive something through one of those doors, and see who's still breathing after the building explodes."

"Let God sort it out," Jimmy whispered back, grimacing.

I nodded agreement, remembering Parker make the same assessment.

"Thanks to me, the police don't have a lot of options."

"Maybe they'll take him out as he leaves the store."

"More than likely," I said, wondering if I would survive that scenario.

"I'm sticking with my original plan," Jimmy said. "Praying I'll get to see my family again."

"I'm with you. I feel like there's a reason I was here. Like God put me in here for a purpose. Some things have happened that are hard to call coincidence."

"As long as we're alive, I'm not losing hope," Jimmy whispered.

I wondered how Suzy was handling the news. Parker must have told her by now that I had done something foolish, in spite of her telling me not to.

Chapter 94

Suzy searched for Kathleen as she digested what she heard. *Someone was knocked out and taken hostage. A man,* Suzy thought, replaying the cadet's words in her mind. *There is only one man in the store who that could be.*

"Where'd you go, sweetie? I was afraid you got run over," Kathleen said when Suzy rolled up.

"I went to see the lieutenant. He wouldn't tell me anything," Suzy said, not divulging the information she literally twisted a young man's arm to get.

"Well, I guess it's in God's hands now," Kathleen said, gazing at the group of prayer warriors.

"I'll be right back," Suzy said, speeding away.

She brought her phone out of hibernation, preparing to call the lieutenant and tell him she heard what happened. She would press him until he told her the extent of her husband's injuries. She noted Steve's number on her recent list and contemplated what would happen if she called it. Would the phone ring in his pocket? No, if Steve were captured, they would have surely taken the phone. And what if one of the captors answered? Would she just click off, leaving them to think the police were trying to contact him?

Then it dawned on her. If the criminals had Steve's phone, they already knew he was communicating with the police. She could beg them for mercy. Suzy scrolled down to her husband's number and hesitated. She worried Tom would find out and be mad, especially if her reasoning was flawed. But then she remembered what Steve always said about it being easier to get forgiveness over permission, and she made the call.

Neither forgiveness nor permission would be required. A woman answered on the second ring. Suzy had no strategy for what to do if Ella answered. She listened as the woman who once had a relationship with her husband, said hello again.

"Is that you, Lieutenant?" Ella said the third time she spoke.

"Can you tell me what happened to my husband?" Suzy asked.

Ella paused, no doubt shocked to find Suzy on the line, finally saying, "You should talk to the police. I haven't seen Steve recently."

"Is this Ella?" Suzy asked, knowing it had to be.

"Yes, Suzy."

"Please, I need to know if he's been injured and taken hostage. I have reason to believe both are true." The floodgates holding back her tears opened up and she covered the phone with her hand.

"I'm so sorry. Yes, that's what I heard. He's alive, but that's all I know."

She took a jagged breath. "I appreciate you telling me. I was beginning to think the worst."

"I wish I knew more. I'm concerned about him too."

"I'm out here with Gary. He's worried sick about you. Would you like me to mention I talked to you? That you're not injured?" Suzy asked, curious how she'd react.

"That's very kind of you, Suzy. Please tell Gary I love him, and I can't wait to see him."

"I'll give him the message. Thank you so much," Suzy said, ending the call.

Don't lose hope. Steve promised he would come back, and he never breaks his promises. Suzy prayed that Steve would run out of that store into her open arms.

"Are you all right, sugar? You keep running off on me. Did I say something to offend you? My big mouth's always getting me in trouble," Kathleen said when Suzy returned.

"I had to call someone," Suzy said, still trying to hold back tears.

"I like it better when you smile. What happened?"

"Something awful," Suzy said, weeping.

"You don't know that. Someone would've come and talked to you. Don't go getting upset for no—" Kathleen said, startled by the sudden appearance of Lieutenant Parker.

"Suzy, I need a word with you," he said.

"I've heard, Tom. Steve was wounded and taken hostage."

"Who told you?" Parker demanded.

"I called Ella," she said, not wanting to get the young man in trouble.

"I wish you hadn't, but that's water under the bridge. I wanted to let you know—" Parker stopped and glanced around. "You might as well hear this as well, Mrs. Duncan. You too, Mr. Thompson. Don't get shy on me now," he said, waving over Gary, who'd been watching intently from nearby.

Parker knelt in front of Suzy and said, "I won't sugarcoat it. This thing is about to get ugly. With Steve captured, we don't have any good options."

"What does Steve getting captured have to do with any of this?" Kathleen asked.

"He's been helping me. That's all I'm willing to say right now."

Gary put his hand on Suzy's shoulder to comfort her and said, "What about Ella? Is she in danger?"

"Everyone's in danger right now, Gary. Currently though, she's in the safest place possible; they aren't even looking for her. I'll try to update everyone when I know more."

"Do your best to bring them out safely," Suzy said as Parker turned and ran to the bus.

"Gary, can I talk to you for a moment, privately?" Suzy asked.

Chapter 95

Suzy climbed out of her wheelchair into the back seat of the Cadillac. Gary turned the key and powered down all four windows, then got in beside her.

"I spoke to Ella and she said to tell you all is forgiven. She means it, Gary," Suzy said, when he settled in.

"That's great—sorry I've been such a jerk."

"I knew Steve would never do what you were thinking. He isn't like that."

"I'm sorry about what happened to Steve. He's tough. He'll get out of this somehow."

"Thanks. I hope so."

"My issues with him go back a long way. I've held a grudge. You probably heard the story."

"Steve just told me you bothered him at work. He only said *that* in case I heard it from somebody else. My husband doesn't discuss his past much. Too painful I guess."

"He never told you how our friendship ended?"

"You were friends?"

"I guess I better let Steve tell the story—when he comes out."

A cell phone rang as Suzy was about to respond.

"That's mine," Gary said, digging into his pocket.

He examined the screen, "Steve's number. Must be my wife."

Gary shook his head as Suzy started to leave. She stared out the window as he got emotional, trying to talk his wife out of doing something. It sounded like they were talking about Steve for a minute—that's when he did break down.

"Please be careful. I couldn't make it without you," Gary said, ending the call.

He gazed out his window.

"You should be alone," Suzy said. "I'll be with Kathleen if you need me."

"Hold on Suzy, I want to say something. I can't believe what an idiot I've been. I may never get a chance to tell Steve how sorry I am."

"Is Steve seriously injured Gary? What did she say?"

"Oh, Suzy no. Ella said the lieutenant just told her Steve's doing better. He's conscious and seems alert."

"Thank God. What is it then?"

"The situation in the store . . . it's bad. The police want Ella to do something. She wouldn't give me details. Sounds like Steve's been doing some scary stuff in there from the beginning. He was likely involved with the shooting we heard. He must have got hold of a firearm somehow."

"Did he get shot?"

"No, one of the bank robbers cracked him with something. Ella told me Steve saved her life. He killed someone who was trying to hurt her—two different times.

"He killed people? Steve never said anything about it. He must have been scared out of his mind," Suzy said, wiping her eyes.

"Good thing Steve was in there instead of me. With my temper, I'd be dead now, and Ella would have been—"

"Stop beating yourself up, Gary," Suzy said. This whole thing is weird. Crazy weird. Everything happened the way it was meant to. I'll be with the others, praying my heart out."

"I'll be over in a minute. I think I'm in shock. Ella didn't mention any of this when we spoke earlier. If I'm not the first one to shake Steve's hand—never mind, I'm an idiot either way."

"What was that about you and Steve being friends?"

"It seems so trivial now, but I'll tell you my side. Maybe someday we can all get together and compare stories. I could never be mad at Steve again."

"Will this make me feel better or worse?"

"It's a sad story."

"I'll stop you when I can't take anymore."

"Steve and I hired in together, back in Michigan. We worked on the same line—before there were teams. We hung out and later even shared a place. We partied hard, both of us. Steve was a hoot to be around . . . most of the time."

"Whiskey made him crazy. He told me *that*."

"Yeah, but that came later, not that we didn't pour a shot now and then. We always had a pony keg in the refrigerator—not much else."

"So when did things go bad?"

"When Ella hired on, not that it was her fault. She was a knockout. All the guys had a crush on her—me included."

"How did Steve win her over?"

"By making her laugh—you know Steve. And probably by not trying as hard. A bunch of us went to this bar after work, if we got out early enough. He would get a few beers in him and have Ella, and everyone else, laughing till our sides hurt, mostly doing impersonations of our bosses and other people, including me."

"And she was hooked," Suzy said, a bit skeptical.

"Pretty much. She asked *him* out. Bought tickets to a Fleetwood Mac concert. The rest of us boys were a little annoyed, I might add.

"And you two were roommates. That must have been difficult for you."

"Not for long. Ella asked him to move in about a month later. They quit going out after work. He toed the line, for a while."

"He wasn't ready to settle down?"

"It appeared he was beyond just a social drinker by then, according to Ella."

"How bad?"

"When Ella moved him in, I didn't think he had a problem. By the time she kicked him out, he definitely had issues. Later, he got *Leaving Las Vegas* bad—worst drunk I ever saw."

"So, he moved back in at your place?"

"I wish. He got a room at a flophouse, barely sobered up for work. You could get away with it back then. Good luck now, coming in with liquor on your breath."

"You couldn't help him."

"He wouldn't let me. Steve wouldn't talk to anyone about it."

"So how'd you and Ella get together? You were 'there for her,' like in that Seinfeld episode I've seen a hundred times."

"I've never seen the show, but it wasn't like that. Ella believed Steve would get his act together and come back. Tough love, I guess. She was a mess too. I'm surprised she didn't hit the bottle. We were both in a lot of pain, and we talked about it. So, yeah, I guess we were there for each other."

"So, why give Steve so much grief at work? I don't understand that. He never bothered you guys, right?"

"I'm stupid. I was worried Ella would break my heart and get back with him. I'm sorry I took it out on Steve. He saved her from a sexual assault in there. I will *never* say anything negative about him as long as I live," Gary said, tears on his face.

"Lieutenant Parker will get them out. You and Steve can be friends again."

"I hope so, Suzy. I swear I do."

Chapter 96

Jimmy told me about the small knife concealed in his belt buckle and, best we could, we discussed how we might use it. The plan was to cut each other loose, overpower our guard, and use his shotgun to kill Bear. Neither of us liked our chances, but at least we'd go down fighting.

Johnny was giving me the stink eye, so I shut my mouth real quick, wondering if he'd heard our conversation. He started pacing in front of the restrooms—still staring at me—then glanced over his shoulder at the bank and after that, scampered over. Dropping to his knees, he laid his shotgun down and came up close to my face.

"I'll be needing that vest," he whispered, the veins in his skinny neck bulging.

He pulled a box cutter and considered where to cut.

"There's a Velcro strap, but you'll have to untie my wrists, I said louder than I intended, causing the convict to flail the razor at my face.

"Shut up, or I'll cut your throat," he said. "You just want me to untie your hands so you can go back to hiding out with that gorgeous babe. She's out there all alone now. I'm gonna see if *I* can find her." Johnny smiled, not making a great endorsement for the dentist at the prison where he was last incarcerated.

He cut the wide strap, then attempted to lift the vest over my head. His smile faded as he realized I was right. He had to free my hands to get them through the armholes.

I waited a moment for him to figure it out, but he looked puzzled. "Untie my wrists. You can retie me after you get it off," I whispered. For a moment, I thought he would do it, then he glanced at the bank and a scared look took over his face. He pushed me over on my side, picked up his weapon, and ran through the checkout. I was relieved he split before Bear came out and killed us both. I'd survived too many battles to die like that.

I was concerned about Ella, with Johnny bent on finding her. I wasn't sure how Parker and Powell would react to Johnny running loose in the store, but I knew what they would have me do if I were still in the game.

Chapter 97

"Ella, how are you holding up?" Parker asked.

"Fine, I guess. Steve's wife called earlier. She knows what happened."

"Suzy told me."

"How's Steve?"

"He seems fine. He's been talking to some of the hostages."

"What are you going to do?" Ella asked.

"Clarence is giving us until sunrise to let him walk out."

"But that's not gonna happen, right?"

"We have an hour to figure something out. I wish there was another way, but I may require your help."

"I'm willing to do anything to help Steve. And so is Snake."

"That's great, but you'll need to leave him in the pharmacy—tied up. He'll have the best odds of anyone in the building."

"I would like to bring him if you'll let me. I can't go out there alone. I just can't."

"Fine, take him along . . . if you trust him," Parker said, imagining Powell's reaction.

"He's standing next to the doorway right now, with a shotgun pointed at it. I trust him. He just wants to get out of here alive like all of—"

"Give me a moment, Ella," Parker interrupted. "Something's going down."

Parker came back on the line a minute later and said, "Ella, I need you to do something for me right now."

"What is it?"

"You've got a guy coming out armed with a shotgun. I think he's jumping ship, but we can't take a chance he'll get in our way. Take him out with the crossbow, if you can, or the rifle if you have to, but I'd prefer Clarence didn't know you were a threat. He's on the main aisle coming your way."

Ella put a bolt in the crossbow. Snake had been playing with it earlier, trying to impress her with his strength. She ended up cocking the bow with his help—and giving him a high-five for the assist.

"Take the rifle and follow me," she whispered.

"I've got a lot of horrible memories carrying a gun like that. I'll take it, but I'm not shooting anybody."

"Great, I've got the only gun-shy bank robber ever, watching my back," Ella said.

Chapter 98

Jimmy slid next to me and whispered, "So much for our idea. Do you think he'll be able to locate the woman?"

"The police are most likely warning her right now," I said, still worried for Ella's safety.

We stared at the bank, waiting for Bear to notice Johnny was missing. Fffft-thuunk was the first sound to break the silence, coming from the direction of the pharmacy. That was followed by what sounded like Johnny's shotgun falling to the floor.

"What was that?" Jimmy whispered, as the rest of the hostages began murmuring.

I was about to respond when I saw Bear drive the scooter out of the bank and turn our way.

"What's all the fuss out here?" he said, driving past us to see if anything was happening outside.

He was turning the scooter around when the customer service phone rang. Bear picked up and listened for a minute without a response. He wagged his head, seemingly agitated.

"It better be there. You've got forty minutes until I start killing people," Bear said and slammed the phone down.

"It'll be over soon, probably not like you hoped," Bear told the hostages. He turned back toward the bank, then abruptly stopped and looked around.

"Yo, Johnny, where you at?" Bear called. "Is he in the restroom?" Bear turned my way, as if I were his secretary.

"He went that-a-way," I replied, tipping my head back to indicate I meant behind me—and opting not to use my John Wayne voice.

Bear stood and tried to catch sight of him. He muttered something about loyalty, got back on the scooter, and sped off toward the bank. Joe inch-wormed over to join us. I had nodded to him several times when he looked my way, but this was the first time we'd been close enough to speak.

I whispered, "New plan. As soon as possible, we need to get your hands free, Jimmy, so you and Joe can get everyone cut loose when Bear tries to leave. Make sure he doesn't hear you. Ella may direct you to wherever the police want you to go. If not, hide in the pharmacy and wait for the police."

I figured they were plotting to kill Bear as we exited the building. If Jimmy and Joe were successful in moving the hostages to a safe place, Parker would know, and he would do whatever was necessary.

Chapter 99

"I need your car," Parker said, trotting up to Kathleen.

She stepped away from Suzy and several others, who were praying with local clergy. He had invited his priest and several pastors to the scene to comfort them in the event of a mass tragedy. Family were now segregated in the far back corner of the mammoth parking lot. Kathleen hesitated a second, looking like she was about to question why he needed it, then reached into her pocket.

"I don't have the keys. Gary has them," she said, as Suzy rolled up.

"Where is he?"

"Gary? He's in the car. I just left him there," Suzy said, pointing to the nearby Cadillac.

Parker tore off without explaining. Gary returned soon after.

"What was that about?" he asked.

"The police need a Cadillac, sweetie," Kathleen said, as Parker drove past.

Chapter 100

Ella and Snake crawled under the counter when they returned to the pharmacy. Ella was wringing her trembling hands as she waited to hear from Parker. She had managed to slip up behind another criminal and shoot him in the back. Snake told her the gunman's name was Johnny. Information she could have done without. Her body jerked when Steve's phone buzzed.

"Nice shot with the crossbow, Ella. You're doing great. I need one more big favor. Are you up to it?" Parker asked.

"I'll probably have a nervous breakdown when this is over, but I want to help."

"Great, our deadline is approaching. I want you to go out there while Clarence is still in the bank. I'm reasonably sure Steve talked a couple of the hostages into setting everyone free when Clarence heads out. They have a knife, we think."

"How can you possibly know that?"

"We've been reading lips. Steve's trying to communicate by miming their intentions to the camera."

"Oh, wow," she said. "Okay."

"The manager is a young man named Jimmy, the only young guy. He and Joe Duncan, maybe you know him from the factory, will need your help."

"Steve's boss. I remember seeing him earlier," Ella said, also recalling him risking his life screaming at her abductor when she was led away.

"If Clarence threatens the hostages, surprise him with the rifle. Don't say a word. Just keep shooting until he can't hurt anyone. Remember, there's a bomb on the door, so don't shoot in that direction. Also, don't get too close until Bear walks away with Steve and they start cutting the hostages loose."

She'd been nodding her head, but then stopped. "He's taking Steve?" Ella asked, fearing for his safety more than her own for the moment.

"No, Ella, they aren't going anywhere."

"Does Steve know that?"

"I'm betting he does. Do you know how to operate the rifle?"

She hesitated. She pictured Bear with his hands around Steve's neck. "Uh, Steve taught me everything he knew about it. Took about five seconds."

"Let's go over it again real quick, okay?"

"Sure, I've got it in my lap."

"First, verify the magazine is loaded with ammunition and fully engaged."

"I checked all the clips—more than once. The mag is in there tight."

"Fantastic, you're doing great. Next, make sure the switch above the trigger is in semiautomatic mode."

"It's pointed at semi," Ella said, without looking. She had checked it when she sat down. Firing a machine gun was on Gary's wish list, not hers.

"Steve was right. You know your way around firearms. Don't select burst because you'll just waste ammo. You have a spare magazine?"

"Two. Snake showed me how to change them out, and I've been practicing," Ella said, as Snake perked up.

"You guys are amazing. Make sure the safety's on for now. You don't want to accidentally shoot your partner."

Ella held her tongue for a moment, determined not to sound defensive. Then she said, "When I shot Steve it wasn't because of the safety. I'll do a better job identifying my target before I pull the trigger next time. I promise I won't shoot anybody but Bear."

"You're all set then. When you have everyone hunkered down in the pharmacy, I'll be able to see, so just wait inside until I come for you."

"Okay, we're leaving now," Ella said, closing the phone.

Snake stood and picked up the shotgun. "Don't worry, Ella" he said, "I'll protect you."

Ella smiled. He had good intentions, and she appreciated the gesture, but she knew they both lacked the skills necessary to pull this off.

Chapter 101

"I have a situation update," Parker said to the family members he'd huddled together. "We promised the leader we would allow him to leave the scene with one person. We're doing everything in our power to bring everyone out safely. Please don't discuss this with anyone outside your group until you are reunited with your loved ones. Keep praying, we could use some divine intervention. That's all I have for now."

"Suzy, can I talk to you," Parker said. By the look on her face he could tell she feared Steve was the hostage chosen for the ride in the Cadillac. "Mrs. Duncan, Gary, come here, please." He took them aside and said, "I don't have much time, but I wanted to give you a heads-up. Your loved ones have roles to play, possibly dangerous ones."

"Just like my old man to volunteer for something," Kathleen said with a nervous laugh.

"I'm praying for you, Tom," Suzy said.

"Bring them out safely, please. Ella's my whole world," Gary added.

"I'll come and find you after it's all said and done. Right now I've got to locate Betty Martin," Parker said, scanning the group.

They watched as Parker stood next to a young woman with three small children beside her. She started crying as he whispered into her ear. Suzy gripped the wheels on her chair, preparing to move closer. Gary attempted to grab the handles to assist, but Kathleen clutched his arm and wagged her finger.

"Who is that?" Kathleen asked.

"Never seen her before," Gary replied.

"I'm not sure what Betty Martin's husband did to get a private chat, but we better go comfort her when Parker is through," Suzy said, propelling her chair in that direction.

Chapter 102

Bear drove the scooter out of the bank. He got to the service counter and glanced at his watch. Like magic, the phone rang.

"You better have my car out there. I'm not playing no more games," he said.

"Someone is dropping it off as we speak. Go check if you don't believe me," Powell said.

Bear powered over to the edge of the block wall and looked warily toward the entrance. The vehicle was there, the drivers-side door facing him. An armor-clad officer got out, leaving the door open. Bear drove back and picked up the phone.

"Nice Caddy, Agent Powell. I can always count on you for a decent set of wheels."

"I'm glad you like it. How about rolling down the windows when you park and leave the car where we can find it."

"I'll leave the motor running and the air-conditioner on."

"Very considerate—you're not getting soft on me, are you?" Powell said.

"If I see anything hinky out there, I'll show you my hard side. I'll make a hole in the ground deep enough to bury all the bodies, maybe even yours."

"We'll find you again. Be sure of that," Powell said and he hung up.

Chapter 103

"Are you sure about this?" Powell asked Parker.

"What . . . having my sharpshooter put a bullet through the glass after the hostages enter the pharmacy?"

"You don't think Steve will try to take him down?"

"His hands will be tied . . . literally. Steve's trusting me to save the day. Probably the best outcome—for the other hostages, anyway."

"Clarence sure is taking his time in there."

"Yeah, if I knew he was going to spend all day in the bank, I might have tried something else. Maybe I should've had Steve disarm one of those bombs. I'd love to be there to see Clarence's face when he comes out."

"Don't second-guess yourself, Parker. That's my job."

"Thanks, I almost forgot."

"I know you're tired of hearing this, but the media is scrutinizing every move we make. They'll be giving hindsight advice for the next six months if we're wrong. Are you sure you don't want Ella to take a shot at him when he comes out? She's only thirty feet away."

"He'll kill the hostages if she misses. And she likely would, just like Steve did. Clarence will know we sent her."

"There's something you aren't sharing, isn't there?" Powell asked.

"I wouldn't feel cheated if Jimmy stuck his knife in Clarence's windpipe. He's been trying to talk Steve into something."

"How do you like his odds of pulling *that* off?"

"Much better than I like Steve's chances walking out the door with Clarence. Maybe he wouldn't take it out on the hostages if Jimmy failed."

"Parker, you still got that ace in your sleeve?"

"Yeah, as a last resort," Parker said, leaving the bus without elaborating.

Chapter 104

I had Jimmy explain the plan to the hostages. Everyone would have to get up and run when they were free. They were also told to make sure they had blood circulating through their legs and feet ahead of time. I was worried about Clara and some of the other ladies, especially after they'd been sitting on concrete for three days.

"Ready?" Jimmy asked, sliding over.

"He's right there behind the teller window doing something. He'll see us if he looks up."

"We won't have a chance, once he comes out."

"Jimmy, does Bear use the bathrooms out here, and when did he go last?"

"Yeah, he goes in there. Shortly after he brought you here was the last time I remember. You think he's going to make a pit stop?"

"I'm betting my life on it."

"Everyone else's too," Jimmy whispered.

Clarence motored out of the bank ten minutes later. He had the rifle in his lap and a black nylon duffel bag in the basket. The same type bag every bank robber on television used for the past twenty years. I assumed it contained the money from the store's safe. The bag didn't appear full enough to hold a fortune. I figured the need for drugs died with the lower-tier criminals. Maybe he had a supply of steroids in there for personal use.

Bear drove up and snarled, "Say your goodbyes people. I don't like your odds of getting out of here in one piece."

Somebody would likely die in the next few minutes. I hoped a sniper would put a round in Bear's skull as he walked me out. I had no doubt the bullet would hit me first—and if that's the way it had to be, then so be it. This was a real SWAT operation, not a television show. On the other hand, if Jimmy managed to clear out the hostages, Parker would have more options. Not that they greatly improved my chances for survival.

I wasn't afraid to die, but I had been looking forward to old age with Suzy. I liked protecting her from further pain. She had seen enough for one lifetime. During the years I battled my addiction, I lived through enough unexplainable events to know there was more to life than we were seeing. I rarely discussed it with anyone—except Suzy.

I didn't know if God would give me another chance to get out of this alive, but he was still on my side. He got Suzy this far, and he could take better care of her than I could anyway. I wanted to fight for my life—win or lose. I said my prayers and made a silent oath to attend church every Sunday—even when the fish were biting—if I was bailed out of another jam. I knew God had a sense of humor. He must have one to put up with me this long.

One of the older ladies began sobbing, and this triggered a chain reaction. Bear smiled, seeming to enjoy the fear he inflicted. I blinked away my own tears. I wouldn't give him the satisfaction. He grabbed the rifle and got off the scooter, then paused a moment and got back on. He drove to the restrooms and tottered into the men's room, leaning on his weapon each step.

"That's our cue," I whispered.

"I won't lie. I was beginning to worry," Jimmy replied.

He maneuvered to put his belt buckle behind my back. I struggled to slide the blade out as Jimmy instructed earlier, not having much leverage in that position. The buckle finally slipped out; it doubled as the handle for the short, two-edged blade.

I held the knife while Jimmy slid the rope against the blade. He was free in no time. I expected the buckle-knife combo to be a cheap novelty item, but the blade proved dangerously sharp. I laid the knife on the floor and Jimmy picked it up.

"Let me cut you loose. We can take this guy. He's going to kill you. He said so, and I believe him," Jimmy whispered.

"He'll see that my wrists aren't tied when he picks me up. He'll kill us all, Jimmy. I'll take my chances out there," I said, nodding toward the door.

The green police signal appeared to originate from a farther-than-usual distance, but was easy to distinguish, even though it was getting light outside.

"Cut these people loose as soon as possible. I expect they'll make some noise to cover for you."

I smiled and nodded at Joe, who was leaning in to catch our softly spoken discussion.

"Godspeed my friend," I whispered, looking him in the eye.

"I'll see you on the other side," Joe said, making me wonder if he meant the parking lot or the pearly gates.

"If not, I'll catch you at work . . . in about ten hours," I answered, making him grin.

Outside, several vehicles were in motion. The police must have been repositioning them as far away as possible considering the likelihood of an explosion in the near future. Parker told me the bus was being used to shield people operating close to the building, including Suzy when she was dishing out food. Seeing it roll by made my heart ache. I hated the chaos my wife must be enduring now.

Chapter 105

As I was beginning to think Clarence was never coming out of the bathroom, I heard the hand dryer turn on. When he finally emerged, he had a cell phone to his ear, the rifle pointed at us, and he was stepping cautiously. From what I could pick up, it sounded like he was apologizing for what happened to his brother. Which meant he was probably talking to his mother. And that was not a good sign he was buying whatever Powell was selling.

"I'm praying for you," Jimmy whispered.

"Tell my wife I love her," I said, my eyes stuck on Bear's every move. "And that I'm sorry."

Bear pocketed his phone and glanced at the scooter, then at me. He pulled the duffle out of the basket. There was no way he was leaving the store in a shopping cart for the mobility impaired, though he certainly qualified. He could even get a blue placard to hang on the rearview mirror of the vehicle being offered—if he managed to live long enough to get to a motor vehicle station.

He braced himself with the rifle and threw the bag in my direction. It landed directly in front of me. There was nothing wrong with his upper body, I reminded myself. I was thinking of a way to take him down if the police couldn't. His damaged leg was his only weakness. The newly-bandaged wound, visible below the jagged cut where he removed the pant leg, wasn't bleeding, but he couldn't put much weight on his leg.

If I could have one do-over in my life, it would be that first shot. I would take a deep breath, then release it as I squeezed the trigger. Maybe I would have yanked the shot anyway. It didn't matter now.

Clarence rode the rifle to the bag and shoved it beside me with the barrel. He knelt down and cut my feet loose with his Ka-Bar, a long fighting knife used in every war movie. I had a rubber version when I was a kid. He opened up my vest and figured out quicker than Johnny that removing it would be a bigger job than it looked.

"That's not going to help you," he grunted.

Jimmy leaned forward and his arms were twitching. I shook my head for him to drop the idea. He might've had a chance, especially if his feet weren't tied, but I liked our odds better with Clarence taking me out of the store. The number of hostages likely to survive certainly improved that way.

"You'll pay for what you did to my brother," Bear said, picking me up by my arm.

I wanted to ask if he'd take a credit card, but I managed to stay quiet. He hung his duffel bag around my neck and turned me toward the exit. As we proceeded, he leaned upon my shoulders, testing how much I could support. My knees sagged with the heft of his massive body.

"Suck it up, buttercup," he said. "I'm going to ride you out of here like a birthday pony."

He still used the rifle as a crutch—on the opposite side of me—the grip solidly in his right hand and ready to go to war. I couldn't see any way to kick it away from him.

"I'll kill them all if you try anything," Bear said, reading my mind as we passed the last hostage on our way out.

I held my tongue. I was at peace. I did my best, whatever that was worth, and now it was out of my control. I was scared, but I had confidence Parker would find a way to get me out alive. If not, I was about to see exactly what *was* on the other side. I wouldn't be in the same tunnel of light with Bear. He'd almost certainly be riding an express elevator going down.

"Hold on," Bear said. He drew me in front of him as we stood below the archway. "I don't think they'll shoot through the glass, but I want you catching the bullet if they do."

Sunlight blazed through the doorway. To my left, the woman's mutilated body lay in a heap. The sight sickened me. It wasn't Clara, but it easily could have been. Or any other sweet old lady I knew. This guy was beyond psychopath. He wasn't even human. Bear stooped behind me as we crept forward. He didn't scare me anymore; he could barely walk, and the big mama's boy crouched behind me.

He was the coward, not me.

I couldn't stop thinking about Suzy, which made me long for a chance to fight for my life. If my hands were free, I would try to sweep away his good leg and take away his rifle as he fell. I doubted I could pull it off, but I would've liked an opportunity to find out.

I trusted Parker had a plan, and the green light off in the distance told me I was following it. I knew Parker had something in play when I saw Joe's Cadillac parked out front. I assumed there was a sniper in the back seat, but I couldn't see anyone. I hoped that wasn't the plan because the bullet would have to pass through my head right now to hit the bowling ball behind me. I knew my life was expendable. Parker would do whatever saved the most people.

The butterflies in my stomach were flying like the Blue Angels at an air show. In the movies, the good guy usually lives and the bad guy always goes down. With Parker calling the plays, I expected that to happen here as well. Bear peeked around me toward the door. Bullhorns, distant and unseen, began squawking something about personnel moving to the back of the parking lot—nothing intended to communicate with Bear. I figured Jimmy was starting to cut rope.

"I know they've got a trap set for me," Bear said, as though I cared about his well-being. "You a cop or what?"

I fought the urge to yell *OR WHAT*.

"No, I work across the street . . . at the car plant," I said.

"Well, this will end soon . . . one way or another. Are you prepared to meet your maker, *shop rat*?"

I nodded that I was.

"Don't worry, you're not the only one gonna die here today."

"What do you mean?" I said, breaking my vow to remain silent unless he required a response.

"If I die, everybody dies. I've got my legacy to consider," he said with a laugh."

"Funny. But don't quit your day job murdering defenseless old ladies," I said, no longer interested in coddling him.

I surveyed the army of emergency personnel and their vehicles gathered at the back of the parking lot. Some of the police cars, ambulances, and fire trucks still had lights flashing. One patrol car remained in the vicinity, parked lengthwise about a hundred feet beyond the Cadillac. Parker was leaning against it like James Dean, gazing in our direction.

A couple of officers wearing bomb squad attire stood nearby. One, his arms resting on the roof, held the green light. The bullhorns, which sounded like they were well off to the side, weren't loud. We could hear ourselves talk, but I heard nothing that sounded like fleeing hostages.

"I don't like it. They want me to think I can just walk out of here after what happened last time," Bear said, loosening his grip as we approached the exit.

I jerked my head away, giving a sniper the shot I hoped they were waiting for. Nothing happened.

"SWAT would've shot both of us by now if they were gonna do it. They'll wait until we get outside," Bear said, pointing at the bomb. "Don't you watch television, shop rat?"

"Nothing on but reruns anymore."

I wondered how many hostages were freed. I didn't trust my sense of time. It felt like an hour had passed since Bear cut my feet loose, but it might have been a few minutes too. The green light started blinking. I closed my eyes, waiting for impact.

Chapter 106

Parker watched Clarence standing at the door, not making any attempt to disarm the bomb. The sun rose over the nearby hilltops casting a yellowish-orange glow on the entrance. A marksman two hundred yards out, lay on top of a Humvee with a tarp spread over him that matched the color of the vehicle. With the sun in his eyes, Parker couldn't make out the sniper.

"How many hostages remaining?" Parker communicated to Powell through his headset.

"Three still tied up, and four working like crazy to get them loose. Most of the others are just on the other side of the checkouts. They can barely walk."

They better start crawling then," Parker said.

"Has Clarence done anything about the explosives?"

"He's staring at the car. I don't think he's taking the bait. Let me know when everyone is clear. I'm not ordering the shot until they are."

"I hope you have that luxury. If Clarence isn't coming out, he's going to make sure no one else does either."

"I'm gonna give Steve a suggestion for what to do if Clarence makes a move on the hostages before they're safe. I'll let him decide how this ends for him. I'll take the shot if he doesn't have the heart for it."

"Playing that ace up your sleeve, Parker?"

"More like the four of clubs. We'll see what happens."

Chapter 107

When I opened my eyes, I saw Parker dancing around. He seemed to be acting out some kind of message to me. Clarence was gazing into the parking lot as well, but he appeared to be focused on the open door of the Cadillac.

It was like Parker was playing charades, pretending to be me, with someone holding their arms around his neck. He acted out taking a few quick steps backward. That was Parker's big plan. Push Clarence down and take his weapon. Obviously, he didn't know my wrists were bound.

Parker repeated his improvisation. Bear had a bum leg, but my restraints cut my options to zero. Parker had to be aware of that. I was eager to fight for my life, but I didn't see how this could work. I could probably wrap my leg around his good one and take him down, but when he got up, he was going to kill something, maybe more than *one* something if the hostages were still back there. But maybe the hostages already took off for the pharmacy. With so many to free, I didn't see how that was possible.

Finished with his turn at charades, Parker lifted a bullhorn.

"Disarm the explosive device and step out," he said.

I wondered if Clarence knew how to make the bomb safe. Parker had said that was Flattop's area of expertise.

"Cut my hands loose, and I'll help you disarm the bomb. It's pretty simple, just a tilt mechanism out of a pinball machine," I said, confident in my assessment now that I could see it from two feet away.

"As soon as I make that bomb safe, I won't be. Let me worry about how I go out of here."

"Walk out and get in the car. No one will harm you. You have my word," Parker blasted over the loudspeaker.

I couldn't tell if Parker had his fingers crossed, but I knew he was lying. It appeared Clarence thought so too, because he stood motionless. I scanned the parking lot in search of my wife. I could spot her in a crowded mall from ten stores away. Parker's bus was in the back corner of the parking lot, along with the other emergency vehicles. I pictured Suzy sitting behind it. All at once, every light flashing on emergency vehicles turned off.

It's go time, I thought, remembering the Lloyd Bridges line from a *Seinfeld* episode.

Clarence noticed too. He stared out, putting most of his weight on me. Clarence and I both wore vests, but what we needed were armor-plated helmets. The green spotlight continued to flash. Then three more, spread evenly across the roof of the patrol car. Parker was sending me a message, but what was I supposed to do? Maybe he could have done something if he were in my shoes, but I had no play here.

"I don't like my chances out there, shop rat. You're a bad hostage. The cops know you're a dead man as soon as I get somewhere." Bear's arm trembled. "I should have gutted you and taken that young fella."

I was terrified, but I wasn't shaking.

"I should have waited a few hours. I can't see anything out there with that sun in my eyes," Bear said, using his hand as a visor.

The sun in your eyes isn't your biggest problem here, I wanted to say. *Tom Parker is.*

"I guess it's time to work on that legacy of mine," Bear said, turning both of us around.

I swiveled my head, not thrilled to discover Ella and Snake running up to help the only remaining hostage. Neither of them held a weapon.

"Get out of there, Ella," I yelled, as Bear raised his rifle.

"Go without me," I heard Clara cry out.

But Ella wouldn't do that. Heading out through the checkout, Jimmy had a woman draped across his shoulder. He was looking back, probably pondering whether or not to come back and help the others. Joe was leading the rest of the pack toward the pharmacy. Ella helped Clara stand. Snake, still barefoot, picked Flattop's rifle up from the floor and aimed at us but didn't fire. He would have hit me if he had. Ella put Clara's arm around her neck to assist her.

Bear would have killed them, but I lifted my legs and started kicking to throw him off balance. He flailed for a moment but managed not to fall. He held the trigger down, spraying the ceiling. He lowered his aim but couldn't steady the weapon on his targets. Ella was making slow progress with Clara; they were halfway to the checkout lane. Snake held the rifle on us, looking like he would shoot both of us to protect Ella if he had to.

My attempts at swaying Clarence's aim had less effect now. He controlled me like I was a rag doll instead of a two-hundred-pound human being. The best I'd been able to do with my last try was to make him step back to recover his balance. He groaned when forced to put weight on his bad leg.

What could I do to keep Bear from killing Ella, Snake, and Clara? We faced them now, and he nearly had the rifle steady. I remembered the blinking light. Parker used the signal once before when I was slow to act. Everything became clear as I comprehended what he wanted me to do—and once again, I didn't like it.

I could see Bear's right hand fidgeting as he waited for the right moment to fire a stream of bullets at Ella. I had only one option. I planted my feet, bent my knees, and dug in hard. It seemed like we were moving in slow motion as I drove Clarence toward the door. Ella and Clara were almost to the checkout lane when Snake figured out what I was doing. He turned and ran, diving into the two women. Clarence's leg buckled, and we fell backward. I tucked my head down, praying his immense torso would allow me to survive the self-inflicted injury I was about to suffer when the bomb detonated.

Six Days Later

"Well, look who finally got here," Suzy said, wheeling over to greet Tom and Jennifer, both in uniform, as they entered the crowded room.

"I've never seen a hospital let so many people occupy a patient's room," Joe Duncan said, sitting next to Kathleen under the wall-mounted television at the foot of the bed.

"Luckily, this is a Nashville hospital. We flashed our badges to get in," Parker said.

"If anyone asks, we're here to do a supplemental interview, whatever that is," Jennifer said, looking at Parker.

"That's all I could think of," Parker said. "I'm not a very good liar."

"I'm glad you could make it," Suzy said, a wad of damp tissues in her hand.

Parker hemmed and hawed for a second before saying, "I feel bad for the timing, Suzy, but would you mind if I make an announcement—about something on a lighter note."

"I told you, Tom, there isn't going to be a pity party. What is it?"

"I'd like to introduce Mrs. Jennifer Parker. We stopped off at the JP after the service. Jenny had to call in a favor to get him out on a Sunday."

"Not very often both of us are sporting our parade-dress uniforms, Suzy. Still, we should have waited," Jennifer added.

"It's like my pastor said earlier, 'This is a day for celebrating life.' I'm glad that you chose today to tie the knot," Suzy said, holding back tears.

The newlyweds squeezed by Joe and Kathleen. They took a seat on the window ledge, where the vents were blowing cold air into the already chilly room. Suzy returned to her spot next to Kathleen.

"How's our girl doing?" Parker asked Gary, sitting in the patient's lounger next to the bed.

"Ella's not feeling any pain at the moment. She was awake earlier, but they gave her another shot, and now she's back in dreamland." Gary teared up as he reached under the sheet to hold her hand.

"She's one tough broad," Parker said, causing Jennifer to smack his arm.

Gary broke the awkward silence that followed.

"The doctors say she'll be good as new . . . eventually. She has a concussion and a broken arm . . . also a couple of broken ribs. She'll be out of work for a while. I'm going back tomorrow—all out of sick days. I don't know how I'll take care of her, but I'll figure something out. I just want to get her back home, hopefully in a couple of weeks according to her doctors."

Joe fidgeted in his chair and then Kathleen jabbed him with her elbow.

"Spill it, Joe."

"I wasn't going to say anything today . . . the funeral and all. I was supposed to return to work tomorrow too, but I put in my retirement papers Friday. They're giving me a few weeks medical leave—mental distress. So I'm done."

"We're going to Michigan for a month as soon as my new car comes in. The Cadillac was a total loss," Kathleen added.

"The insurance company will only cover the rental car for a week, or we'd be on the road right now . . . my old pickup would never make it," Joe said.

Suzy stopped wiping her bleary eyes and smiled. "I've got an idea. Why don't you take Steve's truck? It's at the glass shop ready to go. I can't drive it, and my van is almost new. Use it as long as you like."

Kathleen leaned over and hugged her. "Oh sugar, you're the sweetest thing I have ever known."

After they broke their embrace, Suzy said, "I'm serious, Joe. I'll tell them you're picking it up. Nothing's owed, Steve always bought the best insurance."

"Sounds good to me. I'd even be willing to buy it . . . if I like the test drive," Joe said, wiping his eyes.

"I'll make you a great deal," Suzy said, choked up. "By the way, Tom, thank you so much for the beautiful ceremony today. What did you call it again?" Suzy asked, reaching for a fresh handful of tissues Kathleen pulled out of the box for her.

"That was Metro's honor guard ceremony. We only perform that service for fallen heroes such as your husband. I have to give the credit, though, to my lovely bride. She signed the paperwork to make Steve an honorary member of the police force—posthumous."

"It was my privilege, Suzy," Jennifer said, her chin quivering.

"I got chills watching those officers fire their guns in the air . . . the bugler playing taps. I know Steve was watching from heaven."

The only dry eyes in the room were Ella's, but she was beginning to rouse from all the commotion in her room.

"Suzy, will you be okay . . . on your own?" Gary asked.

"Because I'm in a wheelchair? Gary, please, I can take care of myself. Steve always planned to stay here and start a business when he retired, but I'm thinking . . . down the road . . . a ground-level condo near a beach might be nice."

"Sounds like you'll be okay financially then," Kathleen said.

"You had to go there, didn't you," Joe said, turning to face her.

"What . . . I'm nosy."

"It's okay, I appreciate everyone's concern. After his surgery, Steve signed up for all the life insurance he could get without having a physical. Everything's paid for, and I earn decent money. I'll be fine."

"So, Steve had a heart condition?" Joe said. "He told everyone he was having his appendix removed when he took that sick leave. He certainly appeared healthy."

"He *was* healthy, but according to the autopsy, there was a blood clot near his heart that probably would have killed him if the impact didn't. I'm trusting he didn't feel any pain," Suzy said, dabbing her eyes with a tissue.

Parker peered up at the muted TV.

"The news is coming on. I released a short clip of the video our people took, showing Ella at the time of the explosion. Steve's out of the frame by the way," Parker said.

"Why did you do release it?" Gary asked. "You don't normally see that kind of thing on the news."

"Bank robbers don't normally do something heroic. News outlets around the country were asking for the clip. John Snakowski—AKA

Snake, was the recipient of a bronze star for valor in Vietnam. His funeral is tomorrow, and I wanted to set the record straight. I'll be standing in the back—out of uniform, with dark sunglasses on."

Ella surprised everyone when she grabbed the remote on the table straddling her bed and increased the volume.

"Tom, what exactly are we about to see, I'm not sure I can watch," Kathleen said as the commercial aired.

"There's nothing gory. It shows Ella trying to help the elderly woman to safety—Clara Simpson didn't even suffer a scratch by the way—while Snake has a weapon pointed at the exit. Then you hear gunfire and what appears to be debris falling from the ceiling. Snake has his finger on the trigger and never blinked. Ella's assisting Clara into the checkout lane, when Snake drops the gun and starts running, tackling them as the bomb explodes. His body is the only thing between the women and, as you will see, what looks like an F5 tornado."

Ella said, "You're still going to the funeral aren't you, Gary?"

"Yeah, I want to thank his family. I heard he was born and raised in Nashville."

Suzy, sitting off to the side, made no move to be able to view the television, as a teaser announced the video was next.

"I'm going. I've got some work to catch up on," Suzy said, hanging the strap of her purse on the brake lever.

"We don't have to watch it, Suzy," Jennifer said.

"No, go ahead. Maybe I'll catch it on the news tonight," Suzy said, spinning her chair around.

"I'll walk you out," Gary said, squeezing by the others.

"I'm okay. I don't need your help," Suzy said, as Gary stood beside her while she waited for the elevator.

"I need to talk," he said. "May I walk you out? I promise I won't touch your chair."

Suzy laughed through her tears, then nodded her approval. As they reached her van, Gary got up the nerve to speak.

"I heard you tell Kathleen that a weird thing happened right after the explosion."

"Yeah, it was probably my imagination, but I could have sworn someone poked me in the ribs . . . same place Steve always did. It's the only place I'm ticklish."

Gary was quiet for a moment, then said, "I haven't told anyone yet . . . but right after . . . I thought I had a bug in my ear. I'll tell you what it reminded me of. Steve used to sneak up behind me and put a slobbered finger in my ear—a wet Willy. I hated it, but Steve would be laughing so hard I had to laugh too. And when I tried to get that fly out of my ear, I felt a little moisture. But that might have been all in my head. One thing I am sure of: I haven't had a civil conversation with Steve in far too long, but I miss him already."

"Hey Gary, I know this sounds petty, but did Ella mention anything weird like that happening to her?"

"She was barely conscious when I got to the hospital, but no, Ella hasn't said anything."

"If you don't mind, I'd prefer you keep this between the two of us."

"I'm with you. If it *was* Steve, I'd like to believe he forgot to stop and say goodbye to my wife on his way out of here."

"And Gary, if you find out otherwise . . . don't tell me, okay?"

Made in the USA
Columbia, SC
29 November 2019